Cutie in Camo

By: Rebecca Gulley

Identifiers: ISBN: 979-8-9930840-1-5 (trade paperback), 979-8-9930840-0-8 (ebook)

1st edition 2025

Contents

To the girls who love the outdoors, that obsessed hunter is out there craving to have you in his tree stand. Hunting down the love of your life takes patience; sometimes, it's just like sitting in a tree stand waiting on a deer.

Jackson and Raven's Playlist

Listen on Spotify!

Found You by Kane Brown

Yours by Russell Dickerson

The Good Ones by Gabby Barrett

Wanted by Hunter Hayes

Here For The Party by Gretchen Wilson

Mean To Me by Brett Eldredge

Huntin', Fishin', and Lovin' Every Day by Luke Bryan

Somethin' Bout A Truck by Kip Moore

Promise You That by Trevor Martin

Craving You by Thomas Rhett, Maren Morris

Anything She Says by Mitchell Tenpenny (ft. Seaforth)

The Way I Loved You (Taylor's Version) by Taylor Swift

Slow Dance In A Parking Lot by Jordan Davis

Sleigh Ride by Lindsey Stirling

Girl In Mine by Parmalee

Gotta Be Somebody by Nickleback

Better Together by Luke Combs

Trigger Warnings and Contents

This novel contains mature and potentially sensitive themes, including explicit sexual content; a threesome involving non–main characters; depictions of toxic relationships involving mental and physical abuse (not between the main characters); mentions of domestic violence; sexual assault involving the female main character and a non–main character (Chapter 18); infidelity (not between the main characters); references to cancer and the loss of a loved one; and hunting-related topics. Please note that while hunting is discussed, no graphic details of animal processing are included. Reader discretion is advised.

Chapter 1
Jackson

Adrenaline courses through my body, and my heartbeat quickens.

Standing up quietly, hoping to stay unnoticed. Keeping my eyes on the whitetail deer that has his snout to the ground, I reach for my bow that rests on the bow hook, screwed into the tree holding my tree stand. My body freezes, my arm halfway to grasping onto my bow, as he lifts his head swiftly, flicking his tail, looking around before inching further down the trail. My heart pounds through my chest, shaking my body as I fight to steady my breathing, white plumes slipping past my lips. The deer walks behind a tree, creating a barrier between him and me. When my hand finally makes contact with my bow; I slowly bring it around to get ready to take my shot. As everything seems to move in slow motion, I wait for him to walk the remaining 20 yards to finally be directly in front of me. Hunting deer takes patience. There could be days you didn't see a single deer. And there could be days you could see plenty of deer, and they just never got close enough to shoot at one.

Getting into the stance, I place the stock of the crossbow between my body and my shoulder. Adrenaline continues to pump through my body, causing my hands to tremble. I lower my face to look through the scope, waiting for the deer to appear in my line of fire. Seconds before the deer is directly in front of me, I peek over my scope and notice him looking directly at me.

Before I know it, the deer runs off, blowing at me with its white tail straight up, warning any other deer nearby that it's not safe.

You could be mere seconds from taking a shot, but when a deer spots you, your chances of shooting can evaporate instantly. Patience, dedication, and the time you spend sitting in the woods will give you a higher chance of shooting a deer. Hunting is not just a hobby; it's a lifestyle. If only love for the outdoors was just as easy as loving someone. Both need commitment and time. Spending time in the stand will hopefully give you a higher chance of hunting down that whitetail deer. Just like spending time in our relationship will ensure happiness, right?

Chapter 2
Raven

The leaves were falling from the trees, floating gently to the ground here in River Valley, Ohio. It was the first of October. The weather was a little chilly—perfect for a crisp fall day. It was also the ideal time to snuggle up with my dog, Rex, and dive into one of the many books on my never-ending TBR list.

As I tap the screen of my Kindle to turn the page, I occasionally steal glances at Rex. His head rests across my lap, his lips flapping slightly as he lets out soft snores. Looking away from the words on the screen, I gaze outside and watch the tree branches dance in the wind. Each time they move, leaves flutter down to the ground.

I moved here from the big city about a month ago. I was tired of the long commute to and from work. By the time I got home, there was barely any time left for myself. My only free time came on weekends, holidays, or the occasional snow day. So, what did I do? I quit my job as a school administrator and accepted a position at a local school here in town. My commute became significantly shorter.

I was so excited when I got the job that I immediately began house hunting. After scrolling through countless local listings, I finally found a charming two-story home just outside of town. I felt a wave of relief when the owners accepted my offer. Built in the 1920s, the house is full of character. Its exterior is wrapped in multicolored brick, with each window framed by deep hunter-green shutters. One of the larger bedrooms boasts a beautiful bow window overlooking the front yard, while another upstairs room at the back of the house offers a stunning view of the backyard through a wide, sunlit window.

The yard is perfect. A six-foot privacy fence runs from the house to the tree line, where it gives way to a chain-link fence that encloses the rest of the property. The nearest neighbor lives nearly half a mile away.

My mom tried to talk me out of moving here, but I needed this. I needed a place where I could finally breathe, where the commute was shorter and the stress lighter. The people in town—and at my new job—have been incredibly welcoming. In the month I've lived here, I've savored every moment. Rex, my German Shorthaired Pointer, loves it too—especially our walks through the woods behind the house.

My sister Hannah fosters dogs until they find permanent homes. The day before I moved to River Valley, I stopped by her house for a visit. Before I even had both feet through the door, I was greeted by my two nieces, Abby and Sami, along with five dogs. My sister and I sat on the couch while the kids and dogs ran wildly around the living room. We talked about how I was moving out to "the boonies," and I could tell she was a little jealous. She even mentioned how nice it would be to have a bigger yard for the kids and dogs to run around in.

One of the dogs climbed up on the couch and plopped down next to me. Don't get me wrong—I've always loved dogs. We had a few growing up, but I never imagined myself owning one. That all changed when I met Rex. Hannah talked me into adopting him that very day. When I left her house, I didn't leave alone. The next day, it wasn't just me moving to River Valley—it was Rex and me, together, starting our new life in our permanent home.

Over the past month, I've given a few of the rooms a fresh coat of paint. The kitchen has a rustic charm, with dark blue checkered wallpaper featuring cows and chickens. Upstairs, there are three bedrooms. The smallest one became my office. It holds a desk and a cozy lounge chair—well, it's supposed to seat two people, but Rex usually claims it. I also had a custom window seat built beneath the large window overlooking the backyard. It's wide enough for both Rex and me to sit comfortably. He's a very affectionate dog and always wants to be close.

With each little update I've made to the house, it's become more perfect—for both of us.

I shift my legs to get off the window seat, and Rex lets out a low growl, as if he isn't ready to stop snuggling.

"Want to go for a walk, Rexy boy?"

Rex perks his ears, then bounds off the window seat and bolts downstairs to the door. By the time I follow, he's already sitting patiently, tail wagging. He loves our walks in the woods behind the house.

I lace up my gym shoes and pull on my green fleece jacket before stepping outside. A chilly breeze hits my face as I open the door, tossing my hair into the air.

"Let's go, Rex."

As soon as I say the words, he dashes into the yard, circling with excitement. I step off the porch and follow the stone path toward the woods. Rex darts ahead, nose to the ground as he sniffs through the fallen leaves.

The wind whistles through the trees, making them sway and dance.

As I walk, I kick up a pile of leaves and watch them scatter in front of me.

A week after I moved in, I followed this path until it dead-ended at a creek. I ended up having a gazebo built that was half-enclosed, with a bench seat covered with a cushion—next to the creek.

In the gazebo, Rex stretches out on the dog bed I'd brought. Still, I couldn't believe it had taken me this long to move out here. I should've done it sooner.

A few hours and a few chapters later, Rex and I head back toward the house. He's already slipped into his usual routine—circling the trees with his nose to the ground. More than once, he freezes and points at birds perched in the branches. Rex is such an intelligent dog. It's a shame he doesn't get to use more of the skills typical of his breed. Still, he seems content. Maybe our daily walks through the woods are enough for him. At least, I hope they are.

Back at the house, I push open the back door. Warmth envelops me, and the lingering scent of chili fills the air. I walk into the kitchen, set my Kindle down, and feed Rex. While he chows down, I grab a soup bowl and ladle some from the crock pot. Plumes of steam dance across the surface, and my mouth waters as the smell reaches me. I crumble a few crackers on top, sit at my little table, and eat.

Then my phone rings.

I glance at the screen—of course, it's my mother. I'm not looking forward to this conversation; I already know how it will go. Dreading it, I slide my finger across the screen to answer.

"Hey, Mom," I say, blowing on my next bite before slipping it into my mouth.

"Hey, sweetheart! How's everything going over there? How's the new house? And how's Rex?"

"I'm doing fine. Rex is good too—we've been enjoying the outdoors. How are you and Dad?"

I take another bite while waiting for her to respond.

"We're doing just fine. We've been playing bingo at the community center. Your father won two hundred dollars last week—he looked like he'd won the lottery."

She pauses, and I catch my father mumbling something in the background.

"When are you coming home to visit? I see your sister every weekend, but you haven't been over since you moved out there."

I roll my eyes. Thankfully, we're not FaceTiming. She always tries to guilt-trip me. I live a whole forty-five minutes away. My sister lives thirty minutes away—on the opposite side of the city. My parents are both retired, yet somehow that fifteen-minute difference makes visiting me "too far." They always manage to visit her or attend festivals in the city, though.

"I plan to come visit soon," I reply.

"You and Dad still haven't seen the new house. I think Dad would enjoy the trail through the woods—he could bring his fishing pole and fish in the creek. Rex and I watch the fish surfacing in the evenings from the gazebo."

"We'll see. Your father doesn't like to drive far anymore."

Here we go again. I bit my tongue as aggravation bubbles within me.

Then she says, "Just let me know when you're planning to visit so we don't make any plans."

Noted. Because clearly, I wasn't trying to *invite you* to come here or anything. Why do I even bother?

"Okay, Mom, I will."

I hear some shuffling and realize she's now holding the phone between her shoulder and ear. I've watched her do that for over thirty years—probably walking through the house to hand my dad a beer while he watches TV in his recliner.

"Oh, Raven, I met the sweetest man last week at church. He recently moved to the area—he's a hospital physician. His name is Andy. Handsome, too!"

Oh no. No, no, no. This cannot be happening.

She continues to ramble.

"I told him I have a daughter who's single. I even showed him a picture of you."

Someone, please put me out of my misery.

"He said he'd like to take you on a date sometime."

Seriously? It's one thing to mention a single guy to me—but *showing him my picture*?

That's next-level matchmaking. Now I look *desperate*.

It's not surprising. She's been hounding me for years to settle down and start a family since my last relationship ended.

"Mom, seriously?"

I pinch the bridge of my nose.

"I'm not looking to start a relationship right now. I just moved, and I'm enjoying my free time."

"Well, Raven, we aren't getting any younger," she huffs.

"I still hope to have grandchildren from you someday. Your sister gave me two—I'm hoping you'll give me two... or five."

Five?!

Oh, absolutely not. She'd be lucky to get *one*.

I sigh.

"Mom, I know. Maybe one day I'll meet someone. But I don't want to make the same mistake again and end up with another dud."

I take a deep breath, trying to stay calm.

"Please don't say anything else to that guy. You're making me look desperate. He probably thinks I'm some kind of charity case."

"Oh, sweetheart, if anyone's desperate, it's me," she says with an awkward laugh.

"I just want more grand babies. Your sister says she's done."

Wonderful. Now she's joking about her desperation.

"Well, I'm going to get off here and work on my puzzle. Sweetheart, I'll talk to you later. Bye!"

"Bye, Mom. Talk to you later."

Click. The loud slam of the phone landing on its base echoes in my ear.

I can't believe they still have a landline. She complains about telemarketer calls all day long, but refuses to give it up.

Her parting words stuck with me, though. They aren't going to visit me. That much was clear. All they care about is visiting my sister—because she has kids. I haven't given them grandchildren, so apparently, I'm not a priority.

After I adopted Rex, I told them they had a grand-puppy. That didn't go over well with my mom. She insisted grandchildren had to be human—not dogs. I tried to explain that a lot of my friends' parents consider pets grand-puppies or grand-kitties, but she didn't want to hear it.

Eventually, I just dropped the subject. There was no convincing her. Rex may not be a grandchild to her—but to me, he's family.

The temperature drops after the sun sinks behind the trees. I grab my coat and a blanket, tuck my Kindle under my arm, and step outside. Rex follows close behind as I light the path with my phone's flashlight.

When we reach the gazebo, I aim the light at the switch and flip on the twinkle lights strung across the ceiling. Soft, warm light fills the space. I spread the blanket across my lap, and settle onto the padded bench seat. Once I'm cozy, Rex curls up at my feet.

The steady chorus of crickets fills the night air, creating a peaceful soundtrack as I get lost in a spicy romance novel by Siena Trap.

Time slips away. When I finally glance at the time, I realize it's after 10:00. We've been out here for nearly four hours. I reach down and gently pat Rex, who's snoring lightly. He stirs, lifting his head to look at me.

"Let's go inside, buddy. Time for bed."

He jumps up and bounds off, running around the gazebo. All I hear is the shuffle of leaves as he darts through them. Occasionally, I catch a glimpse of his white fur weaving between the trees.

I pull out my phone again, turn the flashlight back on, and flip off the twinkle lights. Together, we make our way back up to the house.

Upstairs, I change out of my clothes, tossing them into the hamper before slipping into pajama shorts and an oversized T-shirt. When I return to the bedroom, Rex is already stretched out across my bed like he owns the place.

I slide under the sheets, setting my phone and Kindle on the nightstand. With a contented sigh, I close my eyes and drift off to sleep.

Chapter 3
Jackson

It's finally Friday—the start of my week-long vacation. I've been counting down the days since Monday. The hands on the clock kept inching closer and closer to 5:00, but my supervisor kept trying to make conversation as I was packing up my things to leave.

Don't get me wrong—I know exactly what she's doing. She wants me to come in for half a day instead of taking the full week off. As a supervisor, she already has enough on her plate each week; she doesn't want to cover for me.

I kept telling her I couldn't commit to coming in for just a half day. She knows what happened the last time I tried that—the day I was supposed to go into the office at noon, which turned into *maybe later,* and eventually turned into *not coming in at all.*

That day, I shot a deer and had to track it for quite a while because I made a piss-poor shot—barely clipped its lungs. I eventually found the deer lying in a creek, but it felt like I walked forever before I did. After tagging it and dragging it out of the woods—deep into a 60-acre property—I still had to field dress it and take it to the butcher. By the time all that was done, going to work was pointless.

So when I look back at the clock and see it's after 5:00, I finally put my foot down and tell her, it's only a week. Before leaving my little office, I remind her I'm already caught up, and if anything comes up before I return, she'll only need to handle it if it's urgent.

Being a social worker at a small-town nursing home has its perks. Not much happens, and when I'm not filling out patient paperwork, I'm usually out chatting with the residents. I'm always available to listen and offer support, making sure they know they can reach out whenever they need to.

I've always enjoyed hearing them talk about what they call their "younger days."

My supervisor seems a little more relieved when I tell her to only worry about the urgent cases before she leaves my office. She does this every year, or anytime I take off a week for deer hunting. I always take a week off the first week of October to hunt deer. I was looking forward to spending quality time in the woods listening to the squirrels sound like deer running through the woods. With the cooler temperatures, the rut was starting. That means there would be more chances of seeing deer run out before me. I hope Turkey Foot will walk out in front of me this year.

Yes, I nickname my deer; I have a trail camera that sends pictures and videos directly to my phone. Each time I see a new buck on my camera app, I nickname them based on the shape of their antlers. Turkey Foot has an antler shaped like a turkey foot. We also have a buck that I call Nutsy. He has a drop tine that looks like well—a nut sack.

Pulling into my driveway, I can't help the memory from almost a year ago flooding my mind. It's been a year since I found out my ex-girlfriend, Gina, let another man penetrate her with his cock.

That weekend, I had planned to go out and buy a ring to propose to Gina. After she left my life that day, I called my buddy Tanner to talk. Tanner has been around the block with multiple women and might not have been the ideal person to turn to for relationship advice—but at least he's never cheated on anyone.

My other friend, Mitch, has had a messy relationship with his now-fiancée, Lacy. I can't even count how many times she's cheated on him. Every time he came to us with another story, Tanner and I offered the same advice: leave her and move on. I think he eventually got tired of hearing it, because it's been a few months since he's mentioned whether she's done him wrong again.

We only wanted the best for him. He's been my best friend since elementary school—both he and Tanner have.

I remember them both giving me a hard time about Gina, too. They told me I needed someone who supported me and didn't try to change who I was. I always brushed it off. I never thought Gina was trying to change me.

I love hunting. It's something my father and I did together before he passed away. He took me out for the first time when I was nine years old, and we made some of our best memories out in the woods. After he died, a few years back, I bought out my sister Luna's half of our family home, since she lives in Tennessee with her boyfriend, Lucas.

Gina moved in with me a few months after we started dating. The house was the only thing she really changed. She said it "reeked of masculinity." So, I let her change a few things here and there. I had a few deer heads mounted in the bedroom, but as soon as she moved her things in, those were the first to go.

She tried going hunting with me a few times, but she constantly complained about the cold and said she wished she were doing something more worthwhile than sitting in a tree stand for hours. Eventually, it got to the point where she resented even hearing me talk about hunting.

She always had something negative to say about what she called my "hobby." I told her I was stocking our freezer so we wouldn't have to buy overpriced beef at the grocery store. Besides, venison is much leaner and healthier than beef.

Still, it got to the point where I just stopped talking to her about it all together.

With the wind beating against my truck, snapping me back to reality, I push hard on the door to get it open. Climbing out, I barely touch it before it slams shut from the gust whipping through. I flip my hat backward to keep it from flying off and make my way toward the front porch and into the house.

As soon as the door creaks open, Nala—my black lab—barks before realizing it's me. The second she sees me, her tail starts wagging like crazy as she darts over. She might be getting older, but she still has her puppy moments.

I hang my keys on the hook by the door and head upstairs to strip off my work clothes. After changing into a pair of shorts and my old Luke Combs concert T-shirt, I flop back onto my bed, already thinking about the upcoming week in the woods.

Just then, my phone buzzes on the dresser. Before I can grab it, it vibrates right off the edge and smacks face-down onto the hardwood floor. I pick it up and see a fresh jagged crack stretching across the screen.

Great.

I swipe my finger across the screen to answer the call. Loud country music—probably coming from the bar in town—blasts through the earpiece.

"Hey, Tanner," I say, putting the phone up to my ear as I walk back to the bed.

"Hey, bud, you ready for deer season to begin?" The music fades as Tanner steps outside.

"I sure am. Just got home a little while ago, but I still need to get all my gear together so I'm not rushing in the morning. You heading out early?"

Tanner chuckles.

"Yeah, we'll see. If I don't stay out too late tonight, I might go in the morning. If not, maybe I'll head out in the evening."

I smirk, already knowing what keeps him out late.

"You know, if you didn't bring a girl home every Friday night, you might actually make it out for a morning hunt."

"Well, maybe I'll take that into consideration," he says, half-laughing.

"But I can't seem to leave the bar without someone following me to my truck. I guess I'll just have to rail them in the bathroom."

I toss my head back, laughing.

"Okay, buddy. I'm gonna get off here and get my stuff ready for tomorrow. Text me if you decide to go out in the morning?"

"Sure thing. Oh—did you hear the Danielson place sold? I heard some chick bought it."

"Yeah, I heard it sold. Haven't paid much attention to see if anyone's moved in yet, though. I'm surprised you don't know her name. Or do you and just not telling me?"

I hear someone singing in the background before he answers.

"No, seriously, I don't. Just heard it through the grapevine. I think—she works up at the school here in town. Wonder if she's a hot teacher... or a sexy secretary."

Then, with mock disgust, he adds, "Or what if she's a janitor?"

Chuckling, I put him on speaker as I walk into the hunting room.

"Being a janitor doesn't mean she can't be pretty. Women can look sexy working a mop, too."

Sounding unsure, Tanner replies, "I guess you've got a point. Find out who she is—maybe you can get hunting permission there again."

He pauses for a beat, then says, "Well—I'm heading back inside. I'll text you, bud."

We say our goodbyes before hanging up. I really hope Tanner settles down someday. It's been a few years since he's been in a committed relationship.

After Andrea passed away in that horrific accident, I watched a piece of him die. I never thought he'd be able to move on from her.

When I got the call that he was on his way to the hospital to see her, I knew I had to be there. I stood by his side when the doctor came out and delivered the news he never wanted to hear. That day, I watched my best friend fall to his knees and weep. I had never seen him cry before—not once in all the years I'd known him.

It was a year later when I started noticing the random hookups. I never questioned him about it, aside from cracking the occasional joke. Tanner's like a brother to me. And if I'm not giving him crap, do I even care?

I still remember the day Gina left. Tanner was the first person I called.

Without sugarcoating anything, he told me she wasn't the right one. He said he hoped I'd find someone who truly appreciated me—someone who shared my love for the outdoors.

Someone who'd never want me to change.

Is there someone out there like that? Does she exist?

After all of my hunting clothes are in my scent crusher closet, I turn it on so it takes away the scent of my home so the deer don't catch wind of me if there is a breeze tomorrow. I grab my bow off the wall and sit it down in its case before closing it up. Once all of that is done, I grab my backpack and put my face mask and gloves in it before sitting it down next to my bow case. When I get down to the kitchen, I scoop some of Nala's food out for her before starting my dinner.

Before going to bed, I pull out my phone and open the auditor's site to look up the new property owner who just moved in down the road from me. I enter the address into the search box, and the name *Raven Catz* pops up on the screen. Tanner was right—she's definitely new to town. I've never heard her name before.

Hopefully, I'll get to hunt her woods like I used to with my old friend Peter.

Before Peter moved away, we hunted every day after school. Sometimes, we'd get in trouble with our mommas for staying up late doing homework instead of getting it done right after we got home. Hunting coursed through our blood. We were as obsessed with it as video gamers are with video games.

After Peter moved, I introduced myself to the new neighbors. Don't get me wrong—the Danielsons were nice—but at ten years old, hearing them tell me no, that I couldn't hunt their woods, made them seem downright mean. Looking back now, I realize how foolish that was. The new owners did hunt, so it makes sense now—they didn't want some ten-year-old kid hunting on their property when they were out there hunting too.

I made a mental note to stop by on my way home from hunting to introduce myself—and, of course, to casually feel things out and see if she might allow someone to hunt her property. Around here, very few people give out hunting permission.

I've heard stories about some hunters giving the rest of us a bad reputation. There were some good, honest hunters in this world. But then there were some that did some illegal shit, like poaching deer—trespassing on private property or improper tagging. Those type of hunters ruined it for those like me.

I've been hunting on a small farm for years. The farmer has known me since I was a little boy. I always offer to help whenever he needs it, and I keep an eye on his property. Since I watch over the place, I even bought him a trail camera to put on the tree next to his driveway so he can see who's pulling in and out.

Part of me wishes I had just sold my father's house and bought a piece of land with woods of my own. That way, I could walk out back to hunt instead of driving down the road. But I just couldn't see myself letting go of my parents' home. Did I keep it for sentimental reasons? Probably.

Setting my phone down, I drift off to sleep.

Getting out of my work clothes, I hear a car pulling into the driveway. Shuffling down the stairs, I reach the bottom step just in time to see Gina getting out of her car. Her face is unreadable. I've been waiting for her to get home so we can either order dinner or decide whether we're cooking tonight.

Instead of meeting her at the door, I sit in my recliner and wait for her to come inside. The screen door creaks open and slams shut behind her as she walks in and removes her coat—without even acknowledging that I'm sitting less than ten feet away. She hurries up the stairs, and I can hear constant movement above me.

I start toward the stairs, ready to ask what she's doing, but then I notice Nala at the back door, ringing her bells to go outside. As I pad toward the back door, the sound of Gina shuffling down the stairs reaches me. I let her out, then head into the kitchen, where I find Gina putting away dishes from the drying rack.

"So, how was your day today?" I ask.

She pauses, setting a plate in the cabinet, then turns slightly, her expression unreadable.

"Jackson, we need to talk."

That's not what I expected.

"What about?" I ask, unsure of where this is going.

Her hands grip the edge of the countertop. She won't look at me.

"What is it, Gina? What's wrong?"

She shakes her head and covers her mouth, still avoiding my eyes.

"We're done, Jackson. I can't do this anymore."

What did she just say?

"What do you mean, we're done? Why? Did I do something wrong?"

I rub a hand down my face, irritation rising with the silence hanging in the air.

"Tell me, dammit!"

Gina jumps at my raised voice and moves toward the doorway. She turns sharply, throwing her hands up.

"I'm in love with someone else. I'm sorry, but I'm just not happy with you anymore. I tried to support your hobby and get into it with you. But I hate that we never go out on dates. I hate that everything revolves around hunting. You're obsessed."

There's not a single trace of regret in her voice. The woman I thought I loved just admitted she cheated—and fell in love with another man.

My mind reels with what she's said, but only one question breaks through the noise.

"Who is it?"

She storms out of the kitchen and heads upstairs.

Oh no. She's not walking out without telling me.

I chase after her. She slams the bedroom door behind her, but I push it open. She's already moving around the room, throwing her things into a suitcase.

Furious and devastated, I raise my voice.

"Who, Gina? I need you to fucking tell me who it is!"

She turns to face me, her arms full of clothes, suitcase dragging behind her.

"Does it matter?" she snaps.
"He loves me. He pays attention to me. With him, I feel wanted."

She pushes past me and bolts down the stairs, leaving me standing alone in the doorway of what used to be our bedroom.

Feeling defeated, I lean against the doorframe. Why would she cheat on me? I thought we were happy.

A tear hits the floor at my feet. Then another. I shut my eyes and try to wipe them away, but they keep falling. I feel something wet nudge my hand.

I open my eyes to find Nala by my side.

I look around the room. Her dresser drawers are wide open—empty. On her side of the closet—empty.

I instantly sit up in bed, my heart beating faster than lightning as I struggle to catch my breath. It was only a nightmare. I just hope Gina's actions will stop haunting me. Maybe someday, I'll move on—and find someone who loves me for who I am.

Chapter 4
Jackson

Woken by my alarm, I grab my phone from the nightstand and silence it. Running a hand down my face, I lay my head back on the pillow and stretch out my arms and legs.

Today is the first day of deer season, and I'm more than ready to be out in the tree stand, waiting for a deer to walk by. I unlock my phone and turn off the backup alarms I set—just in case I shut the first one off in my sleep. I definitely don't want to oversleep. The night before opening day feels like Christmas Eve when you're a kid. I glance toward my window; not a speck of light shines in yet, the sun still below the horizon.

Sitting up, I let my feet hang over the edge of the bed and stretch my neck before heading to the bathroom.

Tugging off my clothes, I turn on the shower and let the water heat up. I reach in and test the stream with my hand, making sure it's nice and hot before stepping in. As I stand under the showerhead, the hot water runs down my body, relaxing my muscles.

It was going to be a great morning out in the stand. Even if I didn't see a single deer, I would enjoy the sounds of nature surrounding me. Hunting never got old. In fact, if you ever go hunting and you don't feel the adrenaline pumping through your body anymore after shooting a deer, then you're best to hang up your camouflage and bow. After every deer I have harvested, it always takes me about an hour to calm down. The thrill of shooting a deer after waiting patiently for it to walk out in front of you is unexplainable in terms of how it truly makes me feel. And no, I don't go out and throw a party. However, I am providing food for myself, and that's something to be proud of, right?

I grab the Dead Down Wind body wash, lather it onto a washcloth, and scrub from head to toe before rinsing clean. Next, I work the shampoo through my hair, then stand under the hot water, letting it wash over my face. I've trusted these products for years—no way I'd risk using regular "manly" shampoo and let a deer catch my scent in the stand. That'd ruin the hunt before it even began.

When I shut off the water and step out of the shower, warmth clings to my skin. I reach for the soft green towel hanging on the rack and begin drying off.

After hanging up the towel, I pad into my bedroom and grab a fresh pair of boxers from the drawer. Then I head into the hunting room to put on my camouflage clothes and boots. I tie the laces tight, then pull out my phone to play some music while I finish getting ready. Tucking my phone into my pocket, I grab my backpack and bow case and walk out to the truck. It's peaceful, my boots breaking the silence as they shuffle through the gravel in the driveway.

Setting my bow case down next to my truck, I lower the tailgate to slide my bow case and book bag into the bed of my truck.

Closing the tailgate, I climb into my truck and turn the key over. The smell of crisp autumn air, pine needles, and wood smoke wafts in as I roll down my truck windows.

It was going to be a great day out in the woods. I had about 30 minutes before sunrise, which meant I needed to be in the stand before the sun rose over the horizon. The property I hunt on is only about 10 minutes away, giving me just under 20 minutes to get to my stand. I've always found it best to get to my tree stand or blind before the sun breaks over the horizon, so I don't spook any deer that might pass by.

There were some mornings I'd make it all the way down there—sitting in my truck—when I'd get a notification from my trail camera. Anytime I got a picture of deer right in front of my stand, I would either wait or turn around and head back home. Deer movement always determined when I'd head out to the woods in the evening. If the deer started moving before 4:00, I'd leave around 2:00 to get there in time. Sure, that meant a long time in the woods, but if the chances of spooking a deer were slim to none by going out early, it was well worth it.

Maybe I'll swing by Raven's house to introduce myself after I am done hunting for the day. I was about to sit my phone down in the cup holder of my truck, but a notification on the screen caught my eye. Making a note to myself to make sure my cell phone is in silent mode. Deer have excellent hearing—we don't need them to hear my cell phone vibrating in my pocket.

Smiling—it was a text from my little sister Luna.

> Luna: Hey, good luck today. Don't kill the first deer that walks out in front of ya. It definitely needs to be bigger than Nala to shoot.

> Jackson: You know me. I will sit out there until the big buck walks out in front of me.

> Jackson: Don't worry, I will come home to sleep at night before doing it all again.

Luna and I had a special relationship. We were close growing up—well, at least after she turned five, because she was pretty annoying before that. Could you blame me though—there was a ten year age gap between us.

But after our mom passed away, I made sure my sister knew I was there for her. Yes, we fought; I've never heard of siblings who don't. But in the end, we got along. Whenever she needed something or someone to talk to, she knew she could come to me.

My phone vibrates, and I can't help but laugh at what she just sent back.

> Luna: Bub, I wouldn't be surprised if you set up a tent and camped out there.

> Luna: Gotta get to work. Text me if you kill anything.

> Jackson: Will do. Have a good day at work.

Tossing my phone onto the seat beside me, I shift my truck into drive and head down the road. As I pass Raven's house, I notice a light glowing through one of the large bow windows centered on the second story. If I remember right, that's the main bedroom.

I wonder what she's doing up this early on a Saturday. Does she work a second job on the weekends? Maybe she's heading out of town for the day—or the weekend? Endless thoughts burrow through my mind as I continue down the road.

As I approach the driveway to the farmer's house, I ease off the gas, letting the truck slow down. After passing the driveway, I press the brake and pull off onto the grassy path that runs between the cornfield and the tree line. The path is bumpy, but I finally reach my usual parking spot—tucked away and hidden from the road. I shift into park, turn off the engine, and shut off the lights before quietly opening the door.

Trying not to make too much noise, I step out and tiptoe to the bed of my truck to grab my bow. I pull my face mask and gloves from my backpack, then sling the bag over my shoulder. Sliding the bow case to the edge of the tailgate, I open it and carefully take out my bow. I attach the sling and hang it over my shoulder before closing the case and sliding it back into the truck.

With everything in place, I head toward my tree stand nestled in the woods. It's so peaceful out here in the morning—I can hear nothing but my breathing and the occasional crunch of leaves underfoot, which I try to avoid. I walk in slow motion, carefully placing each step, but it's nearly impossible not to make noise; it hasn't rained in over a week.

When I reach my tree stand, I hook my bow onto the bow rope and climb the ladder. Once I'm on the platform, I grab the rope tied to the shooting rail and pull my bow up. When it's within reach, I untie it and hang both my bow and backpack on the hooks I've screwed into the tree above my head.

Now I just have to sit here and wait for the sun to rise, hoping a deer walks by. The only thing I don't like about sitting in the woods for long stretches is having too much time to think. Sure, sometimes great ideas come to mind—but what happened a year ago with Gina still haunts me.

I keep replaying the moment I noticed the change in her. It shattered my heart the day I found out she was cheating. I still don't understand why. I truly believed we were meant for each other. Hell, I thought the next step was marriage. But damn, was I wrong.

Looking back, I'm just glad I never went out and bought that engagement ring.

Gina never enjoyed hunting or hanging out with my friends, but I always thought we got along. I treated her well—or at least I thought I did.

I try to shove the thoughts aside and focus on what's in front of me. She's not my future anymore.

And honestly, I'm just fucking glad I never changed who I was for her. I never expected her to change, either—I accepted that she didn't care for the things I loved. She knew from the start that I spent a lot of time in the woods. It's not like she could claim otherwise.

Jesus, Jackson, stop letting her live rent-free in your head. You deserve someone who accepts you for who you are.

I just hope I can think about something else—because if I don't, it's going to be a long morning. Especially since it's not even daylight yet. My mind won't stop racing, and I've got hours ahead of me.

Chapter 5

Raven

I wake to Rex licking my face as he lies next to me in bed. Rolling over, I look into his green eyes and ask, "Ready to get our day started, Rex?" He just keeps licking any part of my face his tongue can reach.

As I get out of bed, Rex leaps gracefully to the floor and bolts down the stairs. I feel stiff as I stand, so I raise my arms and stretch before slipping on my pink, fluffy slippers. It's still dark outside, but I've always been an early riser. Even if Rex hadn't woken me, I would've been up in the next ten minutes. My internal alarm clock goes off around the same time every morning.

Heading down the stairs, I start thinking about what I want to do today. Maybe Rex and I could try something different. We usually just walk in the woods behind the house on Saturday mornings. But as a few ideas float through my mind, I settle on one.

Today, we'll check out the farmer's market they set up on Saturday mornings. Every Friday after work, I see them putting up tents across the street from the school, in the church parking lot.

Padding into the kitchen, I start a cup of coffee in my Halloween mug. Rex waits by the pantry, tail nub wiggling. I scoop food into his dish and set it down for him before grabbing pumpkin spice creamer from the fridge.

A splash swirls into my coffee, and I take a sip, already feeling more awake.

I drop a bagel into the toaster, set out butter and strawberry jelly, and pull a plate from the cabinet to wait.

When the toaster pops, I pull my bagel out and spread butter across it with a knife. It melts instantly, and I add a layer of homemade jelly. After putting everything away, I carry my coffee and plate to the table and sit down to eat.

I glance out the window just as the sun begins to rise. By the tree line, a few deer graze peacefully in the grass. Definitely not the view I had in the city. Thank God I don't live there anymore.

Sometimes, when Rex and I walk the trails, we catch glimpses of them in the woods. I love watching them so much that I ordered a deer feeder—along with a few bird feeders. When I picked it up, I stopped by the local shop in town to buy bags of corn and birdseed to keep them filled.

Now, the same group of deer visits every morning and evening, stopping by for the corn I put out.

After setting up the bird feeder out back, I bought a bird guide so I could identify the different species showing up in the yard. Every time I spot a new one, I post it in the local birding group on Facebook. I've seen so many already—different kinds of woodpeckers, bright little finches, and even an eagle once.

I eventually picked up a pair of binoculars for bird-watching while sitting in my gazebo, which has become my favorite little escape outside the house. It's quiet, calm, and entirely mine—a happy place where time seems to slow down.

A notification goes off on my phone. I pick it up from the table and see a text from my sister, Hannah.

Hannah: Hey, sis! Are you up for a visitor today?

Hannah: Henry is taking the kids fishing. I would like to see your new place today.

Raven: Sure!

Raven: Rex and I were going to head into town here in a bit to walk around the farmer's market, and I can wait until you get here to ride over there with us.

Hannah: Ok, sounds like fun!

Hannah: I will leave my house here in a few minutes.

My first visit from a family member—of course, it had to be my sister. We've always been close, but since I moved out here, I've actually heard from her more often than when I lived in the city.

I wonder what she'll think of River Valley, this little town tucked away in the middle of nowhere—and of the house I bought that feels even more remote. It'll be nice to spend time with someone other than Rex for a change.

I've made a few friends at work, but outside of work, we mostly just text. They've invited me out a few times, and I keep saying I'm still unpacking and enjoying all the free time I've gained since moving here. Which is partly true. But honestly, I think I've just been savoring the quiet.

A few weeks after I started my new job, one of the teachers—Dean Wilton—asked me out on a date. I told him I wasn't looking to get into a relationship right now, but I did say I'd be open to being friends. Ever since we exchanged numbers, he's been texting me nearly every day.

I'm not going to lie—he's extremely handsome. He always shows up in black slacks and a short-sleeve button-up shirt that fits just right across his biceps. His black-framed glasses frame those dark blue eyes, and he has a habit of running his fingers through his curly, dirty blonde hair. He keeps his beard clean-shaven but leaves a mustache. Usually, I'm not a fan—most guys' mustaches feel rough when you kiss them—but Dean's looks soft, just like his hair.

I'd be lying if I said the thought hadn't crossed my mind—maybe I *do* want to go out with him, even though I told him no. Maybe next time, I'll say yes.

I really enjoy talking to him. He keeps me in the loop on all the local and school gossip, and believe me—there's plenty of it. It doesn't matter whether you live in a small town, or the middle of nowhere with only a handful of neighbors—there's always going to be gossip. Dean's a bit of a flirt, especially with some of the other teachers and staff. Maybe I'm overthinking it, but it felt nice to be the one he asked out. Still, I can't help but wonder—does he text any of our coworkers as much as he texts me?

If he does, maybe I should steer clear. I'm not ready for a relationship—not yet. Right now, I just want to make some friends and ease back into dating, maybe a year or two from now.

After I finished eating, I sat at the table for a few more minutes, watching the deer slowly disappear back into the woods. Once they were gone, I picked up my plate and coffee mug, set them on the counter, then opened the dishwasher and loaded them in.

Back at the table, I pick up my phone and notice a new text message notification. I can't help but smile when I see who it's from.

Should I ask if his ears were burning? I probably shouldn't. I don't want to give him the wrong idea.

> Dean Wilton: Good morning, beautiful!

> Dean Wilton: What are you up to today?

Smiling as I roll my eyes after I read his text. Once again, the thought runs through my mind. Does he tell all of his friends who are girls they are beautiful, or is it just me?

> Raven: Good morning! My sister is coming to town, and we are going to walk around the farmers' market with Rex.

> Raven: What are you up to today?

I head back upstairs to my room to get dressed. Tossing my phone onto the bed, I walk over to the closet and pull out my gym shoes and a pair of dark blue boot cut jeans. As I sift through hangers in search of a shirt, Rex rushes over with his leash in his mouth, tail wagging with excitement.

He loves going into town and walking around—he knows what's coming.

I slide the hangers along the rack until I spot the sweater I want to wear today: my favorite purple one, the one with little pumpkins and black cats stitched across the front. It's cute, festive, and just cozy enough for a crisp morning like this.

I pull it over my head just as my phone dings from the bed.

> Dean Wilton: That sounds like fun. I was going to see if you wanted to go up there and walk around with me.

> Dean Wilton: I would love to walk around with you ladies if it's alright.

I stand there grinning at Dean's last text. Maybe there *could* be something more between us. Still, I definitely want to take things slow—get to know him better before jumping into a relationship that might fizzle out too quickly.

Grabbing my socks and shoes, I sit on the edge of the bed to put them on. As I lace them up, my mind drifts, imagining what it might be like if Dean and I were more than just coworkers and casual friends.

I imagine us taking turns picking each other up for work, sharing quiet lunches in the teachers' lounge when he's not stuck with lunch duty in the cafeteria. I picture us curled up on the couch, watching our favorite movies, or sipping coffee together in the gazebo on a crisp fall morning.

The thought of being close to him—of him holding me like I mattered, touching me with purpose and tenderness—sent a shiver through me. He strikes me as the kind of man who pays attention, the kind who knows how to make a woman feel wanted.

I'm instantly pulled back to reality when Rex jumps up on the bed and starts licking my cheek. I scrunch up my nose and laugh.

"Hey, boy! You're ready to go, aren't you? Let me finish getting ready—Hannah should be here soon."

At the sound of her name, Rex perks up his ears, then starts bouncing around on the bed like a bunny. Suddenly, he gets a wild burst of energy, zipping around my room before bolting down the stairs like he's running a marathon.

Silly Rex.

I finish lacing up my gym shoes and pick up my phone to check if I've missed any messages from Hannah. Just as I'm unlocking the screen, I hear a car door shut outside my bedroom window. Peeking through the curtains—sure enough, there's my sister walking up to the front door.

I hurry downstairs and open the door right as she's about to ring the doorbell. The second it swings open, Hannah throws her arms around me in a tight hug, like we haven't seen each other in years.

"Hey! Ready for some small-town fun?" I ask as she steps inside and starts glancing around the house.

"Yes! I've been dying to get out of the house and have a kid-free day. Henry wasn't too happy about it, but he'll survive. He could use some quality time with the kids—and the dogs."

I grab Rex's leash from the hook by the door and clip it onto his collar. He immediately trots over and sits patiently by the door, waiting to bolt outside. Hannah leans down to pet him.

"You're such a good boy, Rex," she coos with a smile.

"Wow," she says, looking around.

"Love the new place, Raven. The drive out here was so relaxing. How are you liking life out in the boonies?"

"Oh, I love it. It's so peaceful compared to the city. Quiet. Simple. Just what I needed."

I grab my keys from the side table—the one that always seems to collect mail and other random odds and ends—and open the front door. Hannah follows me out as I lock up. We walk to the car, and once I slide into the driver's seat, I turn the key in the ignition.

"Just need to send a quick text before we hit the road," I say, pulling out my phone with a smile.

"So, have you met any guys since you moved here?"

Narrowing my eyes at her, I snap back, "Nope! I'm not looking to date anyone just yet. I have made a few friends at the school. We are actually meeting one of them there."

Hannah shifts in her seat to face me.

"Oh my, it's a *guy*, isn't it? Is he cute? Does he seem interested in you?"

"Hannah! Geez! Yes, he's a guy friend. Yes, he is good-looking, and to answer your last question, he's interested in me, but I told him I wanted to stay friends since I just moved to town."

"Raven Elizabeth, what is wrong with you? It's been 5 years since your relationship with you know who ended. I know the relationship with him was toxic, but I think that it's time to get back into the dating world!"

"Well, I know how long it's been, and I'm not quite ready to date yet. I just moved here; I don't want to seem desperate to find someone or attract too much attention."

Hannah shrugs.

"Yeah, I guess you have a point there. Tell me about this mystery guy who is meeting with us today."

Leaving my driveway, I drive down the road towards town. I roll down the window in the back for Rex before telling Hannah about Dean.

"Well, his name is Dean; he's a teacher at the school."

She leans over the center console, resting her face on her hands as if she is so intrigued with what I have to say about Dean.

"What subject?"

"Shh, let me finish. So anyway, he's a teacher at the school. Freshman biology is what he teaches. Umm, he's a couple of years older than me; he grew up here. He's constantly texting me flirty messages. He is always calling me beautiful and asking me out on dates."

I glance over at my sister because suddenly she is quiet—giving me one of the "Oh my gosh" face, as if she couldn't believe what I just said.

"Well, say something."

"Oh, I thought I would wait for you to finish talking before I proceeded."

Rolling my eyes as she continues to talk.

"But anyway, give the guy a chance to see where things go. Biology sounds like fun, and I'm sure he could give you some private lessons."

"Hannah!"

"What? All I'm saying is give him a chance. If it doesn't work out, I'm sure there's some other country boy out here just waiting for a big-city girl to fall into his lap. And hey—what better way to get over what's his face than to get under someone else? You know what I'm saying?" She says, grinning as she nudges my elbow resting on the center console.

"Maybe; I guess I'll let you give me your opinion of him when we get there."

"You got it. Based on what you told me, I'm sure I will approve of him. I've got your back!"

Tapping my fingers on the steering wheel, I try not to laugh as we roll into town. The closer we got to the farmers' market, the more nervous I felt—wondering what Dean might say, and what Hannah might say *to* Dean.

At the four-way stop, I turn right, heading toward the school, where the market is set up across the street. Turning down a side road I find a spot behind a car already parked along the curb. As soon as I shift into park, Rex starts bouncing around in the back seat, his tail thumping against the upholstery. We don't come into town much, so I'm curious to see how he handles being around this many people.

I open my door and step out, then walk around to the back seat. Rex sits patiently, watching me with those eager eyes. I clip the leash to his collar, and the moment it clicks, he jumps down and tugs me toward the curb, nose already buried in the grass. I pull out my phone and send Dean a quick text.

> Raven: Hey we are here.

His reply came almost immediately.

> Dean Wilton: I see you. Heading your way now.

Hannah, Rex, and I stay where we are, just off the sidewalk, waiting for Dean to make his way over.

Hannah leans toward me, cupping her hand to her mouth.

"Is that him? If so—damn, Raven. You should definitely give him a chance!"

"Shh!" I hiss, eyes wide.

"Hey, ladies!"

Dean calls out, a cheesy grin plastered across his face.

"You must be Hannah—Raven's sister! Nice to meet you. I'm Dean."

Hannah shoots me a mischievous look before turning her attention to him.

Oh dear God, I thought. *What is she going to say?*

"Nice to meet you too, Dean. I heard you're a biology teacher," she said casually.

Dean's face lit up at her words. I could practically see the gears turning in his mind, probably thinking he had a real shot now that he knew I'd been talking about him. Who knows—maybe he's right. My sister approves, and she just met him. But honestly, I barely know the guy. Then again, isn't that the whole point of dating? To *get* to know someone?

"Shall we walk around, ladies?" Dean asks, flashing me a wink.

We stroll through the small farmers' market, which had fewer than ten pop-up tents, each one more charming than the last. Hannah picks up a jar or two of local honey and gives me the whole rundown on how it helps with seasonal allergies. Rex, meanwhile, is soaking up every bit of attention from the kids who run over asking to pet him.

Each time, he'd sit up tall and proud, his little nub of a tail wagging like crazy. Occasionally, he'd give a kid a big, sloppy kiss across the face, which always ended in giggles.

Dean stays close beside me, and every so often, his hand brushes against mine—just lightly, as if testing the waters. I'd glance at him and give him a small smile, then go back to browsing the tables.

At one of the booths, Rex tugs me over and sniffs a table covered in bags of homemade dog treats and a small pile of natural chew bones. An elderly woman sat behind the table in a faded lawn chair that looked like it was from the '90s. She smiles warmly at Rex, then looks up at me, her eyes twinkling.

"Ah, I see your dog found the deer antlers. My grandson finds them out in the woods behind our house, and we cut them up to sell. Dogs love chewing on them. They are pretty expensive in the stores, but we sell them at a reasonable price," the elderly lady says as she looks back down at Rex.

"You should get Rex one of the deer antlers, babe."

I turn my head quickly and give Dean the "What the fuck did you just say" look.

He's grinning from ear to ear, not even acknowledging the look I just gave him.

Did he just call me *babe*?

We aren't together. Did Hannah's words from earlier go straight to his dick? Did he really think that just because I said a few words to my sister that I changed my mind about giving him a chance?

How am I going to let him down easy?

How will I tell him he can't call me babe?

How will I tell him I want to remain friends for a bit longer?

Should I just give in and see where this goes?

Tell him *one* date, and we will go from there.

My mind is just racing with so many thoughts and scenarios. What would one of my favorite female main characters do in this situation? It's been *five* years since I went out on a date with a guy.

Was my previous relationship the reason why I hadn't dated in five years?

It sure was.

I feel Hannah's arm drape around my shoulder, bringing me out of my head, which feels like a tornado is swirling around in it.

"Earth to Raven—did you hear what Dean asked?" Hannah teases, nudging me gently.

"Yeah," I reply, snapping out of my thoughts.

"I think I'll get Rex a deer antler and maybe a bag of the peanut butter bacon treats. How much for those?" I ask, already digging through my purse for my wallet.

"I've got it, sweetheart. It's on me," Dean says smoothly.

I glance at my sister, who was grinning from ear to ear, clearly enjoying every second of this.

Dean pulls out his wallet and hands over some cash once the woman gave him the total. She counts out his change, reaching to hand it back, but he holds up his hand with a kind smile.

"Keep the change."

The woman's eyes light up as she clutches the bills to her chest.

"That's so sweet of you, Dean."

Dean reaches for the bag as she hands it over, shooting me a wink as he says, "Oh, it's no problem, Mrs. Fanning. Thank you for coming out and setting up today. My girl's dog deserves the best treats made in River Valley."

I grab the bag from Dean's hand, and we move on to the next tent, where a table is covered in homemade soaps and lotions. While Hannah and Dean browse and sniff the different scents, I take a moment to scan the small crowd gathered at the market.

As my eyes move through the crowd, I spot Jessie—one of our coworkers from school. She notices me too and starts walking in my direction. But the moment she sees Dean standing between Hannah and me, she pauses.

Her eyes flick between us, her finger subtly pointing back and forth as if silently asking, *Are you two together?*

I shake my head quickly—no.

She visibly relaxes. Her shoulders drop, and the tightness in her expression softens. Then she closes the gap between us.

"Hey, Raven," she greets me, pausing just long enough for Dean to turn and face her. The second he does, her whole face lights up.

"Hey, Dean. What are you two doing here?"

Dean grins, the kind of grin that stretches ear to ear, and without hesitation, wraps an arm around my shoulders.

I tense under the sudden embrace, my heart skipping a beat. The warmth of his arm against me sends a flutter through my chest, and I have to remind myself to breathe.

"Oh, just hanging out with Raven and her sister, Hannah," Dean says casually. "Find anything good, Jessie?"

Jessie lifts a small paper bag and gives it a shake.

"Just some sweet treats," she says with a smile.

Dean begins absentmindedly rubbing small circles on my arm. The light touch sends little tingles across my skin, and while it feels oddly comforting, I feel Jessie watching like a hawk. Her gaze shifts from Dean's hand to his face, calculating.

"So, Dean," she says, her voice suddenly a touch more upbeat, "what are you up to next weekend? My folks finished setting up the cabin for fall. A few of the girls from work are going up there with me."

Oh great. Was she just inviting him, or spelling out that she wanted a cozy weekend hookup? Her tone hinted at more than just s'mores and cider.

Jessie kept going, casually tacking on, "Some of the girls' husbands will be there too. It'll be fun. Would you like to join us?"

Dean slowly lowers his arm from my shoulder, his fingers trailing lightly down my back before falling to his side. I notice Jessie's eyes track every inch of that movement like it means something.

"I don't know, Jessie," Dean says, glancing at me for just a second before turning his attention back to her.

"I think I might already have plans that weekend."

Jessie lets out a soft scoff.

"Oh. Okay. Well, I guess I'll see you two at work on Monday."

"See you then," I offer with a small wave.

"Yeah, take care," Dean adds.

Jessie gave a tight nod and turns on her heel, speed-walking toward the line of parked cars.

I watch her go, a knot forming in my stomach.

Was she mad at me?

Her reaction made it feel like she was. But then again, Dean's arm around me, the way he touched me in front of her—it felt like he wanted her to know he wasn't available.

At least, not to her.

Oh, dear goodness. This is *not* how I wanted things to go when I moved here. I didn't come to River Valley to make enemies.

After making our way past the rest of the vendor tables, we turn around and head back toward my car. As we walk, Hannah is chatting with Dean, completely at ease. I knew the second we got in the car and pulled away, she'd start in with twenty questions—probably beginning with why I hadn't gone on a date with him yet.

Don't get me wrong, Dean's a great guy. He's kind, thoughtful, and clearly interested. But the truth is, I barely know him. And from what I *do* know, we don't seem to have all that much in common. That doesn't mean it couldn't work, but... it's something I can't ignore.

Since Kevin and I broke up years ago, I haven't really considered jumping back into the dating world—at least not seriously. Sure, I still wanted to settle down and start a family someday, but after what I went through with Kevin, trusting another man wasn't something that came easily.

I know not all men are like him. I see healthy, loving relationships all around me all the time. Still, it took me a long time to truly under-stand how much damage that relationship caused. About a year after the breakup, I finally started therapy. That's when I began to untangle everything—what happened, what I tolerated, and how deeply it affected me.

It took multiple sessions before I could fully accept that what had happened wasn't my fault. My therapist helped me see that Kevin had held a toxic level of control over me. He constantly made me feel like no one else would ever love me. He avoided my family at all costs and tried to talk me out of attending every gathering. I thought I was content, but the truth was, I had simply convinced myself to settle.

After the breakup, my family became my biggest support system. They were relieved to have me back, and I finally understood just how isolated I had been. The day our relationship ended might have been the only time he physically hurt me, but the emotional damage he caused was real—and lasting.

So, no, I haven't really dated since then. I needed time. Time to heal. To grow. Maybe now, though... maybe this is the year I give someone a real chance. Who knows—maybe that first someone will be Dean.

I pull out my keys to unlock the car and turn around to face Dean and Hannah as they catch up to Rex and me. My sister slows her pace, grinning like a fool as she mouths, *"Yes, yes!"* and points dramatically at Dean. I roll my eyes and give her a half-smile.

Without saying a word, Hannah walks past Dean, grabs Rex's leash, and hops into the car—clearly giving us a moment alone.

Dean shifts his weight slightly and gives me a soft smile.

"So... I'm really glad I got to hang out with you today. Maybe we could go out to dinner sometime?"

Oh, crap. What do I do? Just go for it? See where it leads? No wonder he told Jessie he might have plans. This was what he meant. Now he was standing there, looking at me with those dark blue eyes, waiting for my answer.

The biggest risk? If it didn't work out, I wasn't sure we could go back to just being friends. But maybe it was time to take a chance.

"Sure," I say, surprising myself.

"How about next Saturday? I'm free all day."

You'd think I just handed him backstage passes to see Taylor Swift. His grin stretches from ear to ear, lighting up his whole face. Behind me, Hannah hoots and hollers like she's in the front row at a concert. I twist around to glare at her, but she only beams and throws me two enthusiastic thumbs up.

Oh, *dear goodness.* I thought the ride home would be full of twenty questions. Now I knew she'd be planning my wedding by the time we hit the first stop sign.

"That sounds perfect," Dean says, stepping a little closer.

"Actually, would you want to do brunch instead of dinner? I know how much you love breakfast. There's a little diner on the outskirts of town—it's cozy, with great food."

"That sounds great. Just let me know what time."

He nods, looking downright giddy. Then he leans in and hugs me. When he pulls back, he presses a gentle kiss to my cheek.

It was just a simple kiss, but I felt it all the way down to my toes. *Why am I smiling like an idiot over a kiss on the cheek?* I hadn't felt this kind of giddiness in a long time. Maybe... just maybe, there was something real brewing between Dean and me after all.

As soon as I climb in, shut the door, and buckle my seatbelt, I close my eyes and draw in a deep breath, exhaling slowly.

"Raven, it's just a date. It's not like you're going to marry the guy next weekend."

We had only been in the car for five minutes, and that's all Hannah had wanted to talk about. At least she hasn't mentioned any wedding plans.

Part of me wished I had just told Dean I wanted to stay friends. There was too much at stake if things didn't work out. But my sister—well, she was over the moon, clearly ecstatic. I knew she worried about my dating life, or rather, my lack of one.

"I know," I sigh.

"I just think maybe I should've stayed in the friend zone with him. If things go south, I don't think we could go back to being just friends."

She shifts in her seat to face me.

"Raven, you need to stay positive. Dean seems like a really nice guy. I'm sure if it doesn't work out, he'd still want to be your friend."

She had a point. I just hoped she was right.

Changing the subject, I ask, "So, did you enjoy the farmers' market?"

"I did! And I love your house—you'll have to give me a full tour when we get home. I love that it's out in the middle of nowhere."

It really was nice having my sister here. I wasn't sure I would've survived going to the market with just Dean. With Hannah there, I didn't feel like Dean's focus was solely on me.

She had good judgment. I mean, she found a good one. Henry might be a little on the quiet side, but he made her happy. That's all that mattered.

I just hoped that if Dean wasn't *the* one for me, then somewhere down the line, I'd find the person I was truly meant to be with.

Chapter 6
Jackson

Well, I'm done hunting for the day. I sat out there all morning waiting for a deer to walk by, and the only thing I saw was a little squirrel jumping through the leaves. For a moment, I thought it was a deer—those little guys may be small, but they sure sound like one crunching through leaves in the woods.

I probably need to take a morning off from deer hunting and go after some of these squirrels instead. Some squirrel dumplings sound pretty tasty on a chilly October day. Sure, deer chili would be better, but I need to actually *shoot* a deer first to make that happen.

I harvested enough deer last year to fill my freezer, but since Gina never ate venison, I had some of it processed and donated to families in need.

I used the last two pounds of meat just last week when I made walking tacos for a lunch carry-in at work. The guys always enjoy it when I bring in dips or walking tacos made with deer meat.

Continuing my walk through the woods toward the path where my truck was parked, I pull out my phone to check for missed calls and texts.

Cell service out here is always spotty. Usually, I don't get signal until I get closer to the wood line. That was another thing that used to get on Gina's nerves whenever I went hunting. She'd get irritated if I didn't text her back right away or call her as soon as she tried reaching me.

I explained to her over and over that cell service out here wasn't reliable, and that I'd respond as soon as a message came through. Sometimes, the text wouldn't even show up on my phone until I was pulling into my driveway. On those days, she'd be so furious she'd give me the cold shoulder for hours. Even when I showed her the timestamp proving when the message finally arrived, she wouldn't budge from her sour mood.

Eventually, I stopped trying to explain. Her attitude over something I couldn't control just became background noise I learned to ignore.

Once I reach my truck, I open the tailgate and set my bow into its case. After securing it with the straps, I close the lid and slid the case into the bed of the truck. I grab my camouflage Crocs from the back seat and set them on the ground so I could take off my muddy boots. After kicking them off, I toss the boots into the truck bed and closed the tailgate.

As I walk around to the driver's side, I heard twigs snapping behind me. I turn slowly—just in time to see the biggest buck I've ever laid eyes on bolt out of the woods and head toward the creek.

Figures.

That monster probably passed right by my tree stand not long after I climbed down. I've followed that deer path before; it runs practically underneath my stand.

Oh well. There's always tomorrow. Maybe I'll stay out longer. With the forecast calling for colder temps, I'll definitely need to pack my portable hand warmer. My gloves do a decent job, but not when I'm constantly taking them off to use my phone. I usually read to help pass the time while I'm up there.

Honestly, I need to invest in a Kindle and one of those clamp-style holders for the tree stand. Maybe even one of those page-turning button remotes. That way, I wouldn't have to take my gloves off at all—just press a button and keep reading while I wait for a buck that hopefully shows up a little earlier next time.

Once I get home, I will go to Amazon and order the Kindle, holder, and page-turner. My buddies would make fun of me when they would see me reading at work. Gina didn't complain; I think it's because it made our time in the bedroom more interesting. Typically I read romance, thrillers and romance-fantasy novels. Actually, I just finished reading a romance-fantasy novel by Madison Renee.

Anyway, I climb into my truck and turn the key, listening to the engine roar to life. Cold air burst through the vents of my truck—making me wish I had a remote start for this bad boy. It's almost paid off, but I have been itching to get me a newer truck.

Shifting into drive, I roll down the path that leads to the main road. My fingers tap against the steering wheel as I glance over at the clock on the dash. It wasn't too early. Maybe I'd swing by Raven's place and introduce myself—seemed neighborly enough.

Last night, before heading to bed, I pulled up her Facebook profile. I just wanted to get an idea of who this Raven was. From what I could tell, she'd moved out here from the big city and worked in the school office. Her profile picture caught my attention right away—a beautiful woman sitting in a gazebo tucked into the woods, her German Shorthaired Pointer resting at her feet.

I kept scrolling through her photos, picking up on little things. She looked close to her sister—there were tons of pictures of the two of them smiling and goofing off. But then I got to some photos from about five years ago. There was this guy in a lot of them—dark hair, green eyes, always with his arm around her. One picture looked like it had been taken at a wedding. Raven wore a formal dress and carried a half-smile on her face that didn't quite reach her eyes. As I looked through more photos, I realized something: in the ones with this guy, she never looked genuinely happy. And I didn't see any pictures of her with her family during that stretch either.

It wasn't until I saw a picture from her college days—standing on bleachers at a football game, surrounded by friends—that I saw a completely unique version of her. That Raven—was smiling wide, radiating pure joy. Beautiful.

Curious, I clicked over to her relationship status.

Single.

I'm not sure why that made me feel relieved. It's not like I know her or have any genuine interest in getting to know her. My only reason for reaching out was to hopefully stay on her good side—maybe even get hunting permission if I played my cards right. That's all.

Still... something about that photo with the guy rubbed me the wrong way. She looked miserable. And even though it's none of my business, it bugged me.

After making a few turns, I found myself on the road Raven and I both lived on. Up ahead, I notice a car pulling into her driveway. I instinctively ease off the gas, curious to see who it was. If she had company over, I didn't want to intrude. It'd be better to stop by when things were quiet—no distractions, just a neighborly introduction—and to ask about deer hunting back in her woods.

But as I got closer, I recognized her. It was Raven stepping out of the driver's side, her sister climbing out on the passenger side, and that German Shorthaired Pointer—Rex—bouncing out of the back seat like he owned the place.

I should've kept driving. I told myself I would if she wasn't alone. But by the time they made it inside the house, I realized I was already turning into her driveway.

Stepping out of my truck, I take a moment. Adjusted my Mossy Oak hat backwards on my head. Smoothed my Camouflaged shirt like that would somehow pull my nerves together. Then I made my way up to the front porch and rang the doorbell, forcing a breath through my lungs while I waited. Wondering whether I should have waited until she was alone or another day.

I could hear laughter behind the door—light, carefree. It made me hesitate again. But then the door opens, and there she was—the same woman from that gazebo photo, only better in real life. Her chocolate-brown eyes under her long lashes met mine, curious and warm. Her dark hair was twisted up into a messy bun, with a few strands falling loose around her cheeks. She wore a purple Halloween sweater—oversized and cozy—but her jeans clung to every curve like they were sewn onto her body.

Damn it, Jackson. You didn't come here to gawk at the woman—you came to introduce yourself and ask for hunting permission.

So why the hell can't you find your words?

"Hi, my name's Jackson," I say, my voice surprisingly steady considering the way her eyes were locking mine in place.

"I heard someone moved in here and figured I'd come introduce myself. I live just down the road—house on the right-hand side with the big red barn." I nod toward it, but couldn't look away from her.

She brushes a loose strand of hair behind her ear, her cheeks blooming a soft pink.

"Oh, I'm Raven. Yeah, I just moved here from the city."

Her smile was gentle, a little shy.

"It's nice to meet you, Jackson. Would you like to come in? My dog Rex is out back, but my sister is about to let him in, and I don't want him running out the front door. He's a—"

"A German Shorthaired Pointer," I say quickly, cutting her off without thinking.

"Yeah, I saw you two getting out of the car when I was driving up the road. Great breed for hunting. Do you hunt?"

Damn. That came out faster than it should have.

Nervous, maybe?

I tried to reel it back as I waited for her response. My brain, on the other hand, was already painting pictures I had no business imagining—Raven in camouflage, crouched beside me in a tree stand, her hair tucked under a cap, cheeks rosy from the cold.

She'd be a cutie in camo—sexy as hell.

But then, her voice brought me back to the present.

"Actually, no," she says, offering a small laugh.

"But I do take him on a lot of walks in the woods."

She glances back toward the house, then turns her gaze back to me, a little more guarded now.

"I'm guessing you do hunt?"

"I do," I say, shifting my weight slightly.

"That's actually the other reason I stopped by—to ask if you'd be okay with me setting up a tree stand in your woods."

I knew the answer before it came. Her smile faltered, her expression thoughtful, lips pressing together.

"Um... I'm not sure I'd like that right now. I spend a lot of time out there. I totally support hunting, don't get me wrong—I just wouldn't want to worry about walking in the woods or fishing in the creek if someone is out there hunting."

She crossed her arms. The movement was subtle, but it told me she wasn't closed off—just careful.

"Do you hunt for sport, or do you actually use the meat?"

Fair question. And I appreciated it.

"I aim for the older bucks, mostly—but yeah, I eat what I harvest. Last year, I filled my freezer and donated the extra to families around town. Made walking tacos for a work lunch not long ago—huge hit."

That earns the hint of a smile. Not a full one, but the kind that crept in without permission. The kind that meant I wasn't striking out just yet.

We stood there in an easy quiet for a moment. The fall breeze rustled the trees around her porch. For a second, I didn't want to leave.

I clear my throat, breaking the silence.

"Well, if you ever change your mind or need anything, don't hesitate to reach out. I'll give you my number—just in case you ever have an emergency or, if you ever need anything."

Her lips curl again, and this time, the smile stays.

I pull one of my cards from my wallet—the ones I hand out to folks who need nuisance animals trapped—and offer it to her.

She took it without much thought and tosses it onto the entryway table just inside her door. I thought she was about to say something, but then her attention snaps toward the back of the house.

The sound of toenails tapping against hardwood hit the air right before a brown and white blur came barreling into view.

"Rex!" she yells, stepping in front of the open door to block him from bolting past me.

That dog was fast, but she caught him by the collar just in time.

And that's when I made the mistake of looking. Not on purpose, at first—it just kind of happened. But the way those jeans hugged her from behind? I swear they were designed by the devil himself.

I wanted to look away. I should've looked away.

Hell, I should be focusing on getting out of here with some hunting permission, not standing here thinking about how her ass would look with a red handprint on it. Jesus, Jackson. Reel it in.

She enjoys the outdoors. She fishes. And she's got that soft, calm energy that just pulls you in without trying. But now is not the time to be imagining her in a fishing shirt and cutoff shorts—knee deep in the creek.

I forced my eyes back up—just in time to realize she was already turning around.

Shit.

I know my eyes didn't move fast enough. She saw. No doubt about it.

Way to go, genius. First visit and you're already caught checking her out like some high school kid seeing a girl in yoga pants for the first time.

Good job, Jackson. Real smooth.

Her sister came to grab Rex, giving me a quick glance before scooping him up like a toddler. I wasn't surprised—those dogs love to be held like babies. My buddy has one, and every photo he posts, that dog's either curled up in his lap or being cradled in his wife's arms like a newborn.

Raven leans against the doorframe, slipping her hands into the back pockets of her jeans. That little move alone almost knocked the wind out of me.

"So..." she says, clicking her tongue.

"Well, it was nice to meet you," I reply, giving her a nod.

"I should get going. Be sure to reach out if you ever need anything."

"Okay—yeah. It was nice to meet you, too. I'll put your number in my phone, in case of an emergency."

We exchange polite smiles before I turn and make my way back to the truck.

Once I was out of sight of the front door, I quickly adjust myself. Glad she didn't notice—thanks to multiple layers of clothing that I had on.

I open the truck door and pause, glancing back at the house.

I remembered wanting to buy that place when the listing went up. It had only been on the market a few days before it disappeared. I was disappointed at the time.

Now?

Now, I think maybe that was a good thing.

Maybe it wasn't meant for me.

Maybe it was meant for her.

Chapter 7

Raven

After I close the front door behind me, I take a slow breath and exhale before stepping into the living room.   There, Rex is curled up on the couch next to Hannah.

I've barely set one foot inside when Hannah looks up and asks, "Who was that?"

Heat flushes my cheeks instantly, and I fight to keep my face from betraying me. Hannah knows me too well—she always does. She can read me like an open book, sensing when I'm being honest and, just as easily, when I'm hiding something. And right now, I'm doing everything I can to avoid talking about the guy who just stood on my porch less than a minute ago.

"Oh, just a guy who lives down the road," I say, trying to sound casual.

"He says he's stopping by to introduce himself, but honestly, I think he mostly wants permission to hunt in my woods."

Hannah's eyebrows shoot up, and she grins mischievously.

"He was cute too. Maybe if things don't work out with Dean, you could get to know him."

Hell, yes—but I wasn't about to admit that out loud. If I did, Hannah would have me knocking on his door asking him out before I even had a second thought.

I picture Jackson again—camo pants and a long-sleeved shirt that hung loose around his torso but hugged his well-defined biceps. You know that TikTok trend where guys wear baseball caps backwards? Yeah, Jackson had a camouflage hat turned just like that. His chestnut hair peeked out beneath the brim, flaring slightly at the edges. His beard looked rugged, but in a good way—not to short, not too long. But long enough to rung your fingers through. He looked like he'd just stepped out of one of those hunting and fishing magazines. And yes, I may have flipped through those magazines a time or two.

I love the outdoors—I may never have been much of a hunter, but fishing has always been my thing. My dad and grandpa took me out when I was five, and I caught so many bluegills it felt like I won the jackpot every time I reeled one in. I've been hooked ever since—and no, I'm not afraid to bait my own hook. Earthworms, minnows—bring it on. I'm not afraid to get a little dirty.

Hannah nudges me in the side, yanking me out of my daydream.

"Sweet baby Jesus, Hannah! I can't go on a date with every man in this town. I just moved here!"

Hannah raises her eyebrows, waiting for me to answer her question. Chewing on my bottom lip, I tell her his name.

"His name is Jackson."

On the way home from the farmers' market, my sister talked nonstop about my date with Dean. She kept telling me what I should wear and what to do on this so-called date. Hannah also tried to tell me what I should do after the date, which included sleeping with Dean. I told her there was no way in hell that I was going to sleep with Dean. Especially after the first date.

In my last relationship, Kevin and I were together for a few months before we slept together. I would have waited a little longer, but Kevin kept telling me that he loved me. He kept telling me that he wanted to show me how much he loved me in the bedroom.

That night, Kevin took my virginity. Even though I had always planned on saving myself for marriage. At the time during my relationship with Kevin, I thought maybe he was the one. I definitely didn't enjoy it. He wasn't gentle; he got off, and I never experienced an orgasm with him. Occasionally, we experimented with toys. Which is the only way I was able to achieve an orgasm with him. And if I never reached an orgasm—he didn't care one bit. Our sex life wasn't the greatest, and looking back now, I regretted sleeping with him. I never really talked to Hannah about my sex life. She just knew I no longer had my V-card.

I really hoped Dean wouldn't expect to have sex on the first date—and if he did, he could forget about getting a second one. Maybe I was in denial, but I truly didn't think Dean would be that kind of guy. Still, the way he had persistently asked me out so many times made me wonder.

I already knew where this conversation about Jackson was heading. Hannah was going to tell me to keep my options open and that I needed to start dating some of the guys here in town.

"Raven, I know you don't want to hear it, but guess what? It's important to keep your options open. You don't want to grow old and alone in this house, do you?"

Ahh! I knew it. I *knew* she would say that—she can be so predictable sometimes. That's one of the many things I love about her.

"I mean, I'll have Rex. He should live another ten or eleven years. If I don't find a man to settle down with, at least I'll have Rexy boy by my side."

I sat down beside my sister, and Rex climbs across the sofa and into my lap. Who knew a fifty-pound dog could act like such a lapdog? He licks my face before settling across my legs. I hoped Rex would live even longer than ten or eleven years. He's the best thing that's happened to me—aside from moving out here. I love spending time with him when I'm home. He's my best friend, other than my sister and my best friend, Violet.

When I look down at Rex, he is staring back at me with his green eyes, wagging his short tail. Hannah sighs and props her feet up on the coffee table.

"Well, I think you should totally give Dean a chance. He seems like a nice guy, Raven. I'm glad you agreed to go on a date with him next weekend."

Groaning I toss my head back on the couch, waiting for this conversation to be over.

Hannah nudges my shoulder before asking, "So, what do you want to do for the rest of the day? I'm not due to head back home until it gets dark. Henry's taking the kids to his parents', and his buddies are coming over for game night—so we can do whatever."

I have been hoping to enjoy the rest of the day with Rex at our favorite spot in the woods, but I'm grateful to have my sister here. No one else has visited me since I moved out here.

"Hey, we could pack some sandwiches and bring coffee or hot chocolate, then walk back to my gazebo," I say as I head into the kitchen.

"We can grab some blankets from the closet and do some birdwatching—or maybe catch a glimpse of some deer."

Hannah jumps off the couch.

"That sounds perfect. I'll make the sandwiches while you grab the blankets."

With the blankets in hand, I grab my Kindle from the coffee table and join Hannah in the kitchen to help with the sandwiches. I brew some coffee, pour it into a large thermos, and grab a couple of mugs from the cabinet. Once everything's ready, we head outside and stroll through the woods to my gazebo.

Rex runs ahead of us, leaping into his bed and chewing on the toy he left out here the other day. I set the blankets on the table next to my cushioned bench seat and pour coffee into our mugs. We both sit down, cover our laps with the blankets, and sip our coffee.

After we sit there for a few minutes, we watch a vibrant red cardinal fly up to my small bird feeder that hangs off my gazebo. Rex notices the bird but only watches it. He holds a staring contest with it until it flies away from the feeder. Part of my gazebo is enclosed, and a small bookshelf holds a few of my favorite books. Since they are my favorites, I keep two copies of each. My signed copies are kept on a shelf in my house.

My sister jumps up from her seat and wanders over to the bookshelf. She pulls out one of the novels and flips it over to read the back cover. It's one of my favorite spicy hockey romances—a sleek black paperback by Siena Trap, the kind of book you don't leave lying around when company's over. A smirk tugs at the corner of her mouth before she slides the book back into it's place.

Her fingers trail lightly across the spines as she browses, pausing now and then to read a title or admire the detail on the spine. Next, she pulls out a Christmas romance by Breanne Bergie, complete with a light blue cover with mistletoe framing the title. After reading that one, I felt I should have been placed on the naughty list—the spice made me want to go out and roll around in the snow to chill myself off. She slides it back into its spot, then turns to face me with one hand on her hip.

"So, have you been to any book signings since you moved here?" She asks, still half-distracted as her eyes continue to scan the shelves.

"You know it! I saw Kate Komula at the little bookstore in town two weeks ago. She writes spicy hockey romance books, too! I had a lovely chat with her about the one I'm reading—she's so sweet. And the ending of her first book? Total twist. I didn't see it coming."

That was one of the things my sister and I had always shared—a deep love for books. Total bookworms, the both of us. Before I moved, we used to go to book signings together, sometimes even dressed in themed outfits just for fun. Occasionally, we'd attend a book club meeting, or buddy-read the same novel and obsess over every twist and swoon-worthy scene.

Now that I've settled out here, maybe we could get back to our buddy reading. I don't plan on attending the book club in the city—especially since I don't live there anymore. Hannah reads her fair share of romance, but she also devours thrillers like candy. I've read a few thrillers here and there, but Amy Tackett's books are the only ones that have truly hooked me. So, I mostly stick to my spicy romance novels—they're my comfort zone.

Hannah pulls a novella by Jessica Booth from the shelf and walks over to sit beside me. I grin. Yes! This is the perfect moment to pull out the Kindle I have tucked snugly in the pocket of my hoodie.

There we are, nestled under warm blankets in the cozy stillness of my gazebo, coffee in hand, surrounded by trees and birdsong—about to do my absolute favorite thing: read.

"Excellent choice, Hannah. If you don't finish it before you head home, you can take it with you—but I expect it back on my shelf within a few days. I don't need you taking it hostage."

"Geez, Raven, don't worry. I'll probably finish it today," she says, grinning.

"I love the cover—it's super cute. Did you know Henry and I did a similar race once? It wasn't on New Year's Eve, though—it was just a random day in July. Christmas in July–themed. It was so much fun."

She pulls the blanket up over her lap and adds, "Now pass me a sandwich while I dive into this book."

I grab two sandwiches from the bag and hand her one. We sit there in comfortable silence, munching on our food while we read. The soft rustle of leaves and distant chirping of birds fill the air—a peaceful soundtrack to our cozy afternoon. Every now and then, one of us giggles or gasps at a plot twist, breaking the quiet with shared amusement.

Rex climbs up and nestles himself between us, his warm body pressing against my side. He always loves to snuggle when I'm out here, and honestly, it helps keep me warm on chilly days like this.

As I turn another page on my Kindle, my thoughts wander back to this morning—specifically, to Jackson showing up at my door.

How could I let him come out here and hunt the creatures I love watching? Don't get me wrong—I understand why deer are hunted. Overpopulation is real, and hunting helps regulate that. But... why *here*? Why my woods? Aren't there other properties he can hunt on? I get that this one would be really convenient for him. It's less than a few minutes down the road.

This is my peaceful place, my refuge. I didn't want to worry about stumbling across him hunting when I'm just trying to walk the trails, read in the gazebo, or if I was fishing in the creek. I know I won't be able to fish much longer unless we get a stretch of warm days, but the cooler weather never stops me from coming out here. Especially not with Rex. He loves it as much as I do.

Jackson seemed like a genuinely nice guy, but part of me couldn't shake the question—was he really being kind, or was it just a strategy to get hunting access to my land?

He'd told me to call if I ever needed anything. Maybe I *will* take him up on that offer—find some small task around the house and see if he shows up. If he doesn't? Then I'll know it was all just an act to get what he wanted. This I will know if he holds true to his word.

It's Monday, and I'm 33 years old today.

My sister can't come over to celebrate—my nieces have a soccer game tonight. And of course, my parents wouldn't dream of missing one of their games, even if it means skipping their own daughter's birthday.

Violet, my best friend, won't be in town until later this month. So, it's just me and Rex tonight—spending my birthday together, alone.

My mom called while I was driving home from work to wish me a happy birthday. Then she quickly added that they were heading to the soccer game. Not once did she mention any plans to celebrate with me, not even a "we'll see you this weekend."

Sure, I'm already planning to stop by on Sunday, but... I don't know. Maybe they'll surprise me then?

Before I moved here, even if we didn't celebrate on the actual day, we always got together the following weekend. Cake. Ice cream. Something.

But I'm not going to get my hopes up. I've learned that lesson the hard way with my parents. Especially now—when they've barely made an effort to come visit me at all.

The first person to text me today—other than my sister Hannah and Violet—is Dean.

Not gonna lie—the closer we get to our date this weekend, the more nervous I get.

I've gone back and forth all day. Should I cancel? Should I come up with an excuse and just get out of it? I could say there's a family emergency—he wouldn't question that. But I know Dean. He'd probably check in later. Ask how things went. Maybe even drive by my place and see that I'm home.

And that's the thing—I don't want to build a spiderweb of lies just to get out of a date I agreed to.

But I also can't shake the urge to cancel it either.

Chapter 8
Jackson

I stopped by Raven's four days ago, and I still can't get her out of my head. The image of her bent over in her jeans imprinted itself on my mind. I was so tempted to compliment her and smack her ass. Hell, her ass in those jeans haunted my dreams. And the fact that she enjoyed the outdoors and fished was a massive turn-on for me. In my 32 years, I have never met another woman other than my sister who enjoyed the outdoors, let alone one who also fished. I wonder if I could get her to go hunting. Not only did I fantasize about this woman out fishing in cut-off shorts, knee-deep in the water. But if she wore camouflage from head to toe and carried a bow or firearm. I don't think I would let her out of my sight. Every morning since the day I met her, I woke up with a hard-on that didn't go away. A few times, I had to jerk off in the shower. She was constantly on my mind. She became a new fantasy that was well out of reach.

I knew it's been a year since my relationship with Gina ended. But was I ready to get back out there and date? Maybe. Or maybe I could just get to know Raven as a friend.

Maybe you should quit fantasizing about her.

Did I want to go out on a date with her? Maybe I will ask her out on a date. Get to know her.

I could take a few days off from hunting. The deer have been traveling at night, so sitting in the tree stand would be pointless.

Shooting deer at night is illegal, so I will have to wait until I get daytime pictures on my trail cameras again. I could always go squirrel hunting, but then I do not want to spook the deer by firing off my twenty-gauge shotgun to kill a few squirrels. Even though I took this whole week off from work to go hunting, I could make the best of it and talk to Raven about going on a date. Even if she doesn't agree to a date, I could always do some much-needed work around the house. Gina had a honey-do list around here somewhere that had some minor repairs I had been meaning to work on since last year. I always put off those tasks until Gina would give me an attitude or shut me out. Her attitude returned to normal once I completed the task, as if nothing was wrong.

I caught myself constantly checking my phone to see if I had a missed call or text from Raven. Feeling disappointed that there were no notifications from her, I sat my phone down on my bed. She has my number, and she knows to call if she ever needs anything. I know part of me wishes she would change her mind about giving me hunting permission. I can't believe she said no. But I also understand why she did.

If I want to see if Raven wants to go on a date, I will need to catch her while she is home. When I gave her my phone number, she didn't give me hers in return. Maybe after I run into town later, I will swing by on my way home to see if she is home.

I look at my phone for what feels like the hundredth time today only to see I had a notification that my Kindle and its accessories were just delivered.

After picking up the package from my front porch, I open it and set up my Kindle. When it was ready to go, I download the next book in the series that I was reading and kick back in my recliner and read.

After a while, I set my Kindle aside and rose to let Nala out through the dog door I'd had installed last year. It was, without a doubt, the best investment I'd ever made. The custom-built door hadn't come cheap, but it gave me peace of mind. I could lock up the house and still give Nala the freedom to slip outside whenever she pleased. I fenced in my backyard last summer, so I knew there would be no chance of her running off, even though she typically stayed within the property lines. Really, the only time Nala would venture outside of the property line was when the mail lady came down the road. Our mail lady always threw Nala a treat if she was out in the front yard. Or when I had a package delivered, she would leave a treat on top of the package.

When I return to the living room, the clock on the wall, catches my eye, and I decide it's time to slip on my shoes and coat before heading out to the truck. I needed to go to the grocery store to pick up a few things; after that, I could swing by Raven's house to ask her about going on a date with me. I kind of hoped she'd say yes. The more I thought about it, the more eager I was to ask her. Raven was special. She enjoyed the outdoors, and I can't help thinking that she moved into the house down the road from me for a reason. It's like she fell into my lap. *Almost literally.*

The drive to the grocery store felt like forever. It was only a ten-minute drive, and the shopping even felt endless. I was trying to kill some time before heading home because I knew Raven would not be home if I left now. The school was dismissing the kids out the doors when I drove by. Knowing the staff didn't leave until around 3:45, I figured I would walk down the rest of the aisles before heading to the checkout line. Maybe I will find something I forgot to put on my grocery list.

As I approach the last aisle in the store, I stop dead in my tracks and back up.

Gina was here at the store.

I had little to no interest in talking to her, let alone looking at her. So I turn around and return to the adjacent aisle, where I had just walked down, to avoid her.

I head to the nearest checkout line and greet the cashier as I load my groceries onto the moving belt. We make small talk while she's scans and bags the items. After a minute goes by, I feel a tap on my shoulder and turn around to see Gina behind me. She looks at me with a disheartened look on her face.

"Hey, Jackson."

I had hoped I could've avoided her. I guess today wasn't going to be my lucky day.

Scoffing, I say, "Gina, what do you want?"

"Oh, Jackson, I'm so sorry for what I did to you. I wasn't happy, but I thought I'd found someone who made me happy. He ended up leaving me for someone else. I messed up. I was in the wrong for what I did."

I roll my eyes as I pull out my wallet, eager to pay and get the hell out of here.

"Um, I don't know what you want me to say. You made me look like a fool. You cheated on me, then just left after dropping that bomb. Sounds like the guy gave you a taste of your own medicine. How does it feel?"

"Jackson, I know I made a huge mistake. If there's any way I can make it up to you, I'll do it."

Shaking my head, I couldn't believe what she was asking me. I stand there in silence while she continues.

"Would you consider giving me a second chance? I'll go to therapy. I'll do whatever you want. Please? I still love you, Jackson."

I'm not sure why she thought she could just waltz back into my life after everything she did.

I watched my best friend Mitch constantly give his woman, Lacy, chance after chance. He even proposed to her, hoping that the last time would be the last. I wished him the best, but I don't think his future is with Lacy—at least, I hope not. He deserves someone who won't do him dirty.

I look back at Gina, who's on the verge of tears. Was she telling the truth—that she still loved me? Or was she just trying to get into my head? Either way, I knew one thing for sure: I didn't love her anymore. Nor was I willing to give her another chance.

"I'm sorry, Gina. I can't. I'm still hurt, and what you did was wrong. I thought I knew you, but I was wrong. Never in a million years did I think you'd go behind my back and start a relationship with another man just because you didn't like what I did in my spare time. Yeah, my time during hunting season was tight, but it's not like we didn't spend time together outside of that."

I pause before adding, "I've actually started talking to someone."

I wasn't really talking to anyone—not seriously—but I had chatted with Raven the other day, and I was definitely interested. So it wasn't the whole truth, but it wasn't a lie either. Regardless, I had no interest in letting Gina back into my life.

"Do I know her? Is she from here?" she asks, searching my eyes, desperate for answers.

"I don't think so, Gina. She just moved here. Goodbye."

I take my change from the cashier, put my bags in the cart, and walk out the door without looking back. How could she think I'd just take her back, just like that? Does she really believe I'd welcome her into my life again after what she did?

I know damn well that if the roles were reversed—if I had been the one who cheated—she would've never given me the time of day, let alone a chance to explain myself.

I put my shopping cart in the corral, grab the bags, and head toward my truck.

As I drive past the school, I notice Raven's car is no longer in the parking lot. Perfect—she should be home by the time I get there. My heart picks up a little. I just hope she says yes.

Chapter 9
Raven

It's been one of those days. I'm so glad to finally be home, lying on my bed.

Today, I had to deal with Dean—he wanted to talk about our upcoming date. Not only did he bring it up, but he also told *everyone* we work with. My co-workers kept coming up to me, saying how nice it was that we were finally going out. Apparently, he's been talking about wanting to date me since the day we met.

And Jessie? I always knew when she was nearby—I could feel her scowl burning into me. She probably hates me for saying Dean and I weren't together that day at the farmer's market. But how the hell was I supposed to know he was going to ask me out? Especially after I told him several times that I just wanted to be friends.

So yeah, I get why Jessie might be pissed. She probably thinks I stole him from her on purpose. I guess in a way I did steal him from her.

Now I'm stuck wondering: what's going to happen at work if things don't work out between me and Dean? I'm the new person in town, and he's lived here his whole life. River Valley is small, and from what I've seen so far, people here really stick together. And they *love* to gossip—especially my co-workers. I swear, I hear more rumors during one lunch break than I used to hear in an entire week back home.

Sighing, I felt Rex jump onto the bed and settle beside me. He always seems to know when I'm having a rough day.

Oh, and as if that weren't enough—guess what else happened today? My mom texted me, asking when I was coming to visit. Then she went on and on about my sister seeing me *and* visiting them all in one weekend—just to rub it in. Her "favorite" daughter. She didn't even try to hide it.

I texted her back and told her I'd come over this Sunday. She probably wonders why I can't make it on Saturday, but I'm not about to tell her I have a date. I told Hannah not to say a word to Mom or Dad. At least I know she can keep a secret—unlike Dean and, well, the rest of the town.

Thank goodness I'm off on Monday. I'm definitely going to need that extra day after this upcoming whirlwind of a weekend.

I hear a vehicle pull into my driveway, but I just continue lying on my bed. It's probably more books I ordered. With the number of books I've been buying lately, I'll need to order another bookshelf soon. After a few minutes, I don't hear the vehicle drive away. Instead, the doorbell rings. I get out of my bed and walk to the window. Oh, my gosh—can this day get any worse? Jackson is here. What the hell does he want now?

I saunter down the stairs and let Rex out the back door before heading to the front to see why Jackson is here. When I open the door, I see that he has already started walking down the steps, heading back to his truck. Rolling my eyes, I figure I must have taken too long to answer—or maybe he thinks I'm not home. He turns around when he hears the door creak open the rest of the way.

Stuffing my hands into my sweatshirt pockets, I ask, "What are you doing here?

He gave me a look as if I'd just driven a knife through his heart.

Maybe I should apologize?

No, I don't think I will—he's probably here to see if I've changed my mind about giving him hunting permission.

"Well, hello to you too," he says, his tone dripping with sarcasm.

He takes off his hat, running a hand through his hair before continuing, "I was stopping by to see if you'd like to have a little picnic at the park with me this Saturday. The weather's supposed to be nice."

He fidgets with the brim of his hat, clearly nervous.

"I hope I didn't catch you at a bad time. I figured I'd just stop by since I don't have your number."

Is he serious? A picnic? Now? Out of nowhere?

Why is he suddenly asking me out? Is this some roundabout way of changing my mind about hunting on my land?

At least I didn't have to come up with an excuse—I already had plans.

"I have a date on Saturday," I say, crossing my arms and leaning against the doorframe.

Raising an eyebrow, Jackson asks, "With who? Is he from around here?"

Oh, my gosh. Is Jackson actually jealous?

I *knew* it—he was totally checking me out the other day when he stopped by.

"Uh, yeah. His name's Dean," I reply.

Jackson scoffs.

"Dean Wilton? Really? That guy's the biggest flirt this town's ever seen."

Wow, I didn't think there was only one Dean in River Valley.

Well... at least I'm not the only one who thinks he's a flirt.

"You know, Dean's a nice guy. I'm actually looking forward to our date."

Jackson throws up his hands.

"Well, don't come crying to me when you realize he flirts with anything with tits. No woman should have to watch her man flirt with other women—it's so disrespectful."

He turns to head down the stairs but looks back over his shoulder.

"I guess enjoy your date with the biggest flirt in town. But Raven—just be careful."

I stand there and watch him climb into his truck. He looks up at me and smirks before putting it in drive and pulling away.

What the heck? He was clearly upset that I was going on a date, yet he tried to act like he cared by telling me to *be careful.* Classic mixed signals.

I close the front door and wander back upstairs, then plop down on my bed.

What a day. Seriously—what's going to happen next?

How could this day *possibly* get any worse?

I pull out my phone and scroll through my contacts until I reach Violet's name. Tapping the message button, I send her a quick text. I wasn't sure if she was too busy to answer a call, but I needed to talk to someone.

> Raven: Hey, I hope you are doing well. Got a second to talk?

Before I can even put my phone down, it buzzes. It's a message from Violet.

That was quick.

I haven't talked to my best friend much since moving here. She was so excited when I told her I was moving out of the city. She has already planned a trip to visit me later this month and during my summer break.

> Violet: Hey Raven! I am doing fantastic. Been keeping busy with work. I have a few minutes. I

> hope it's okay to text. The noise at this airport is
> so loud.

Violet traveled a lot for work. She spent a lot of time in airports and traveling all over the U.S. She worked in the marketing department for Bloopsy, which sold different types of developmental learning toys. When my nieces were younger, Violet always sent me some of the toys they were producing. In return, she asked us to give feedback on how the girls liked the toys. Let's just say my nieces loved playing with the toys that Violet sent me.

> Raven: It's no problem. So I am going on a date
> this weekend.

My phone vibrates before I even put it down.

> Violet: That sounds like fun! What is his name,
> and how hot is he on a scale from 1 to 10?

I shake my head as I text her back.

> Raven: His name is Dean. I work at the school
> with him. I don't know, maybe a 7? I am some-
> what anxious about going on this date with him.
> I don't know him all too well.

> Raven: But I guess that is the whole point of
> dating, right? But my neighbor Jackson warned
> me about him...

> Raven: He said he flirts with anything with tits.

> Violet: Lol! Do you think Jackson is just trying to
> keep you all to himself?

> Violet: Is he cute?

Raven: I don't know, Vi. He just stopped by a little bit ago, asking me out on a date. When I told him about my date with Dean, he seemed jealous, but he also seemed concerned. He is pretty cute. A couple of days ago, he showed up to my house in camouflage. I thought I was going to pass out. I had to hide my feelings that day, though. Hannah was here. She has already been talking to me about my upcoming date with Dean.

Raven: I am going to call him because I want to ask him about Dean. He would be my safer option instead of asking some of the people at work. I don't need people coming back and telling Dean that I am asking questions about him.

Violet: Well, I hope your date goes well. Don't worry too much. If things don't work out with Dean, you could try Jackson. He sounds dreamy.

Violet: But hey, I gotta go. Text me and let me know how your date goes, and I will see you later this month!

Raven: Okie dokie! I will let you know how it goes, and I can't wait to see you later!

I walk over to my dresser and begin searching for the card with Jackson's number on it. I found it buried in a stack of loose papers piled in the corner. Holding the card in my hand, I stare at Jackson's name and the number printed below it.

With a sigh, I sink back onto my bed, holding the card up above me.

After a moment, I grab my phone and add Jackson to my contacts.

Now came the hard part: deciding whether to actually call him.

He *did* say he'd help if I ever needed anything. But would this count as something he'd help with—especially after he just showed up here asking me out?

Chapter 10

Jackson

Well, that conversation didn't go as well as I had hoped. I was really hoping Raven would've say yes. But I just found out she's going on a date with Big Flirt Dean.

Dean and I went to school together, and all he ever did was flirt with the girls in our class. He'd soak up any attention they gave him.

We used to be friends, but once we both started showing interest in girls, I didn't like how he acted around them or how he treated them. We ended up going our separate ways—he started hanging out with the jocks, and our friendship faded.

And of course, now he snags the new girl who just moved here. Hopefully, she'll see what kind of guy he is and won't be interested in a second date.

After I park my truck in the driveway, I grab my groceries and head inside. I set my keys and phone down on the counter. My screen lights up, showing I have a text. I pick up my phone and groan when I see who it's from—the last person I want to hear from: Gina. I don't want to read it, so I set my phone face down on the counter. I'll read it later—or maybe never.

I get all my groceries put away and start making fettucine Alfredo. While the noodles boil on the stove, I feed Nala. The second the lid pops off the food container, I hear her toenails tapping across the hardwood floor. She comes running not just for her food, but anytime I'm eating anything. Hell, she even comes running when I fill my cup with ice.

While I eat my dinner, my mind drifts more to Raven than the food—so much so that my meal goes cold pretty quickly. I keep wishing there were some way to convince her not to go on that date. But would she even believe me? Or would she think I'm just trying to get her to cancel on Dean so she'd go out with me instead? I mean, I'd definitely be the better choice—no doubt about that.

After I finish eating, I set my dirty dishes in the sink and make my way toward the living room to read for a bit. My phone rings before my right foot even clears the kitchen doorway. I swear, if it's Gina, I'm shutting my phone off for the rest of the evening. I need space—I don't want to deal with her right now.

I pick up my phone and see a number I don't recognize. Could it be her? There's only one way to find out. I slide my thumb across the screen to answer.

"Hello?"

"Hey Jackson, it's Raven. You know how you said you'd help me if I needed anything?"

"Yeah, I remember. What's going on?"

What could have happened in the short time since I left? I grab my keys and wallet off the counter and shove them into my pocket as I head toward the front door.

"So don't be mad, okay?" I stop just before reaching the door. There was a brief pause before I ask, "What do you need, Raven?"

I hear her take a deep breath on the other end of the line.

"Well, it's about my date with Dean. Can you tell me more about him?"

What the hell?

What did she want to know about Dean?

Didn't she already know enough?

They work at the same school. She sees him every day.

What exactly is she looking for?

Of course, she'd ask me. I told her to reach out if she ever needed anything. I just didn't think "anything" would mean giving the lowdown on another guy.

I figured she'd ask for help to fix something around the house, maybe an oil change or a brake job—not this. Never in my life has someone called for help just to ask questions about a guy.

But in a small town, everyone knows everything.

This could be my golden opportunity to sabotage their date. I could feed her a bunch of nonsense—embarrassing stuff, lies, things Dean hates that I'd pretend he loves.

Is she really that desperate to impress him? If so, she's wasting her time. She wouldn't need to try so hard with me.

"What do you want to know? His favorite color?" I chuckle, waiting for her response.

"If you're not going to help, I'll just hang up. Maybe I'll call one of the girls from work."

I sit down on the couch and cross my legs.

"No, I'll help. I told you I would. So, you want to know what he likes and dislikes?"

"Yes, Jackson, I'd appreciate it." Relief ripples through her voice, like I'd just agreed to take her final exam for her.

Oh, this might be fun. When the date flops, and she comes back to complain, I'll just say he must've changed since high school.

Technically, I wouldn't be lying—we haven't hung out since then. She can't blame me for not knowing him anymore. Right?

"Well, one thing Dean absolutely loves is the outdoors. He goes on nature walks all the time with his mom. His favorite food is chicken bacon ranch pizza. And he's really into reading."

"Wow, the outdoors and reading? I love both of those things! Do you know what kind of books he likes? I doubt it's romance, but still. At least we have something in common. What doesn't he like?"

Yes, Raven—we have those things in common. If only you knew. Maybe one day you will. Maybe after this date.

"Um, let's see... he doesn't like cats or dogs. He also doesn't like going on first dates without getting something physical out of it. Oh, and he's lactose intolerant."

That one's true—about him expecting something on the first date. I've heard plenty of stories. He really does think he's God's gift to women. But Raven doesn't seem like the type to jump into bed with someone right away.

And thank God for that. I can't stand the thought of him touching her.

Get it together, Jackson—she's not yours.

"What? He doesn't like cats or dogs? That's weird. He seemed to like Rex when we went to the farmer's market last weekend. He even bought him treats and a deer antler. And now that you mention it, he does always put sugar in his coffee at work. I guess that explains the lack of cream. Well, he'll have to forget it if he's expecting anything after our date. I'm not that kind of girl."

Good for you, Raven. Never do anything you're not comfortable with. It makes me feel a little better knowing that this date won't go well. Dean doesn't like to be told no.

"Well, thank you for your help. I'm guessing this isn't what you thought I'd need help with, huh?"

"You're right about that," I reply with a small laugh.

"I figured maybe you'd need something fixed around the house. But it's no problem. I hope your date goes well. I'll talk to you later."

After we say our goodbyes and hung up, a devilish grin crept across my face. This could go one of two ways—either it works out in my favor, or it backfires completely. But it was just too easy to give her all the wrong information. Why should I help Dean win over the girl I want?

Back in school, it never failed—if I liked someone, Dean would magically show interest too. I know that was years ago, and it shouldn't matter now. He's known Raven since the start of the school year. I've only known her for a few days. But when I found out she enjoyed the outdoors, I thought maybe—just maybe—there was a chance to get to know her.

Even if she didn't want to date, I'd be happy just being friends.

Yeah, I'd love something more, but I'd never push myself on anyone.

Sure, I've got my guy friends to do outdoor stuff with, but Raven? She could fit into that world too. I can only imagine how hard it must be to move out here alone.

It hasn't even been a full week since I introduced myself. Jesus, Jackson—get your shit together.

Still... it grates on me. Dean always gets the girl.

I just hope that one day they'll see through him.

Tossing my phone onto the coffee table, I lay back on the couch. Nala trots over, gives me a big slobbery kiss across my face, then climbs up to curl beside my feet.

It's been a day, that's for sure.

Chapter 11
Raven

"You know, Raven, you could practically go in sweats and a t-shirt, and I bet that man would still drool over you," Hannah says through the phone that sits on my dresser.

She insisted on calling me through FaceTime since I sent her multiple pictures of outfits I had picked out for my date this morning with Dean. So, while she was on the phone, I changed into outfits and asked what she thought.

As I take off one outfit to try on the next, she declares, "That one! Do that one, please!"

"But all I have on is a bra and my underwear. I can't go to brunch like this. Pretty sure they would kick me out or point to the sign that says 'no shoes, no shirt, no service.'"

I roll my eyes as Hannah just laughs at me. I pull the next outfit out of the closet, and she just sighs like I am boring her to death.

The corner of my lip tugs into a smile.

I pull on my dark gray sweater that hugs my curves and pull on my skinny jeans. I do a little twirl for Hannah and strike a few poses.

"I think that's the one, Raven. Wear your dark-brown boots with that outfit. Now get in that bathroom and curl your hair, girlfriend. Make sure to use your big curling iron. He can always curl his fingers in your hair to make those curls nice and tight."

"Geez, nothing is happening after this date. I am not one to sleep with a guy after a first date. You should know that by now."

"Well, if you don't sleep with him, you could always have a hot make-out session with him. Besides, maybe after this date, you will realize you have a spark with him. Be sure to take a condom with you, just in case. Remember what Mom taught us?"

"Yes, I remember what Mom taught us. No sex if it's not wrapped up."

Of all the things our mom taught us, that was the one thing that Hannah would always bring up to me when I went out on dates.

"Okay, well, I am going to hop off here. I need to get the kids' breakfast started. Have fun, and be sure to let me know how it went. I will see you tomorrow at Mom and Dad's. Mom said that she is excited to see you."

"Yeah—I will let you know how the date goes tomorrow when I see you. See you tomorrow," I say as I blow her a kiss.

After we both say goodbye, I hit the end button and curl my hair. I don't know why I am so nervous. I see the guy daily at work. Looking down at my phone to see that I have thirty minutes before Dean will be here to pick me up. In the worst-case scenario, this date could go very badly, and we can just go back to being friends, right? And if we don't remain friends, I have the other friends I have made at work.

But wait, what if my other friends make a big deal about our date not going well? Oh no, what have I gotten myself into? After I curl the last bit of my brown hair, I unplug the curling iron and sit it down on the sink to cool. Sliding my brown boots on, I head downstairs to pull my coat off of the hook. I sit on my couch and pick up my Kindle to read until Dean arrives.

I look out of my front window and see a car coming down the driveway. I put my Kindle in my purse—grab my keys off the key hook, and drop them into my purse.

Deep breath in and deep breath out, Raven.

Here I go; hopefully this date goes well.

I open my door just as Dean is walking up the stairs. I turn around to lock my door, and Dean is in my personal space as soon as I turn around. His gaze lingers down on my lips as if he is going to just go for it. Hunger was in his eyes. Like he is ready to take me right then and there. He puts his hand on the door above my head, leaning towards me.

"Good morning, beautiful," he purrs.

"Are you ready for some brunch? I am starving," he asks as he keeps eye contact with my lips.

Hello, my eyes are up here.

"Yes, I am starving!"

I don't know what else to say after that, because he just looks at me like he wants to devour my face.

Offering him a small smile, he grabs my hand and presses a kiss to the back of it—keeping his eyes on me. His mustache brushes against my skin.

It is soft.

He lowers my hand from his mouth and turns while still grasping onto my hand.

This is our first date, and he is already holding my hand. We are only walking to his car. It's not like we are out in public.

What have I gotten myself into?

He walks me to the passenger side of his car and opens the door for me. I slide into the seat and put my purse onto my lap. Closing the door, I watch him do a little jog around the car to get in the driver's seat.

He makes small talk as he drives us into town. And when I say he, that means *Dean* is doing all the talking—about how excited he was that I finally said yes and that he had been counting down to the last second before he could leave to come pick me up.

The drive to the diner feels like we are moving slower than molasses. When we arrive at Lucy's diner on the outskirts of town—he comes around to open my door. He offers me his hand as I get out of his car.

Keeping his hand on the lower part of my back—we walk toward the door. Once we are inside, we are greeted by one of the waitresses, with a name tag that reads: Lacy.

As she smacks the gum around in her mouth, she lets us know we can take a seat and that she will be over to take our orders. Keeping his hand on my lower back, Dean guides me to one of the booths in front of the large window. I sit down first before he slides into the booth on the opposite side. We awkwardly look at one another until I pick up my menu to make it look like I am trying to decide what I am going to order.

"Raven, we both know that you will be getting French toast. That's your favorite breakfast food," Dean retorts as he picks up the menu.

"If you had to choose something else, what would it be?" Dean asks while glancing at the menu.

"I would have to say my second would be sausage biscuits and gravy. And not the canned gravy; it has to be made from scratch."

A rumble of laughter drifts through the air.

"I've never had the canned gravy before—good to know to avoid it," he says, glancing over the menu.

After we decide what we are going to order, Lacy, the waitress, comes over and takes our drink and food orders.

As she is taking Dean's order, she talks to him in a different tone.

Wait, is she flirting with him?

Doesn't she realize that he is on a date with me?

I thought he would shrug her off when he talked back to her, since he was on a date with me. Nope, he is flirting right back at her.

He even gives her a wink before she walks away. Oh, and I watch him as he watches her walk away. His eyes linger on her ass until she disappears behind the counter.

Unbelievable!

I knew he seemed flirty at school, but part of me figured he wouldn't do that on a date. Maybe Jackson was right about Dean. We are here now, so let's see how the rest of this date plays out.

"So, I started reading this romance novel the other day. The author is from Ohio and is one of my favorites."

"Oh, that's nice—so what do you have planned for the rest of the day? I thought about walking around town and going into some of the shops afterward if you wanted to."

"Oh, that sounds like fun. I don't have anything planned for the rest of the day. The only other plan I have for this weekend is visiting my parents. They have been bugging me to come visit ever since I moved here. It's only a forty-five-minute drive; I don't understand why they cannot come my way. The road goes both ways. Even when I lived in the city, I was always the one to visit them."

"Hmm, yeah, that does not make sense as to why they wouldn't want to visit you. Wouldn't they want to see where their daughter is living?" Dean asks while his eyes scan the dining area around us. It's as if he is looking for something or someone...

"You would think so, but I can't figure out my parents' thought process. Anyway, let's not talk about my parents. I was actually going to see if you would like to go to a book signing next weekend. The little bookshop here in town will have a local author signing books. I have read several of her books and wanted to get a copy of her new book that she just released and get it signed."

He messes with the napkin that is folded around the silverware as he replies, "Oh, I don't know, Raven. Book signings are not my thing. Actually, reading is not my thing either. I prefer to play video games."

Wait, Jackson said he liked to read. Why would Jackson tell me he liked to read? What else did he say that wasn't true? I guess I am about to find out. I have my elbows resting on the table and Dean reaches across the table to take my hand. Does he feel like he has to touch me? I would feel differently about this if he didn't flirt with the waitress.

"So, do you have any pets?"

He gives me this look as if I am asking him his deepest, darkest secret.

"Um, actually, I don't. I used to have a dog when I was growing up, but I don't really have an interest in having a pet. They are too much work, and it is nice to leave for vacation and not have to worry about who's going to take care of them while I am away."

Hmm, that's interesting. What else did Jackson tell me? Oh, right, that Dean loved the outdoors.

Jackson mentioned that he often went on hikes with his mom. Is he wondering why I am asking these questions one after another? But then again, I am starting to realize that Dean is just full of himself. He seems to enjoy being the center of attention.

"So, do you like to go on hikes or walks? I thought about taking Rex to one of the nature reserves in the neighboring town. Rex and I normally just walk through my woods, but it is always nice to venture out somewhere new."

Dean shakes his head.

"Actually, no, I hate the outdoors. I don't like having the possibility of running into any snakes or spiderwebs. In fact, I do not like nature one bit."

Well, shoot. I think Jackson told me the complete opposite. Maybe he told me the opposite when he mentioned that Dean gets upset about not getting any action after the first date. I am most definitely not asking him that right now. Guess I will just wait and see what happens after the date is over.

Now I am dreading the rest of this date. Here I was, ready for it to be over, although now I am thinking of every possible way to drag this date out. Going to the shops will definitely buy some extra time.

Hopefully, I will have a plan by then because I do not plan on getting intimate with Dean. After sitting here for a bit, I realized that there was no chemistry between us. If possible, we just need to stay in the friend zone.

"So, how are you liking it here so far? After you sent me your address, I realized that you lived down the road from someone that I went to school with."

Ignoring his first question, I was eager to hear what he had to say about Jackson. I clearly know who he is talking about, but I pretend not to know.

"Hmmm, who is that?"

I pick up my drink to take a sip, keen to hear what he has to say about my neighbor.

"Jackson Kenten, I am surprised he has not been down to introduce himself yet. He is obsessed with hunting and is always asking property owners for hunting permission. That's why his girlfriend Gina left him. She started seeing someone else behind his back and left him for the guy. I tried telling him back when we were in school that he was never going to snag a chick if he sat in the woods all the time."

All I can think about is Jackson. Why should someone have to change who they are for someone else? I am sure there is someone out there who would enjoy hunting just as much as he does. And for his ex to cheat on him, I knew exactly how he felt. Not only did Kevin control me with his narcissistic behavior, but occasionally I caught him sneaking off with random women. I was constantly getting myself checked for STDs to make sure he wasn't giving me anything when he wanted to have sex with me.

The day he found out I was getting tested was the day our relationship ended. He accused me of cheating and was so angry that he physically hurt me. I may have escaped the toxic relationship with some bruises, but it was still one of the best days of my life. I took pictures of the bruises as evidence and called for help. A day later, Kevin was booked in the local jail for domestic violence. Eventually, I was able to obtain a restraining order against him. Now, I don't have to worry about Kevin coming within 100 feet of me.

Disgusted, I stare at Dean as he picks up his drink and takes a sip.

How does he have any room to talk about Jackson's relationship?

He flirted with the waitress while we were on our date. I know I have trust issues with men, but that's a red flag right there for me.

"Oh, yeah, Jackson stopped by last week. He seemed like a nice guy. He asked for hunting permission, but I told him no. I didn't want to worry about whether I could go out in my woods if he was out there hunting."

He chuckles, "You go out into your woods? What the hell do you do out there?"

Well, this conversation is definitely going south rather quickly.

"That's where I take Rex on his walks every day. And I have a gazebo out back that I like to sit in and read. It's my go-to place to relax."

Dean looks at me like I just told him that I like to eat real worms in my dirt pudding. He must really hate the outdoors.

Our food arrives, and once again, Lacy, the waitress, and Dean flirt with one another.

It's like I am not here.

She puts her hand on his arm as he compliments her eyes. After she leaves, he digs right into his food, not even looking at me as I just sit there and glare at him. Doesn't he feel the heat of my scowl? When he looks up at me, I look down, avoiding eye contact as I start eating my French toast.

"Maybe we can get ice cream next weekend. This place has excellent ice cream. Every Saturday night, they make their homemade waffle cones." Dean says as he continues to glance around the room, winking at the other women in the diner.

Is he for real?

I feel like such a fool for going on this date with him. I really wish I had listened to Jackson. A date with Jackson would probably have been better. I just thought he was trying to use me to get permission to hunt in my woods.

Maybe I was wrong?

Chapter 12

Raven

After we are done eating, Dean pays for our food, and we walk out to his car. He opens the car door for me and closes it once I am sitting in my seat. He rounds the car and slides into the driver's seat—the biggest grin plastered on his face.

As he is buckling up, he asks if I want to walk around town and go into some of the shops.

Of course, I tell him yes. I wasn't ready to go home. I dreaded how this date was going to end if Dean expected to sleep with me. My mind started to race. How is he going to react when I told him no.

We walk into every store except the bookstore. When we are standing outside the door, Dean shows no interest in going in. So instead of going in by myself, I tell him I don't want to go in.

It doesn't seem to bother him that I don't want to go in, especially after I tell him I like to read. So we end up walking back toward his car to drive back to my house.

After he pulls into my driveway, he puts his car in park. He sits there for a minute before turning to look at me.

"I had a nice time. Hopefully, we can do this again."

I'm not sure what to say because I sure as hell didn't have a good time.

Instead, I lie, "I had a good time as well. Thanks for brunch."

He cuts me off by grabbing my face and crushing our lips together. Here, I thought the guy would have at least waited until he walked me to my front door. Nope, here he is, trying to shove his slimy tongue down my throat. I pull back, and he still has his hands on my face, as if he's afraid to let go. He looks me in the eye like he wants to lean back in and kiss me again.

"Um, Dean, I think we should just be friends."

He lets go of my face and looks disgusted with what I just said.

"Why do you want to be just friends?" He asks as he sits back in his seat. With a confused look on his face, he mutters, "I thought we had something good going on here."

Should I mention the elephant in the room, or in this case, the car? That he was flirting with the waitress on our date, or the fact that he flirts with any woman that he's around? Obviously, he doesn't notice it. Should I tell him we have little in common? I spend a lot of my free time outdoors or reading. He's a video gamer. The only plus side I would see in dating a gamer is I could read while he plays his video games.

But that's not the point.

I want to find someone who enjoys doing the things I do and who will do those things with me. Or at least supports me?

Is that too much to ask?

"I think it would just be best to stay friends since we work together. If things got serious and ended up not working out, it would just make things awkward at work.

"I hope you understand. I wouldn't mind hanging out with you still, but just as friends."

He sits there for a few seconds, absorbing what I just told him. If he tells me he doesn't want to be friends, I can't be mad at him. I would rather be honest with him now instead of leading him on and make him think that there might be some chemistry between us.

His whole mood has shifted; he now looks angry.

"Why did you even agree to go on a date with me, if you all of a sudden feel that we shouldn't date because we work together? We can try to be friends, but I really like you, Raven, and I thought we could have had something special."

He pauses before looking out his car window.

"I think I am going to the cabin with Jessie."

Was he hoping to get a reaction out of me when he said that he was going to go to the cabin? Honestly, I was more than okay with it. I didn't feel like he was going to continue to push me into going on a second date or pressure me into doing something I didn't want to do.

His jaw tightens—removing his dark blue eyes away from me before looking out the front windshield as he says, "I will see you at work next week." I nod and grab the door handle. I pause, opening my mouth to say something, then decide to just get out of the vehicle.

Guess he's not coming to open my door for me. Must have just been an act. Although I did piss him off since I told him we should remain friends. As I walk up the stairs and into my home, Dean is already high-tailing it out of my driveway.

Rex is lying on the couch when I walk into the living room. I sit down beside him and start telling him about the date. He is such a good listener; he never talks back, and he always looks at me when I talk to him. I told him about Jackson telling me things that weren't true about Dean.

You know what?

I think I might have to have a conversation with Jackson. I want to know why he tried to sabotage my date.

When Dean was driving us down the road to my house, I saw Jackson sitting on a swing on his front porch. He never looked up; it looked like he was looking at his phone.

I grab my phone out of my purse and try to call him. It rings but goes to voicemail, so I try a couple more times and still don't get an answer.

I think I will just walk down to his house with Rex, give him a piece of my mind, and find out why he told me lies. Tucking my phone in my back pocket, I walked to the front door to grab Rex's leash off of the hook and hook it onto his collar. We both head out the front door and make our way down the road. As we approach Jackson's house, I notice that he is no longer sitting on the front porch. Luckily, I know he is home because his red pickup truck is parked in the driveway. We walk up to his front door, and before I knock, I look over to see a Kindle sitting on a small wooden table next to his porch swing. Is that Jackson's Kindle? Does he like to read?

Focus, Raven, you're here to yell at him.

But in a way, I guess I should thank him. Apparently, I am just one hot mess when it comes to guys. I am about to press the doorbell when a black lab barks. I guess I didn't need to ring the doorbell; the dog–bell has let Jackson know that someone is at his front door.

My sister and I came up with the dog–bell joke. One day, I was at her house, and we ordered pizza to be delivered. The second the delivery guy pulled into the driveway, all the dogs barked. We laughed and asked who needed a doorbell when we had a dog–bell. The pizza delivery guy probably thought we were high or on something when he finally made his way to the door. So every time I am greeted by the dog before pushing the doorbell, I think of the dog–bell.

"Nala, hush girl, there's no need to bark."

Right as Jackson tells his dog Nala to stop barking, he walks into the hallway and sees me through the screen door.

"Raven, what are you doing here? Is everything alright?"

He pulls his phone from his pocket and says, "Shit. I didn't know that you had tried to call me."

He looks down to see Rex sitting next to me before looking me over.

Concern flickers across his face.

"No, Jackson, everything is not alright. I just got home from my date. Do you want to guess how it went?"

Jackson raises his hand to rub the back of his neck.

Oh my, I was right!

He tried to sabotage my date with Dean! You have been busted!

"Look, Raven, I—."

I raise my hand to cut him off because I need to get all of this out.

"Look, while I don't appreciate that you tried to sabotage my date with Dean. I felt like the biggest fool when I asked him to go to a book signing and a walk at the nature reserve. I am very upset with you, but in a way, I guess I should be thanking you."

Putting my hands on my hips, I continue, "I guess what I am trying to say is that if I didn't bring up any of those lies that you told me, I would have never known that Dean and I didn't have anything in common. I should have listened to you about him being the biggest flirt. I know he flirts with our coworkers at work, but for him to flirt with the waitress in front of me just proved what kind of man he really is. And I am going to guess that when you mentioned that he likes to get action after the date, it was to warn me. I can only imagine what he wanted to do to me after he kissed me in my driveway."

Jackson looks like he is ready to punch someone.

"Are you okay? What did he try to do to you? I will go kick his ass if you want me to."

I shake my head, "No, I don't need you to go kick his ass. After he tried shoving his tongue down my throat, I pushed him away. I then told him that we should remain friends since we work together. I gave him the excuse that if things got serious and then didn't work out, things would just be too awkward at work."

Jackson looks down at the ground before looking back up at me. He asks, "How did he take that? Dean has never been the guy to get denied by a woman. So I can only imagine that he didn't take it well."

"He didn't take it well at all. Let's just say I saw a new side of him that I was not quite fond of. He acted like I embarrassed him by telling him I just wanted to stay friends. Oh, and Jackson, don't ever lie to me again. I already have trust issues, and I was hoping that when you helped me the other day that it meant I could trust you. Instead I feel like we took two steps back."

Not giving Jackson a chance to speak, Rex and I turn around and walk down the porch steps towards the road to head back home.

I never looked back to see if Jackson was still standing there on his front porch. Just when I thought we were going to be friends, it went up in smoke after I found out that he was trying to sabotage my date. But was he really trying to sabotage it? His false information helped me realize that Dean and I had nothing in common, and I also learned that Dean wasn't respectful to any ladies unless it benefited him.

Chapter 13
Raven

"Okay, spill, how did the date go?" Hannah asks as soon as she gets into the passenger seat of my car.

Since Mom forgot to add Parmesan cheese to her grocery order, Hannah volunteered us to go to the store to get some since I told her I was not talking about my date in front of Mom and Dad.

"Well, there is not much to tell. It didn't go well." I glance over at her in the passenger seat as she adjusts herself in her position to face her body towards me.

"Oh no, you have to at least give me details. Why didn't it go well? He seemed like a nice guy."

I let out a dramatic exhale.

"Yeah, he's nice to all the women," I mumble.

"What was that? Come on, Raven, I had to wait until today to find out how your date went—that you went on yesterday."

"Well, if you must know, we went to brunch. He flirted with the waitress, and all the information that Jackson gave me was false and made me feel like a fool. We don't have anything in common. Oh, and we can't forget him trying to shove his tongue down my throat in my driveway. So when you want to tell me he seemed nice, he was just laying his flirtatious charm on you that day last week."

She covers her mouth as if she is trying not to laugh.

"Wait, you asked Jackson for information about him?" Hannah asks while still trying not to laugh.

"Is that the only thing you heard from that summary of my date? Yes, Jackson gave me his number this past week and told me I could call or text him if I needed help."

I can't believe that's the only thing she heard in the entire sentence.

As if she needs me to clarify, she asks, "So you asked Jackson for help with your date? Didn't you say that he asked you out on a date? And then you go and ask him for help about your date? Don't you think when he says you can call him for help if you need help fixing a leaky faucet or installing something in your house? Not help with your date, Raven."

I fidget with the radio, acting like I am trying to find a new station to listen to. It was probably a bad idea to call Jackson to ask questions about Dean. He probably thought I needed help fixing something, not obtaining information about my date with a guy he despised.

"I can see why it was a bad idea to call Jackson about that, but I barely know Dean outside of work, and I was just really nervous. After my date, I confronted Jackson about trying to sabotage it. I told him that with my trust issues, we took two steps back. I was so furious with him that I left his house after saying the last words. I have never had a man get under my skin and aggravate the crap out of me, especially when his little plan to sabotage my date helped a little. So how can I be frustrated and pleased at the same time with what he did?"

"Oh Raven, I can see where you are confused. I guess you just have to see the positive side of it. At least now you know that you and Dean have little in common."

When we arrive at the store, I pull into a parking spot, and look over towards Hannah as I shift the gear into park.

"You're right. I just felt like a fool the entire time when I was on my date with him."

Hannah grabs my hand and gives it a little squeeze.

"I totally get it. I know Jackson lied to you, but it sounds like he did it only to help you."

She had another good point there.

We climb out of my car and run inside the store. We grab what Mom needs before venturing down the frozen section. I stop in front of the ice cream case and open the door to grab a tub of cookies and cream. After we pay and walk out, we climb back into my car and head toward Mom and Dad's house.

The entire time we were eating dinner, my mom talked about how nice it was to have her whole family home for the day. She just kept telling me that I should visit more often. Not once did she mention that they would visit me. At least my sister doesn't think the same way my mom does. It's not a one-way street. I can't wrap my head around why my parents can't make the trip to visit me. They can drive to visit Hannah and her family, but can't add another fifteen minutes to visit their other daughter. I wonder if they only visit Hannah and her family because Hannah has kids. If I did, would they visit me?

Mom would not let me finish dinner without mentioning the list of suitors she was trying to line up for me. There was no way in hell I would let my mom choose the man that I was going to spend the rest of my life with so that she could get more grandbabies. I wanted to marry a man that I loved, and I wanted someone that loved me for who I was. I wanted a man who would do anything for me and cherish and worship me like I was the best thing in his life. Is that too much to ask? I didn't care that Mom was trying to set me up with a doctor who started attending church with her and my dad. Plus, since our little phone call the other night, I have feared what other men she has talked about me to. Hannah wasn't helping the situation; she tried to contain her composure while covering her face with her glass of wine as Mom rambled about the men she was trying to shove at me.

After eating, the kids beg to play board games with Aunt Raven. They know I won't say no, either. I get into the game just like they do. I am the fun aunt, of course. We played a few board games until it was time for Hannah and Henry to take the kids home and get them ready for bed.

I tell Mom and Dad goodbye as I follow Hannah out the door. I link arms with her as we walk toward my car. Henry is buckling the kids in, giving Hannah and me a moment to talk before we both head home.

"I am glad that you guys came over. I would have dreaded this visit if I had been the only one here having dinner with Mom and Dad. Do you think they will ever come to visit me?"

"I don't know, Raven. I don't understand why they haven't yet either. I am glad we came to dinner as well. I know the kids have been ready to see their Aunt Raven. Maybe during their Thanksgiving break, I will bring the kids over, and we can stay the night at your house. They would love to venture back through your woods."

She hugs me before letting me walk towards my car.

"Yeah, that sounds like fun. I would love to have you guys over, and I know Rex would love that. I will text you this week."

We say our goodbyes, and I hop in my car to drive home.

Chapter 14
Raven

Ten minutes from home, I hear a loud "pop" sound and realize my rear passenger tire had blown.

Great!

I was literally so close to home, and now I am stranded out in the middle of nowhere. The nearest house that I saw looked to be the size of a quarter. Letting off the gas completely, I pull over to the side of the road. Flipping on my hazard lights, I curse under my breath.

Shit.

Of course, this would happen to me.

Frustrated, I shove my car door open, swing my legs around, and rest my elbows on my knees as I run my fingers through my hair, tossing it up into a messy bun on top of my head.

Pushing myself off the seat, I walk around the car—moonlight illuminating the night sky—to check the damage. What's left of my tire is now nothing more than a shredded mess.

I guess I will try to change my tire. That was one of the many life lessons that my dad taught my sister and me. Better to be prepared in case you are stranded and need to change a flat tire. Who knew I would be putting my dad's lesson to good use?

God, I hope I am strong enough to loosen the lug nuts. Eventually, I need to invest in one of those impact guns. That would help get this done in a jiffy. I open my trunk to get out the small jack, the spare tire, and the lug nut wrench. I set everything down next to my car, drop to my hands and knees onto the cold dirt, and place the jack in the right spot to lift my car.

Once I get the jack in place, I try to loosen the lug nuts before jacking up the car. Grunting, I pushed with my entire body, but it's no use. The lug nut doesn't budge. *Really wishing that I had an impact gun right now.*

Standing there for a few seconds, deciding what to do next. I could call someone to see if they could come pick me up or help put the spare on so I can get my car home. Maybe I could call Hannah to see if Henry could help, but they are probably getting the kids ready for bed.

One name comes to mind, but do I want to ask him for help?

He said that I could call him if I needed help.

But—what if he's busy or—doesn't pick up?

I don't want to call Dean; he's the last person I would call. In fact, I think I would rather walk home.

Would one of my other co-workers come to pick me up? Then again, I would hate to call them late at night. It's almost 10:00. Pulling out my cell, I scroll through my contacts and select Jackson's name. At least it's ringing and doesn't go straight to voicemail.

"Raven? Is everything okay?"

Concern laces his voice, and it probably doesn't help that I am calling him this late at night.

"Umm, actually, no, I am about ten minutes from home and stranded on the side of the road with a flat tire. Any way you could help me change the tire or bring me home? I can call and get it towed home in the morning. I just can't wait around for a tow truck tonight. Rex is at home alone."

I hear some shuffling and keys rattling through my phone before I hear a door shut.

"Where are you exactly?"

I put him on speaker-phone and pull up my messenger app.

"I will send you my location because all I know is that I am on the main road that brings you into town."

A rumble of laughter comes through the phone, followed by the sound of his truck starting.

"Okay, I've got the location. I am on my way, Raven. I can stay on the phone with you until I get there if you would like?"

Those last few words made me feel safe, even though I was in the middle of nowhere with a car that couldn't drive me away from danger. The tone of his voice convinces me that he means it.

"Yeah, that would be great, thanks. It is kind of lonely out here on the side of the road, and if someone happens to attack me, then at least someone will know."

I hear a chuckle through the phone.

"Sure, it's no problem. It's important to me to know that you are safe. I want you to feel safe even if you're out in the middle of nowhere alone. We don't have to talk if you don't want to."

Maybe I misjudged him. Maybe he wasn't just out to get hunting permission from me. He seems to care about me. He remains on the line with me, but remains silent. Just him being on the other line helps me feel like I am not alone. The only things that I can hear are the sounds of his turn signal and the soft sound of the radio.

Sitting in my car for the next ten minutes, I think about how my life has been since I moved here. I don't regret moving out here. It was definitely a much-needed change in my life. I love the extra free time I have to do what I want. The life that I lived in the city just seemed miserable the more that I thought about it. The majority of my week was spent in the car or at work. And my weekends always felt consumed by housework or visiting with family. I know jumping back into the dating field probably wasn't the most brilliant idea. But hopefully, since I told Dean I wished to remain friends, that it didn't ruin our friendship completely. But after going on a date with Dean, why was I friends with him? Did I only enjoy talking to him because of the way he spoke to me? Did I fall under his flirtatious spell? I am just glad that even if that friendship crashed and burned, I would still have friends that I have made at work.

I need to visit the bookstore in town and see if they have a book club or know any that meet in town. It's probably best to have friends outside of work, especially since most of my coworker friends like Dean.

I see headlights coming down the road in the direction that I expect Jackson to come from.

I look down at my phone—it has only been five minutes since I had called him. Doubting it could be him already, I broke the silence as a vehicle began to slow, inching closer to where I stood.

"Uh, Jackson, someone's coming down the road... and they're starting to slow down."

Feeling vulnerable as the vehicle gets closer.

"Oh, sorry, Raven, I should have warned you, that's me."

Relief floods through my body—knowing now that it wasn't some random stranger stopping.

Did he speed here?

It takes ten minutes to get home, and he arrived in five?

When Jackson drives past me to turn around, he parks behind my car. Standing there like a deer in headlights, I manage to look down at my phone to end the call before he gets out. The door to his truck swings open with a creak—he steps out and strides toward me, his gaze locked on mine. Keeping his truck running, its headlights cut through the darkness, outshining even the moonlight, illuminating the road past my car.

He starts looking through my trunk, realizing that I had everything he needed and was sitting by my flat tire. He raises his eyebrow and looks up at me.

"You started to change your tire?"

I nod. A smirk crept onto his face.

"Yes, I am not completely helpless, Jackson. I know how to change a tire, but I am not strong enough to get the lug nuts loose."

He chuckles like he is just surprised; I guess it's not every day that you hear about a woman who knows how to change a tire.

I remember shortly after learning this lesson that I used the knowledge. My friend Kayla and I were going to the bowling alley to meet our other friend and her boyfriend. Before leaving the house, my other friend Natalie called to see if I wouldn't mind picking up her boyfriend, who had a flat tire on the side of the road. I agreed to do so and asked where he was stranded. As my friend and I approached his vehicle, we saw him leaning against his car on the side of the road. Kayla and I got out of my car and walked over to his car. I asked if he wanted to put the spare on or tow it later. He said that he was going to try to put the spare on but did not know where his spare tire and changing kit were. At that moment, I felt like a genius. You would think every man would know where to find this stuff and how to change a tire. Instructing him to pop his trunk, I showed him where everything was. Once he pulled everything out, I told him where to put the jack before trying to get the lug nuts loose. It may have taken us 20 minutes to change that tire, since the lug nuts took a bit to get loose. At least he could drive his car to the bowling alley and didn't have to leave his car behind.

Jackson brings me out of my thoughts when he says, "So we can get the spare put on so we don't have to tow your car in the morning, or I can take you home—and can come back out tomorrow and put the spare on so we can take it to the mechanic in town to get a new tire put on."

I am trying to weigh my options promptly. I felt so bad calling him so late on a Sunday night; however, what choice did I have?

"Let's put the spare on. I don't want to take up any of your time tomorrow. I hate that I called you so late for help—I didn't know who else to call."

Jackson walks up to me, leaving only a little room for Jesus. He put his hand under my chin, tilting my head so he could look into my eyes with his ice-blue depths, which glistened in the moonlight.

"Raven, I hope you realize that you can call me anytime. I don't care if it's three o'clock in the morning."

His hand starts to cup my face as he continues, "And never think of yourself as a burden."

Tears pool in my eyes as I lean into his touch before stepping closer to him. He folds his arms around me and rubs small circles on my back. I have always felt like I could never trust a man to hold true to their words. I know Jackson's attempt to sabotage my date did more good for me, and stopping whatever he was doing to drive here tonight to help me realize that he holds true to his words.

When Kevin and I started dating, he made several promises he would never follow through with. Kevin broke me when we were dating. After those first few promises were broken, I would never get my hopes up again when he made another promise.

But with Jackson, he has proved to me just two times that I have called him for help. Not only is he here helping me tonight, but he offers to drive me home and will come back tomorrow to get my car. It still boggles my mind why his ex cheated on him.

I pull away from our embrace and say, "I am ready to go home. We can get my car tomorrow if you're okay with that."

He gently squeezes my arm and says, "Sure, really, I don't mind, Raven. Let's go."

He walks me to the passenger side of his truck and opens the door for me. After he closes the door, he walks over to my car to put the spare and changing kit in my trunk before closing it. Jackson climbs into his truck and buckles his seatbelt. Looking over at me, he gives me a quick smile.

"Ready?"

I nod.

"Okay, let's go home."

I pull out my car keys to lock my car as Jackson pulls off the side of the road heading towards home. During the entire drive to my house, he stays focused and drives the speed limit, allowing me to occasionally glance over at him while his eyes remain fixed on the road. We don't speak as he continues toward my house—the music on the radio filling the silence.

After he shifts his truck into park in my driveway, I realize it took exactly ten minutes to get home. Raising my eyebrow, I ask, "Did you speed when you came to pick me up?"

He turns to look at me and gives me a small smirk.

"Maybe, but not fast enough to get pulled over. Why?"

Why did I want to know? Did I want to know if he was speeding to get to me faster? Or was it because I wanted to know if he only sped so he could fulfill his helping task quickly and get home faster? Part of me was hoping he would get to me faster since I was alone, but I knew I didn't need to get my hopes up.

"I was just wondering. I noticed it took you five minutes to get to me, but ten minutes to get to my house. You didn't have to speed; I felt safe having you on the phone until you got to me."

He runs his hand through his beard and looks around my yard like he's looking for something.

"Raven, I just wanted to get to you as fast as possible, I honestly didn't realize that I was driving that fast. I know I had you on the phone the whole time, but I could not stand the thought of you out there alone. Again, I am sorry if I scared you when I didn't let you know that it was me getting closer."

I move a stray hair behind my ear, feeling grateful, knowing he cared how I felt.

"It's no big deal, Jackson. It made me a little anxious, but I felt safe having you on the phone. Thanks again for coming to get me. And let me know when a good time would be to get my car in the morning."

Before I reach for the door handle, Jackson jumps out of the driver's seat and runs around to open my door.

He helps me down to the ground and leans on the door frame before saying, "Okay, if you want, I will text you in the morning and see what time you want to go. And Raven, I mean it, you are not being a burden. I am happy to help."

I smile at him before telling him that I will see him tomorrow. He doesn't leave my driveway until I am in my house and the door is locked behind me.

Chapter 15
Jackson

I had a hard time falling asleep last night, and getting that call from Raven made me even more alert. For her to call after 9:00 didn't feel right. As soon as she told me what happened, I was already dressed, grabbed my keys—and was headed out the door before she even sent me her location. Knowing there was seemingly no chance of something happening to Raven, I stayed on the phone with her anyway until I physically saw her. With how the world was these days, I was not willing to take a chance of something happening to her.

We didn't talk on the phone while she was waiting for me. But I could hear her breathing periodically through the phone, letting me know she was still there, and that she was safe. It wasn't until she mentioned my speeding that I had no clue I was driving over the speed limit. Getting to Raven was my sole objective; everything else faded into the background. Hell, I don't even remember making sure that I was keeping an eye out for deer. With the rut or deer breeding season being hot and heavy right now, you're more likely to see bucks chasing a doe, and it's not like they stop to look both ways before crossing the street, either.

But after I got back home from dropping her off, I lay awake for hours before drifting off to sleep.

"Okay, Raven, I'll be right there. I'm leaving my driveway now."

Slamming my truck door shut, I turn the key over to start up the engine of my red pickup truck. I can hear her, she's mumbling something to herself while I am driving down the road. I've got my foot on the gas, pushed down to the floorboard. Instead of increasing my speed, my truck slows down.

"What is going on with you?" I ask my truck, knowing damn well that it's not going to respond back.

I start to tap the brake to pull over to look at my truck really quick before proceeding to get to Raven. The second my foot touches the brake, my truck lunges forward. It's as if the pedals have been switched. Every few miles they switch on me, so I am constantly going back and forth between using the gas pedal and the brake pedal.

Tightness forms in my chest realizing that I should be to Raven by now. I'm clearly not. I still have another five minutes.

"Jackson, is that you? Someone is coming."

I feel my heart start to race.

"No, Raven, that's not me. My GPS says I'll be there in five minutes. Get in your car and lock the doors."

But she didn't hear what I just said. Turning up the volume, *I can't hear her breathing anymore. I hear a car door slam shut on the other end. Then I hear someone talking.*

"Jackson, you can turn around. There's someone here to help me. Thanks anyways." She says calmly.

Who the hell is there? Is it someone she knows? I look down at my gps and I am only a mile away. Looking back up at the road, I see a vehicle parked on the opposite side of the road. As I get closer, I still can't tell whose vehicle it is.

When I am less than five feet away my heart drops.

It's the last person I ever wanted to be here.

The last person I wanted Raven to be around.

He locks eyes with me, winking before tossing his head back and fit of laughs rumbles from him. He stretches his arm around Raven's shoulder to bring her in for a hug.

She's been crying.

How in the hell did I not realize that she's been crying on the phone?

She waves me off and says, "You can go home, Jackson. Dean said he can change my tire and take me home."

She looks up at him after she's done talking to me. She looks at Dean like he's the greatest thing that has ever walked the earth. I shift my truck into park. When I go to open my door, it won't budge! I continue to push on my door, watching Raven and Dean kiss on the side of the road. After I try the other door, I resort to beating on the window to get their attention. Now Dean has her shoved up against her car, his hands down her pants as he's kissing her neck. Raven's eyes roll back as she bites her lip.

Fuck.

I need to get to her. He's touching my girl. He messed up their date by flirting with Lacy. He doesn't deserve her. As I continue to yell, feeling so far away, something wet touches my face over and over again. I feel pressure my chest—as if something is sitting on it. Dean looks back at me, opening his mouth. The only sound that comes out of him is a bark. A bark?

When I open my eyes—my body trembles while my heart is trying to calm down. Nala is lying across my chest, licking my face. I am so fucking glad that it was just a nightmare. That nightmare only wanted me to keep Raven close. There was no way in hell that I was going to let Dean anywhere close to her. Well, outside of work at least. I would hope that she would try to avoid him there. I roll over and realize that it's 6:30.

Nala climbs off of me and lies down at my feet. I didn't set an alarm since I am normally an early riser. Thanks to the nightmare I just had, I am up a little earlier than usual.

I check my phone, desperate to see if I had a text from Raven.

Come on, Jackson, she's not going to text you this early. She is probably waiting to text you at a more respectful time so that she doesn't wake you up. Maybe I will text her around 9:00 to let her know I can be ready whenever she is.

Nala gets up and lays her head on the pillow beside me. She puts her paw on my face, letting me know her belly is empty and that she is ready to eat. I push her paw off of my face, and she inches closer and puts the same paw back on my face.

"Okay, Nala, I know you're hungry."

She moves her paw and licks me up the side of my face. Sitting up in bed, I watch Nala make her way downstairs and most likely heading towards the kitchen.

After feeding Nala, she's back asleep in her dog bed. Even though she woke me from a nightmare, she also wanted to let me know it was time for her to eat. The life of a dog, eat, sleep and play.

I return upstairs to take off my pajama pants and boxers so I can get into the shower. As the hot water cascades down my body, I think of Raven. Hugging her last night felt so nice, even though we were in the middle of nowhere. I have never felt so protective of someone like I was with her last night. When I dropped her off and helped her out of my truck, she stared into my eyes like she was waiting for something to happen. Over the past few days, my mind has been on an emotional roller coaster. After hearing that she was going out with Dean, I was in fact jealous that he had taken her from me. I am almost certain she knew it too.

I kept telling myself that she wasn't mine, that I just wished she were. On the morning of her date with Dean, I was on the edge of my seat, waiting for her to return home. I watched them leave her house.

After hours of waiting, my mind ran wild, wondering what they could be doing. Taking her out to eat wouldn't take that long. What else could they be doing? My thoughts instantaneously went to the worst thing they could have been doing. The thoughts of Dean taking Raven to his house and undressing her sickened me.

He didn't deserve her. He's never treated women right unless it was benefiting him. After waiting on my front porch for what seemed like an eternity, I watched them drive by. After seeing Dean pull into her driveway, I went inside my house. I couldn't watch her take him into her home if she decided to do so.

So when she showed up at my house that day to confront me about trying to sabotage her date, I was so fucking relieved that the date didn't go well.

So relieved that she told me there would not be a second date with Dean. I was even more relieved that the only thing he stole from her was a kiss. After she told me he shoved his tongue down her throat, the only thing I could see was red.

Even though she was unhappy that I had lied to her, she thanked me.

She thanked me because she realized Dean was not the guy for her.

I wanted to tell her that "I told you so." But all I wanted to make sure was that she never got hurt. When she told me to never lie to her again—that day I promised I would never do that again to her—even if she didn't hear me say those words when she turned on her heels to go back home; I just hoped that I could earn her trust.

The water in the shower runs cold, bringing me back to reality. Shutting off the water, I reach for a towel to dry off before heading to my room to get dressed for the day.

I saw on Facebook the other day that the small bookstore in town was having a book signing this coming weekend. Maybe I will see if Raven wants to go to it. I don't know whether she has read the author's books or not, but it's always nice to support local indie authors.

I pick up my phone to see that I have a text notification. A smile spreads across my face when I see who it is from.

> Raven: Morning, I am up and ready whenever you are. Just let me know when.

> Jackson: Good morning. I'll be ready to leave here in a few minutes. I'll text you when I walk out to my truck?

> Raven: Sure! Sounds perfect. Thanks again.

I smile as I read her text; it sounds perfect. I get to spend the morning with a gorgeous girl whom I am falling for.

Chapter 16
Jackson

A frown threatens my face when I pull into Raven's driveway to see her sitting on her front porch—waiting for me. When she looks up from her phone, she smiles and I can't help but return one back to her.

Damn, I was a lucky man to be living down the road from this beautiful woman. Before I can get out to open her door, she runs up to my truck and hops in.

"You know you didn't have to wait outside for me. I could have come up to the door to tell you I was here." I say as she buckles her seatbelt.

"I know; I hate to know that people might have to wait for me. So I normally try to be the one waiting for them."

I buckle back up—pull back down the driveway, and start heading towards her car. She's wearing a pair of blue jeans that are faded around the knees that hug all of her curves just right and a red River Valley school sweatshirt. Her hair is tossed up on top of her head in a messy bun, a few stragglers dangle around her face. She doesn't have on a dab of make-up either. And if I am being honest, she doesn't need it. She looks gorgeous without it. She pulls out her purse and rummages through it until she finds what she's looking for. She pulls out a pair of black sunglasses and puts them on, covering those brown eyes that I desperately want to get lost in. Occasionally while we are driving, I look over at her; it looks like her mind is going a mile a minute.

"What is going on in that pretty little head of yours?"

She props her elbow up on the window and leans her head against it.

"Can I ask you something?"

I nod.

"Sure anything? Unless it's about Dean."

She laughs and shoves me in my elbow, that is resting on the center console. I could listen to her laugh every day. Maybe next time I will record it so I can listen to it anytime that I want.

That wouldn't be weird, right?

She looks at me with curiosity before asking, "How did you know that I loved to read?"

I look back at the road, worried about how to answer that question. Is she going to think I am a stalker for looking through her social media? Or will she think I did it to learn more about her?

Tell her the truth.

"Well, I uh—I kind of looked at your photos on your Facebook before coming over to introduce myself. I saw that you have gone to many book signings and seen a lot of pictures of the books you have read. When I came over the other day to ask you out on a date, I was also going to see if you wanted to go to the book signing the following weekend."

She smiles at me.

That has to be a good sign, right?

If she thought I was a creep, I don't think she would be smiling at me. I continue driving, waiting to see what she is going to say next. The ball is in her court now.

"Aww, yeah, I would love to go to the book signing with you. I have one of that author's books and want to get the second book that she just released. I am guessing that you like to read too? I saw a Kindle on your little table next to your porch swing."

Well, thank goodness she doesn't think I am a creep.

"Uh, yeah, I do enjoy reading. I read quite a bit when I am out hunting. It helps pass the time, so I don't get bored twiddling my thumbs or scrolling through social media. You can only look at people's posts for so long until it gets old.

"Actually, I just got that Kindle last week. I used to read on my phone or read physical books. Last week when I ordered the Kindle—I also ordered the page turner and the holder to hook onto my tree stand. That way, when I sit in the tree stand, I don't have to take my gloves off to change the page. Do you have a Kindle holder and a page-turner? If not, I will send you a link for the one that I ordered. The holder should clamp down on your headboard."

Now I feel like I am just rambling. I don't know what it is, but I feel nervous when I am around Raven. It's as if I am afraid that I will say the wrong thing that will send her running. But when I get nervous, I tend to ramble. Focusing on the road ahead of me, I occasionally catch her peeking over at me out of my periphery.

What is she thinking right now?

Does she think it's weird that I enjoy reading—or that I bought a Kindle holder to hook on my tree stand so I can read in the woods?

I can see a non-reader thinking it might be weird.

"I actually have a Kindle holder, well, two holders, both on stands. I keep one in my house and the other out back in my woods."

Curious, I turn to look at her.

"You have one in your woods?"

A smile looms across her face, and her cheeks turn pink before she replies, "yes, I keep it out in the gazebo I had built when I first moved here. I sit out there and read. It's nice to have it on chilly days like today. I wrap myself up in a nice, cozy blanket and turn the page with the page-turner. Those two things were the best inventions ever for readers.

My mom told me that those were so unnecessary. I told her it was the best way to keep my hands and arms warm. Plus, when I use them while I am lying in bed, I don't have to worry about dropping my Kindle on my face or the ground. The wristband for the page-turner was a nice feature, so it doesn't get lost in my sheets."

I let out a laugh. No, I am not laughing at it being ridiculous. I am laughing because I can relate to the whole Kindle falling on my face while sleeping. It's not pleasant to have my Kindle hit my face if I fall asleep while reading. The feeling was like falling out of bed when you really aren't. It startles you, your heartbeat starts racing, so what do you do? You read some more until it happens again. Eventually, you learn your lesson and put your Kindle or book down and go to sleep, or it lands somewhere else without waking you up.

"I might have to get another Kindle holder for my bedroom. I tend to fall asleep with my Kindle still in my hand. And it's not very pleasant when it hits you in the head after you doze off. So—what do you have planned for the rest of the day today?"

I drive past her car and drive the extra distance to turn around in the driveway down the road. I would be lying if I said I was ready for her to leave the passenger seat of my truck. Spending time with her was starting to feel like a necessity—like breathing.

"I actually don't have any plans for the rest of the day other than taking Rex for a walk. If you don't have plans, you and Nala can join us."

I look over at her, the corner of my lips quirks into a smile.

"I would love that."

I shift my truck into park behind her car, and we get out to start working on removing the shredded tire and replacing it with the spare.

I loosened the lug nuts; it took a lot, but eventually I got them loosened. Raven puts the wrench in the jack socket to raise her rear tire into the air. I don't know what it is, but knowing that a woman can change her tire is hot. She may have been unable to loosen the lug nuts, but I had a difficult time getting them loose myself. After getting the tire off the ground just enough, she stands up to kick the bottom of the tire to knock it loose.

How is this girl still single?

I have to keep adjusting myself to keep her from noticing how she affects me. She walks around me to retrieve the spare from the trunk—we didn't want to risk it getting stolen last night. My eyes fixate on her as she bends over, the denim of her jeans tightening around her curves while she reaches into the trunk to grab the spare. I pull off the bad tire and toss it to the side. She hands me the spare, and I line it up with the holes. Raven picked up all the lug nuts and hands them to me one at a time.

Typically, women would just stand to the side while a man did the job, or they would be sobbing their eyes out because they had no clue what to do. Raven, on the other hand, was special. She was helping me get the task done quickly. Although I didn't want to finish this task quickly, at least my time with her today will not end anytime soon. When all the lug nuts are tightened down, I let Raven know it is okay to lower the jack. I toss the old tire in the bed of my truck, and Raven puts the jack and wrench in the trunk of her car.

"Do you feel okay driving with the spare, or do you want to drive my truck, and I'll drive your car to the mechanic?" Her eyebrow raises after I ask her that question. She opens her mouth to say something and then closes it.

"I'm only asking because it feels different driving on a spare and can feel unstable. My truck sits up much higher, but you might feel more comfortable driving it."

She bites her lower lip and looks at my truck.

Shifting to look back at me, she says, "I will drive your truck if you don't mind driving my car. I have never driven on a spare tire before.

"This was the first time I was putting my dad's life lesson to good use. Thanks again."

We walk over to my truck, and I open the door to the driver's seat and let her climb in. She turns the key over, and the engine drums to life. I shut the door, and she lowers the window and smiles at me.

"This feels totally weird, but I think I like this."

She pulls her sunglasses off her head, and she gives me a wink before she covers her eyes. If I hadn't already had feelings for this girl, I would now. Seeing her in the driver's seat of my truck was imprinted in my mind. Would it look weird if I pull my phone out to take a picture? Or would she think that it's hilarious?

"Follow me, and when we get into town, I will have you find a spot along the street. The parking lot at the mechanic's is typically full. After I go inside to drop off your key and tell them we want a new tire put on, I will come find you. Okay?"

She nods, "Okay. You have no idea how much I appreciate this."

I can't help but wonder if there was a deeper meaning to those words.

"Alrighty, let's go," I say with a nod, turning on my heel and making my way toward her car, the gravel on the side of the road crunching beneath my boots as I walk.

Sliding into the driver's seat, I adjust the rearview mirror just enough to catch a glimpse of Raven in my truck, her head is bobbing to the rhythm of the music pulsing through the speakers. I roll the window down, letting the warm breeze mix with the beat of music. My girl is jamming to Gretchen Wilson in my truck. I start her car and don't even have to mess with the radio, because the song blaring in my truck is playing in her car right now. We pull off the side of the road and slowly make our way through town—her back wheel with the spare causing the vehicle to vibrate.

Occasionally, I looked in the mirror to see that she was still singing the words to Gretchen Wilson's *"Here For The Party"*.

No woman has ever driven my truck. They were typically the passenger princess. And come to think of it, no woman has ever asked to drive my truck. I never asked if they wanted to. Knowing that the situation was a little different with Raven, I could see myself telling Raven she could drive my truck anytime she wanted. I could get used to the view of her doing so.

I glance back at her again once the song ended—she seemed relaxed while driving my truck—one hand on the steering wheel and the other hanging out the window. Right then and there, I decided that I was not going to let her get away. Hopefully, no other man will get in my way.

Chapter 17
Raven

I want a truck. Don't get me wrong, I like my little car; it's great on gas and gets me from point A to point B—but I like the feeling of sitting up higher. Jackson has a fancy radio in here, too. When Jackson got into my car, I turned the radio on and found a station playing Gretchen Wilson's *"Here For The Party"*.

Turning the dial, I belted out the words as the bass thumped through Jackson's truck. I knew for a fact that if he rolled down the window in my car that he could hear the music blaring in his truck.

Swaying side to side, I felt downright sexy in his truck. And the look on Jackson's face when I winked at him before putting my sunglasses on just had me melting. He boosted my confidence and made my self-esteem rise through the roof.

As we made our way into town, I could have sworn that I saw him glancing back at me in the rearview mirror a handful of times. If he did, then he got a show of me jamming in his truck. When the next song *"Somethin Bout A Truck"* by Kip Moore came on, I pretended to hold a microphone and sang every word of the song until we reached city limits. The only one I wanted to see me singing was Jackson. I would just be giving the town something else to gossip about. Especially since I was still the new girl in town.

As we approach the mechanic, I watch Jackson park on the street in front of the building. Driving down the road, I pass the mechanic and park along the street. I am glad Jackson is here helping me. I have limited knowledge of cars. So, when he offered to talk to the mechanic about getting a new tire, it was a blessing. The last time I went and got new tires put on my car, the guy talked me into getting the most expensive tires out there when I could have had a cheaper option—that was just as good. The guy kept giving me the runaround when I asked him about the difference in cost. After the new tires were installed, the total cost shocked me. I thought my day was already bad enough after being taken advantage of. But when I got home that evening, Kevin started yelling—blaming me for letting it happen, as if I had asked to be taken advantage of at the tire shop.

Over the past few days, I have realized that Jackson isn't like Kevin. Especially when he offered to drive my car, Kevin would have made me drive my car or told me to find a way home.

Jackson cared and wanted to make sure I drove a vehicle that I was comfortable with. Yeah, his truck and my car were very different, but I don't know if I would have felt comfortable driving my car with the spare on it, especially if something happened on the way to the mechanic.

The light tap on the window startles me. Jackson waits on the passenger side, motioning for me to unlock the door.

Unlocking the door, he climbs into the passenger side and sits down.

"Hey, sorry, I didn't mean to scare you. Before we head to your house, do you mind if we pick up Nala?"

I give him a puzzled look. He wants me to keep driving his truck?

"Sure, you don't want to drive? I can hop in the passenger seat so you can drive your truck."

He shakes his head.

"Nah, I want to be the passenger princess for once, plus I am enjoying the view."

I can feel my cheeks turning red. Covering my mouth, as a small giggle escapes my pursed lips. Never have I heard the term *passenger princess* before. And when he mentioned enjoying the view, did he mean me? Or did he mean being able to look out the window without focusing on the road?

Shifting the gear into drive, I glance over my shoulder and ease onto the road, heading to his place to pick up Nala before going home.

As I drive, he talks about Nala—how she can't stay out of creeks, ponds, or puddles, always running straight into the mess without hesitation. But when it rains? She won't even go outside. And baths are a battle—unless he smears peanut butter on the walls of the tub.

There's something in the way he talks about her—a softness, a smile tucked into every word. It's the kind of love that doesn't need explaining. And I get it. Because that's how I feel about Rex.

I tell him how Rex barged into my life like he was always meant to be part of it. He smiles and says how impressed he was when we showed up at his door the other day—how calm and well-behaved Rex was. Said most German Shorthaired Pointers are wild, always bouncing off the walls.

And hearing that... it does something to me. My heart swells. Rex may not have started his life with me, and it might not have been easy for him in the beginning, but he's mine now. He's gentle. He listens. He's love in its purest form.

And I still can't believe I get to call him mine.

After we pick up Nala, we head down the road toward my house. On the way, he asks where we'll be walking. I tell him we can just go out back, through the woods behind my place. The look he gave me was like I'd handed him the keys to a candy store—pure excitement lighting up his face at the idea of a walk in the woods.

I drive Jackson's truck down my driveway, shift into park, and glance back at Nala, sitting perfectly still in the back seat. She doesn't move until Jackson climbs out, strides around to my side, and opens my door—then hers.

He helps me out of the truck, but instead of simply holding out his hand, he lifts me up and slides me gently down to the ground, my hands resting lightly on his chest. Just as I'm about to pull away, I look up into his eyes. Something unspoken passes between us—a flicker of something real—until Nala breaks it, wagging her tail furiously and kicking up gravel, sending tiny rocks scattering in every direction.

Rex greet us as soon as we step inside my house. He sniffs Nala, and the two of them returns the favor by sniffing each other's behinds. I cover my eyes, laughing.

"Can you imagine if humans greeted each other like dogs do?" Clapping my hand over my mouth, surprised that I'd asked that out loud.

Jackson snickers. Well, at least he thought it was funny.

"You know," he says with a grin, "I can't say I've ever thought about that. But I sure wouldn't want to see humans doing that when they're just meeting someone. Glad I didn't do that when I came over last week."

I gave him a playful shove because of the joke he had just made.

We make our way through the house and out the back door. Rex and Nala bolt toward the woods, stirring up a commotion as they tear through the fallen leaves. It hasn't rained in days, so the dry leaves crunch loudly underfoot as we follow them along the trail.

Jackson points out the deer paths weaving through the woods and stops at a tree with a rough, scraped up patch of bark.

"That's how big bucks mark their territory," he explains. "They scrape the trees to show they're the dominant buck around."

"I'd never noticed it before."

He goes on to say that at this time of year, it's common to see bucks chasing does.

"If you're ever driving and see a doe sprinting across the road, a buck is probably not far behind."

"Good to know, I can only imagine the damage it would cause to my little car."

"You got that right. I always recommend driving under the speed limit, especially at night. And always be aware of your surroundings. If you happen to see eyes light up in the field next to the road, slow down, just in case it's a deer."

As Jackson talks about where he hunts and how many deer he's taken down in the past few years, I can hear the passion in his voice. I can't help but smile at how alive he gets when he talks about it.

We walk down to my gazebo, and I'm eager to show Jackson my little sanctuary. The moment he steps through the doorway, I catch his eyes wandering over the space—taking in the cozy seating area and the small bookshelf holding my collection of favorite reads. A slow smile tugs at the corner of his lips as he moves closer to the bookshelf, clearly appreciating this quiet corner of my world.

I watch his eyes scan the titles of the books on the top shelf before going down to look at the ones on the bottom shelf. He smirks.

"So, from what I can tell from your little collection, you like spicy romance books. But when I looked at this shelf, I noticed this one is a low-spice romance novel."

He pulls the light purple book out from the bookshelf and holds it up for me to see. It's by EM Chandler.

I walk over to where he is standing and take the book from his hands. I brush my fingertips along the title and smile.

"You know, Jackson, this story is beautiful. Yeah, it's low spice, but the male main character loves every bit of the female main character for who she is. He's determined to make sure she knows that, and he is also determined to do whatever it takes to make her smile."

I hand the book back to him so he can slide it back onto the shelf.

As he starts to put the book back in its place, he turns to me and says, "I know. I've read this one on my Kindle the other day. Everyone deserves someone who makes them happy and loves them for who they are."

Who is this guy, and where has he been?

He is exactly right; no one should have to change themselves for someone else.

If they can not accept you for who you are, they aren't worth your time because the person who will accept you for who you are is out there waiting for you.

Reading provided a safe haven after my breakup with Kevin. The men these authors write helped raise my standards of men. And I would be lying to myself if I said that Jackson didn't meet the same standards as the men I read about.

I know he is probably hurting from his past relationship, but I am glad he didn't change for her. I am so happy he didn't change because he probably wouldn't be standing here with me in my gazebo in the middle of my woods, talking to me about books or hunting.

Heck, who knows if he would have come and introduced himself last week if he were still with her. And if he did, would he have just asked for hunting permission and left after I told him no? Would he have offered to help even if he had a woman he went home to every night?

If I had never asked him for help with my shitty date with Dean, I would have probably learned the hard way. And my car would have sat there until I called a tow truck or eventually broke down to call Dean. This man knew what he wanted in life and set his own standards that he would not change for anyone. Why should he? He seemed perfect to me in my eyes.

Chapter 18
Raven

It's been a few days since I last saw Jackson. We've texted here and there, but not as much as I'd hoped. He's sent me a few selfies from his tree stand—some pictures of deer grazing in front of him, and one of his Kindle propped up in the holder attached to the stand.

One of his selfies was adorable. It looked like he'd smeared the black makeup football players wear under their eyes all over his face. When I asked why it looked like a toddler had drawn on his face—he said he smeared it on so he wouldn't have to wear a camouflage face mask on the milder days.

Yesterday, he sent me another photo that had me laughing. At first, it looked like a funky guy sitting in a tree stand. I zoomed in and realized it was a scarecrow—dressed like a hunter. Jackson explained it helps the deer get used to seeing something in the stand, so they're less likely to get spooked when he's actually sitting there.

He said his buddies had just thrown an old camo shirt over the seat, but he thought making a full-blown scarecrow hunter was way more fun. I had to agree—it sounded fun. I even caught myself wondering what the scarecrow's name was.

As if he could read my mind, Jackson texted: *"His name's Billy Bob."*

"Yes, Hannah, I am still planning on having the bonfire later this month. And no, I don't plan on inviting everybody from work."

I tell my sister while driving home. She called me when I was heading home from the hardware store in town. I needed to get some bulbs for my house. Some of the lights kept flickering, letting me know they were about to go out.

"Are you going to invite Jackson?"

Hannah has been asking me questions non-stop about Jackson—since she found out that he came to my rescue the other day. I told her it was no big deal. He told me he would come help me whenever I needed him. She thought it was so sweet that he stayed on the phone with me until he got to where I was stranded. I tried to shrug it off, but she just kept telling me I needed to hold on to Jackson. With all the things that Jackson said and did, she could tell he was one of the good ones.

"I thought about it. That way it's not just you, Henry, Violet and me there. I will have to see if he is hunting that evening. Maybe he could swing by afterwards."

Hannah snickers through the phone. "Maybe he will wear his camouflage there."

"Maybe." Wait, did I just say that out loud? My cheeks heat, and I know that they are turning red. There was no way in hell Hannah was going to let that comment slide.

"I knew it! You do have feelings for him. You need to just tell him, Raven."

"I don't know Hannah. What if he doesn't feel the same? I really enjoy hanging out with him and talking to him."

"All I am saying is that I think you should. But I totally get if you need some extra time. Just don't wait until it's too late."

As I continue to drive down my road towards my house, I look to see if Jackson is home. Maybe I could swing by and see if he wants to go for a walk—or just hang out and talk. I see a few other vehicles parked in Jackson's driveway and see him and another guy lifting a deer into the bed of his truck. A burst of excitement courses through me.

"Hannah, I will call you back later, I am going to swing by Jackson's before I head home."

"Okay, just keep in mind what I said."

When we hang up, I hit my brakes and back up into his driveway. I jump out of my car and walk over to the guys. Jackson is currently posing with the deer—his eyes lock on mine.

"Do you always smile that big with all of your ladies?" I ask as I stand side by side with the guy who is taking the pictures.

Have you ever seen those pictures where the wife shares the image of the guy with the big fish, and the guy's smile is so huge? Then, the wife shares a picture of them on their wedding day, and the guy has a slight smile or a serious face. Jackson's grin that stretched from ear to ear made me think of that.

He laughs.

"My smile grew bigger when I saw you pulling in. I was about to call you to see if you were home." He rests the doe's head back down on the tailgate. "Oh, Raven, these are my friends Mitch and Tanner. Guys, this is my neighbor Raven."

Mitch reaches his hand out to me but then takes it away before saying, "It's nice to meet you, Raven. We have heard a lot about you. I would shake your hand—but I don't think you want blood on you."

Tanner, who was taking pictures of Jackson, extends his hand for me to shake.

"Yes, it is finally nice to meet you, Raven. Jackson talks about you all the time."

I look over at Jackson, whose cheeks are pinkish from his friend's comment about him talking to them about me. And by the look on his face, he doesn't speak a little about me; he talks about me a lot. The butterflies in my stomach flutter, and I feel a little nervous, but it's a happy feeling.

"Well, Tanner, I think we should head out. We will see you later, Jackson. And Raven, we hope to see you again." Mitch gives Jackson a wink before they turn around and get in their vehicles to leave.

Standing in Jackson's driveway, looking at the dead doe in the bed of his truck, he says, "The next stop for this deer is the butcher. Do you want to ride along?"

Smiling, I say, "Sure, I'd love to."

I walk to the side of the truck, where he has my door already open.

Before I climb in, he asks, "Do you want to be the passenger princess today, or do you want to drive?"

I climb into the truck, leaving my legs dangling outside.

"I think I will be the passenger princess today, especially since I don't know where I am going. It's not like I am following someone who's watching me from the rearview mirror today while I sing my heart out."

Did I call him out on him watching me the other day singing while driving his truck?

I sure did; the words just flew out of my mouth.

He smirks.

"Pretty girl, you can drive my truck anytime. Like a GPS, I'll be there to guide you. I am not here to let you crash and burn."

I swing my legs around so he can close the door.

We pull out of his driveway and head to the butcher shop. Jackson tells me about the deer he killed this morning and how long he had to wait until it was in shooting range. He talks about only being able to shoot his bow out to sixty yards—that if the target is really far away, just the slightest movement can cause you to miss what you are trying to shoot.

When we arrive at the butcher shop, Jackson backs his truck bed up next to the garage door. As the garage door opens, a man ducks under the garage door and opens the tailgate.

I stay in the truck while Jackson gets out to drop off his deer. The man waiting for him carries a heavy chain with a hook, the metal clinking softly as he moves. With practiced ease, he pierces the deer's leg and secures the hook in place. The chain rattles as he lets it fall, then he presses a button, and the deer lifts slowly into the air, swaying above the bed of the truck. Once it's suspended, the man takes a saw from the table, its teeth glinting under the harsh light, and cuts away the parts of the legs above the hook. When he's finished, he pushes the carcass into the freezer, the heavy door groaning shut behind it. Meanwhile, Jackson stands at the counter, filling out paperwork. When the man returns, he hands Jackson a receipt, and the two of them exchange a few easy words before Jackson climbs back into the truck beside me.

We head back to Jackson's house to rinse out the bed of his truck before the blood has a chance to dry into the grooves of the truck bed. I stand beside the truck, leaning against the bed rails, my arms folded over the cool metal as I watch him spray the deep crimson streaks from the truck bed floor. The water hits the blood, thinning it into red rivulets that snake across the metal and spill into the grass, soaking into the earth.

"Can I go sit with you sometime?" I ask. It sounded like fun—and honestly, I just wanted to spend more time with Jackson. Who knows, maybe we could even sit together in the woods and read.

I'd been Googling hunting regulations and found out I'd need to complete a hunter's safety course. So, I signed up for the online version and passed it with flying colors. If he said no, I'd accept it—but something told me he'd be all for it.

The only problem?

I didn't own a single piece of hunting gear.

Jackson gave me a look, like I'd just asked him a trick question.

"You want to sit in the woods with me? And go deer hunting?"

I nod.

"Yeah. But I don't have any camouflage... unless I borrow Billy Bob's clothes for the day."

He lets out a chuckle before saying, "My ex-girlfriend's clothes are here. She never wore them—still has the tags on 'em. When she went out with me that one time, we just sat in the box blind, so she didn't need camouflage. I bought the clothes for her two years ago, but I never took them back after she told me she was never stepping foot in the woods with me again."

This ex-girlfriend of his just keeps climbing higher on my shit list.

I looked up camouflage clothing online last night—it's not cheap. If she had no interest in hunting, why didn't he return the clothes?

Did she tell him to return them?

Or maybe... maybe he hoped she'd change her mind. I'm not thrilled about wearing his ex's clothes, but at least she never actually wore them.

"Yeah, that'd be great," I say.

"I browsed online last night but haven't ordered anything yet."

Once Jackson's truck bed is clean and shows no trace of the deer's blood, he hops down and walks over to shut off the water.

"I'll send you the link for the hunter's safety course," he says.

"They offer it online now. Super easy—I took it when I was nine."

I nod, hiding my smile. He's in for a surprise.

"Actually, Jackson, I already took the course and passed. Just let me know when I can go with you."

He stumbles back a step, like I just hit him with a shockwave, then comes over and scoops me up, spinning me around.

"That's awesome, Raven! Not that I doubted you'd pass—I'm just surprised you already took it."

I shrug and smile down at him.

"I figured I'd take it before I even mentioned wanting to go. I would've felt awful if I'd asked to join you and then failed the exam. But I have to admit—it was pretty easy. Especially if a nine-year-old can pass it."

He lowers me to the ground and pulls me into a hug.

His arms tighten around me as he leans in close and whispers, "I don't know why it took you so damn long to fly into my life, but I'm thankful you're finally here."

I follow him up to the house and settle onto the porch swing beside him. The cool October breeze carries a bite, but I can feel Jackson's warmth beside me. I scoot a little closer, just enough that our legs and sides are barely touching.

He notices my shiver, his eyes flicking to mine before he reaches for the blanket on the small table beside the swing. When he drapes it over our legs, his hand lingers, fingers brushing against my thigh as if by accident—but the way his touch trails says otherwise. The blanket traps the warmth between us, but it's his closeness, his deliberate nearness, that steals the breath from my lungs.

I think I'm going to have to get one of these swings for my own front porch someday. But for now, I don't mind coming here to sit on Jackson's.

Something about being near him brings me peace. Like we speak the same language without needing to say a word. Like maybe—just maybe—we're two halves that finally found their way back to each other.

Chapter 19

Raven

"So what is the latest in your dating life, Raven? You and Jackson have been hanging out a lot here lately."

I roll my eyes dramatically while video chatting with my sister.

"Raven, don't you dare roll your eyes at me. You're lucky I don't just randomly show up at your house and interrogate you. It's bad enough that you don't send me daily updates."

"What is there to know? We are friends and have just been hanging out quite a bit. We went to the book signing up in town last weekend and talked about all the books we'd read, along with the ones we have on our TBR. Or do you want to talk about the time that we stayed out late talking on his front porch swing? Or do you want me to give you updates on when he takes me out hunting?"

Her mouth opens, but I quickly cut her off.

"No, Hannah, nothing happened—at least, nothing you'd call exciting. We took our Kindles and sat in the woods, although I saw a few deer walk behind us while we were sitting in the tree stand. It was pretty cool to watch them from the stand instead of from my gazebo or through the window in my backyard."

She looks so disappointed, as if she is hoping for something else to happen between Jackson and me.

"Well, why don't you see if he wants to date you? You two have quite a bit in common, and he likes you. Wasn't he the one who asked if you wanted to go to the book signing?"

She had a point there, but I would not let her think she was in the right. My stubbornness prevented that.

I hear the crunch of tires on my driveway and move to the window to see who it could be. I wasn't expecting Jackson for another thirty minutes—not yet, not this soon.

"Hey Hannah, I've got to go. Someone is here. I'll text you later?"

Sounding annoyed, she says, "Sure, I guess. I expect a full report of your evening with Jackson."

I let out a long exhale.

"Okay, I will text you later with a fully detailed report."

Hitting the end button on my phone, I walk downstairs to see who was knocking at my front door.

I should have looked a little closer at the car pulling in because when I opened the front door, I saw Dean standing on my front porch. I haven't seen Dean much at work. He seemed to be avoiding me. Apparently, just being friends wasn't going to work for him.

I want to ask him why he had been avoiding me, but I couldn't bring myself to spit the words out.

"Hey, Raven, can we talk?" he asks, slurring his words.

Is he drunk?

Why the hell is he here—drunk—wanting to talk to me? He's had plenty of chances to talk at work, especially during lunch.

I step out onto the front porch and pull the door shut behind me.

"Dean, are you drunk? And what are you doing driving like this?"

He doesn't answer. He can't even stand still. His body sways, shifting unsteadily from side to side, as if he's struggling to stay upright.

"I want a second date with you, Raven. We would be so good together, baby."

Is he being serious?

Do women always say "yes" to this man?

Why?

I guide him down the stairs and out to my driveway. All I can think about is how I am going to get this man out of my driveway without him getting back in the car and hurting himself or someone else.

Or worse, killing someone or himself.

"Dean, where's your phone and your keys? I am not letting you drive home drunk."

Walking ahead of him—approaching his car, I feel his clammy hand grasp my arm. He whips me around, slamming me against the side of his car, his weight caging me in as he forces his face into the curve of my neck.

He's definitely drunk. The stench of tequila is hot and heavy on his breath.

I try to squirm out of his grip, but his hard body that is pressed against me is keeping me from moving. He brings his mouth up to my ear and sucks on my earlobe.

"We could be so good together, baby. I think you should give us a chance. Let me show you how much I like you."

I feel his hard cock pressing into my belly as he starts to grind it into me. Feeling sick to my stomach at the feeling of his hard length pressing into me, my mind is racing—wondering how I am going to get out of this situation.

As he tries to run one of his hands up and under my shirt, I knee him in the groin and shove him out of my way. Clearly, I am not fast enough.

He grabs my wrist and yanks me back in front of him—using his other hand to slap me across the face as he shoves me down into the gravel.

He paces back and forth, his glossy eyes filled with hatred as he looks down at me.

"You are such a fucking whore, Raven! I have seen you with him." He spats, raising his hand to point at me.

"You fucking humiliated me. No woman has ever told me no until you."

Well, they need to start telling you no, that's for sure.

"Don't come running to me like his ex-girlfriend did. You will get tired of him being obsessed with hunting."

What did he mean about Jackson's ex-girlfriend running to him?

As I scramble to get to my feet, Dean yanks me up by my hair, a bolt of excruciating pain ripping through my scalp and down my spine. I cry out, but he doesn't stop. He drags me toward his car, each step jarring, disorienting—then slams my back against the side of it, the cold metal biting into my skin through my shirt.

He plasters his mouth onto mine as his other hand tries to snake its way into my pants.

"You see what you do to me, Raven?"

He grinds into me while he keeps yelling, "I tried to move on and sleep with another woman, but I can't seem to get fucking hard. I could have fucked Jessie the other night at her cabin. But it seems I can only get hard when I am alone and thinking of you. You fucking ruined me, Raven. So—I guess we are going to have to get this over with, and hopefully, I can fucking move on. I need to fuck you to get you out of my goddamn system."

The rage in his voice has me so terrified. Feeling paralyzed, unable to move. My heartbeat feels like it's going to beat out of my chest.

Closing my eyes, I have no clue what my next move will be.

However, I know I am not strong enough to fight him off. The pressure of his body against my chest isn't helping my breathing; I can't seem to catch my breath. As he keeps my other arm pinned to the car, I try to push against him, trying to shove him away.

But it's no use.

I am not strong enough.

My vision blurs as tears trail down my cheek and onto Dean's River Valley school sweatshirt, causing the red cotton fabric to turn a darker shade of red.

Feeling defeated, I stop trying to push him away as he continues to put more pressure on me with his chest along with the erection that is being impaled into my stomach.

I only hoped that someone would eventually drive by. Someone had to see. If only Jackson would just look down the road. If only he could have heard my screams.

With the amount of pressure Dean is putting on my chest my breathing becomes restricted. I can't seem to yell for help. I am to the point of giving up as Dean's other hand snakes his way back into my jeans, shoving his fingers down to the center that doesn't ache for him. But he does it anyway because it's what he wants. It doesn't matter what I want.

Dean groans against my neck.

"Fuck. Yes, I can't wait to sink my fucking cock into this pussy. I have been dreaming of it since you moved to town, Raven." He says as I feel his hot thick breath coat my skin.

He brings his hand out and grabs my chin with a grip that I know I won't be able to break free from.

Jerking my face up, he yells, "This could have gone a lot smoother if you didn't fight me. Want to go in your house, or am I going to fuck you against my car?"

Giving it my all, I squirm to get out from between him and his car.

He takes the hand that once gripped my chin and clamps it around my throat, still holding me pinned against his car. His filthy palm presses tighter, cutting off my air. My lungs burn, my vision blurs, and I know in seconds I'll lose consciousness. My strength is gone. I can't fight anymore. He will win. He will take what he wants.

Black spots start to coat my vision from the lack of oxygen.

He crashes his lips onto mine, and snakes his hand back down to my jeans, popping the button. Dean rips the zipper down before wrenching down my jeans, exposing my underwear.

A deep gruntal groan rips from his throat as he dips his fingers in my pussy.

"After I fuck you, Raven, I am going to taste this pussy that will have my cum dripping from it. It's going to be mine," he whispers into my ear.

He brings his hand in front of my face, and he plunges his fingers into his mouth like it's his last meal. He groans as he sucks his fingers before reaching for his jeans.

My body starts to go limp, but the only reason I am still standing is because Dean has me pinned to the car. I feel him unbuttoning his jeans. Now, the only barrier between his cock and me is his boxers. He tugs down his boxers, freeing his cock.

Please, someone help me.

I feel his hand trace my underwear before he tugs it to the side. I close my eyes, wanting this to be over. Unable to fight—unable to breathe.

He's going to get what he wants.

Before my vision goes completely black, the pressure against my neck and chest withdraws.

Gasping for air, I open my eyes to see that Jackson is here; he pulled Dean off of me. I never heard Jackson's truck pull down the driveway, but I am thankful he is here.

Pulling my jeans up, I race towards the steps to my porch and turn around to see Jackson laying punches into Dean.

Parts of my vision blur into black spots from the lack of oxygen, but I force myself through the haze and make it inside the house to grab my phone—desperately needing to call the cops.

By the time the cops arrive, Dean is unconscious—most likely from the amount of alcohol he consumed prior to coming here.

The cops have Jackson and me each give our statements about what happened. When I finish sharing my story, Jackson's face falls, the color draining as heartbreak fills his eyes.

After gathering what they need, the officers tell me someone would be out to tow Dean's car away.

Jackson slips his arm around my waist as the cops walk back to their car, driving off with Dean slumped over in the cruiser's backseat. I lean into Jackson's warmth, and he gently wraps his other arm around me, holding me close. His hand rubs soothing circles on my back, and that quiet comfort was all that I needed for the dam of tears to break free.

If Jackson hadn't shown up when he did, Dean probably would have succeeded in what he threatened to do to me. My body shook with trembling sobs as I clung to him. I lift my eyes to meet his, seeing the deep care shining through his watery gaze, before burying my face against his chest. Jackson was my safe place. When I was with him, I finally felt truly protected.

Chapter 20
Jackson

I was looking forward to seeing Raven this evening. We had planned to sit in the box blind instead of the buddy tree stand. When I walked out of my barn, about to head inside to grab my bow and our hunting clothes, I looked down the road toward Raven's house and spotted a car. I saw a man pushing someone up against it. Squinting, I realized it was Raven.

Acting fast, I jumped into my truck and drove down the road toward her house. As I got closer, I saw it was Dean. The red I saw burst into an inferno.

I tore down the driveway and slammed on the brakes, gravel skidding under my tires, before throwing the truck in park. I shoved the door open and ran toward Dean—who was trying to force himself on Raven.

Her eyes were closed when I ripped him off of her.

What did I do next?

I started beating the shit out of him. How dare he touch her like that? Who the hell does he think he is?

Before I knew it, I had Dean on the ground. The stench of alcohol reeked on his breath as I drove my fists into his face, rage taking over. When I realized he'd gone limp—passed out—I stood up, chest heaving, adrenaline pulsing hard through my veins.

I looked around, searching for Raven. Her body was trembling, shaken from what Dean had just put her through.

Fuck... I should've been here sooner.

I could've stopped him. I could've been here when he showed up.

The sound of sirens grew louder as the cruisers approached Raven's house. When the cops arrived, I stood beside her while one officer dragged Dean off the ground and the other asked for our statements.

After Dean was cuffed and stuffed in the back of the cruiser, and the officer finished taking our statements, they let us know a tow truck was on its way for his car.

Listening to Raven tell them what happened broke my fucking heart. Hearing her voice crack, seeing her hold herself together just enough to get the words out—it gutted me.

All I could think was that if I had just stepped outside a few minutes earlier... maybe I could've stopped all of it.

When the cops pulled out of her driveway, I wrapped my arms around her, silently telling her she was safe now. Tears welled in my eyes as she sobbed into my chest. She looked up at me for a moment before burying her face again, and I held her tighter.

I didn't want to let her go. I wanted to hold on to her forever, to make sure she knew she was safe with me—always.

"Do you want to go inside?" I ask softly.

She nods against my chest.

"If someone needs to talk to the tow truck driver, I'll handle it."

She didn't say anything as we went into her house, except for a few soft sniffles.

"Jackson," she whispers as we step inside, "will you come upstairs with me? I want to get out of these clothes and into the bathtub." Her lip trembles.

"I really don't want to be alone right now."

A tear slips down her cheek. I reach up and gently wipe it away, nodding.

"Of course."

We make our way upstairs, and I tell her I'll hang out in the room—what she calls her reading area slash office—so she could have some privacy.

I settle into her oversized reading chair and pick up the book sitting on the small table next to it. Most of Raven's book collection consists of romance novels, but this one was different—a thriller by a local author. I'd heard of her books but hadn't read any yet. Word is, she's known for her unexpected twists.

I crack open the book and start reading the first chapter while waiting for Raven to finish in the bathroom. The story hooked me quickly. As I kept reading, I pull out my phone and add it to my Kindle—figured I'd support the author and avoid asking Raven if I could borrow her copy. Besides, it's always good to support indie writers.

A few minutes later, I hear the bathroom door open, followed by another door closing. The thought of closing the book crosses my mind, but I keep reading, telling myself I'll stop when Raven finds me.

"I see you found my current read," she says, her voice soft.

I look up from the book. Her damp hair is braided and draped over her right shoulder. She wore black shorts and a baggy T-shirt, casual and comfortable. She walks over and sit beside me in her giant reading chair. Honestly, I'm pretty sure she bought the biggest one they make. I wouldn't be surprised if Rex wandered in and sprawled out on it while she reads.

"Yeah," I say with a smile.

"I didn't know you read thrillers—although I *did* notice you have quite the collection of spicy romance novels in here."

I mentally note what page I'm on and set the book down on the table.

"What can I say? I have a favorite thriller author," she says with a faint smile.

She reaches behind us, grabs a blanket draped over the back of the chair, and lays it across our laps before resting her head on my shoulder. Her damp hair soaks through my T-shirt, but I don't care.

I had planned to tell Raven how I felt about her tonight. But Dean got in the way of that—he hurt the girl I'm falling for.

This isn't something she'll recover from quickly. It'll take time. And I'll be right here, by her side, for as long as she needs me.

"Thank you for being here, Jackson," she whispers.

"I'm sorry for ruining your evening. I know we were planning to go out hunting. If you want to leave and go on your own, I completely understand. I don't want to be the reason you miss out."

After what just happened, I had no plans to go hunting. There was no way I'd be able to sit still in the woods, knowing Raven was here alone—especially after what I saw... and what she told the police.

Hunting could wait.

I was needed here. With Raven. Making sure she felt supported. Making sure she felt *safe*.

"Raven, I have no intention of going hunting tonight," I say gently.

"I'm here for you, and I'll stay as long as you need me. I know Dean won't be showing back up anytime soon, but making sure you feel safe—that's my number one priority."

She lifts her head from my shoulder and looks at me.

"Do you mind staying the night, then?"

I give her a small smile and kiss the top of her forehead.

"Sure. I'll either need to head home to open Nala's dog door or just bring her down here."

I'd do anything for this woman. She made me want to be a better man.

Although we're just friends, she accepts me for exactly who I am. She doesn't try to change me or tell me I should live my life differently.

She sits up and gently lifts my arm, guiding it over her head so she can lean against me again.

"You can bring Nala here," she says softly.

"I'm sure Rex would love that. It might get a little chaotic in the house, but eventually, they'll both want to snuggle with us."

I smile at the thought of our dogs curled up beside us—chaos and all.

I know I'll go get Nala soon, but not just yet. Right now, I want to soak up every moment of peace I can with Raven.

There was only an hour of daylight left, and I figured I would head home to get Nala and a few things so I could stay the night at Raven's.

"Do you want to come with me to get Nala, or do you want to stay here?"

We are still in her reading room, her legs draped over my lap while her head rests against my chest.

"I think I'll be okay. Just lock the door before you leave and knock five times when you get back, so I know it's you," she says, letting out a small giggle that made me feel slightly better about leaving for a short time.

"If you're hungry, I'll call and order pizza on my way to my house." She rubs her belly.

"Pizza sounds great. Pepperoni is my favorite."

I bop her on the nose before standing up.

"You got it—pepperoni pizza coming right up. They take a bit for delivery, but I'll be back before it arrives."

Downstairs and out the door I went, locking it behind me. While driving my truck home, I call to order the pizza.

I quickly gather my things for an overnight bag, grab a small container for Nala's food, and walk back out the door with Nala.

Within ten minutes, Nala and I were back at Raven's. I grab Nala's food and my bag and head into the house. Before I could reach the last step, the door flies open, and Nala runs inside, as if she owns the place. Raven must have been watching out the window, waiting for me to return.

"I thought I was supposed to knock five times," I smirk.

She closes the door as I walk toward her living room to set my bag on the couch.

"I came downstairs to fill my water bottle and saw you pull in, so I figured we could save the knocking for another day."

She spins on her heel and walks toward the kitchen to fill her bottle up.

Since I didn't want to stay long at home, I pull out Nala's food bowl and pour some of her food into it. I hear Raven dumping food into a bowl for Rex in the kitchen. Probably a good idea. I'd never seen a dog sit and watch another dog eat. My buddy always had to feed their dogs at the same time. They would lock themselves in a room with all the food bowls, fill them up, and then set them down in front of each dog. Dogs remind me of kids—if one kid is eating something, the other wants the same.

Returning to the living room, I unzip my overnight bag, grab my gray plaid pajama pants and a t-shirt to change into for the evening. Next, I pull out my Kindle and set it on the coffee table in front of the couch before tossing my bag on the floor next to the couch where I'd most likely be sleeping tonight. Sitting down briefly, I grab my night clothes and head to the downstairs bathroom to change.

When I open the bathroom door to head back to the living room, I see Raven under a blanket on the couch. Only her head is visible because the blanket covers her entire body. She has her Kindle on its stand, reading. Raven looks up when she hears the floor creak as I enter the room. A gentle smile appears on her face.

I grab my bag and put the clothes I'd worn today into it before sitting down next to her on the couch.

"Well, don't you look cozy?"

She pulls the blanket up around her neck and giggles.

"I would share my blanket with you, but then I'd have to unravel myself from it. There's another blanket in the hall closet. I'll bring some pillows down here before we go to bed."

She pushes on the couch pillow next to her.

"These are too soft to sleep on."

Grabbing a blanket out of the closet, I return to the couch. Since I didn't have a Kindle holder like Raven, I couldn't copy her, so I settle for covering my lap and hugging the blanket under my arms.

We just sit there and read; occasionally, she would tell me about the book she was reading. She seems surprised that I was interested in what she is reading, especially when I ask questions or make small jokes about the characters.

After we eat our pizza, we get ready for bed.

Raven heads upstairs to her bedroom, and Nala—the traitor—follows her along with Rex, leaving me downstairs by myself. I flip off the light switch and lay down on the couch.

Instead of closing my eyes to fall asleep, I imagine Raven upstairs in bed with my dog Nala. Wishing I were Nala right now.

What would I give to have Raven in bed next to me, cuddling all night long?

Anything.

My bed has felt empty since Gina left. Nala occasionally lies in bed with me at night but prefers her dog bed in the living room.

Since I didn't feel I would fall asleep soon, I pick my Kindle up off the coffee table and read for a bit. As my eyes start to feel heavy, I set my Kindle down, roll onto my side facing the couch, and fall asleep.

I jolt awake at the sharp creak of the floor. My heart spikes as I sit up, eyes locking on Raven at the bottom of the stairs. I've never been a heavy sleeper—unless I've had one too many—but right now, every nerve in my body screams alert.

My mom told me she had to get creative with the tooth fairy when I was little. She could never sneak into my room and reach under my pillow without me waking up. I don't remember any of this, but my mom said the one and only time I did wake up, she told me she was just making sure I put the tooth in the right spot.

The next morning, I woke up to a note from the tooth fairy beside my bed. The tooth fairy claimed my head was too heavy and that I would need to put my tooth in a small box next to my bed. Later that night, I followed the directions given by the tooth fairy. And after that night, that's what I did for the rest of the teeth I lost.

"Is everything okay, Raven?"

Looking around the house to make sure I didn't see anything out of the ordinary. She pads over to where I am sitting on the couch—I move to the other end so she can sit down.

Instead of sitting at the opposite end, she sits beside me and lays her head on my shoulder.

"I had a nightmare and couldn't fall back asleep. Can I stay down here with you, or can you come up and stay in my room? I know you're in my house, but I don't want to fall asleep alone."

I put my hand on her leg and nod.

"But if it makes you feel better, we can put a pillow in the middle of the bed."

The way she says it, she sounds unsure, like she's worried she's made me uncomfortable.

Grabbing her hand, I place my other hand over hers.

"Raven, I want you to understand one thing—I'm here for you. Don't hesitate to ask for anything. You could ask me to skinny dip in your creek out back just to make you laugh your ass off."

A smile appears on her face before I continue my little speech.

"I would do anything for you. I can promise you that, pretty girl. You deserve to come first—."

She looks down.

"Hey, look at me, please."

Placing two fingers under her chin, raising it up so she looks at me when I say this next part.

"You deserve to come first, Raven. You might have entered my life like a tornado, whipping my life upside down the day I showed up on your porch, but I wouldn't change it for the world. There's no other person I've ever wanted to spend time with—until I met you."

A tear strays down her cheek. My heart broke for this woman. I just kept wishing I could have been here to prevent it all—to prevent her from experiencing this traumatic event. Wishing I could have stopped her from going on that date with Dean.

Although if she had never gone on that date, they would probably still be mutual friends. But if she continued to deny him, would he eventually come after her? I shudder at the thought.

We both get up and head upstairs to her bedroom to lie down. I laugh when I see both dogs sprawled out on the bed.

I couldn't help but joke, "You know, we could just use one of these dogs as a divider. They're trying to take over your bed."

She laughs as she tells Rex and Nala to get down. I shuffle to the other side of the bed and pull back the covers to lie down. I would love to pull her in and cuddle while we both sleep, but I need to focus on what she needs right now.

She only wants me close so she can feel safe—like she trusts me not to make a move on her, and I thanked God for that.

I wanted to be her rock, her everything.

A few hours later, I wake up to Raven screaming and flailing her legs. After a few seconds of becoming more alert, I realize she is having a nightmare. I pull her in close, rub my hand up and down her arm, and whisper that I am here and everything was okay. She stops screaming—now awake and crying. Raven rolls over and buries her head in my chest.

I continue rubbing her arm, letting her know she is safe. A muffled sound vibrates my chest as she tries to say thank you before she falls back asleep in my arms.

My other arm, trapped under her body, was falling asleep, but I couldn't bring myself to move her or shift my arm up under her neck. I ignore the tingling, numb feeling and eventually drift off to sleep.

I wake a few times as Raven shifts here and there, but thankfully, she has no more nightmares while sleeping in my arms.

Chapter 21
Raven

The nightmare from yesterday replayed over and over in my head. I don't know what I would have done if Jackson hadn't come when he did.

However, I know that if Jackson hadn't shown up, I probably would have passed out while Dean raped me. Would Dean eventually realize I wasn't fighting anymore and relieve the pressure around my neck? Or would he have kept his hand clamped around my neck until he finished? I'm relieved I'll never find out the answers to those questions. All I knew was that I felt violated and could have died yesterday. I always thought Kevin broke me, but if Dean had got away with what he wanted to do with me, it would have shattered me into a million pieces if I regained consciousness.

I guess I will call my therapist Monday morning, whom I haven't spoken to in a couple of years. She told me that when she saw significant improvements, we could have sessions as needed. I already know that my therapist will recommend that I set up weekly appointments with her after what happened. But I would rather talk to her about it than let it fester and eat at me for years.

When I asked Jackson to stay, I thought I might have been overstepping. Especially since we were just friends. But having him in the house with me last night made me feel safe. Well, at least until I had that terrible nightmare. Not only did Dean traumatize me yesterday, he also traumatized me while I was trying to sleep. Jackson was in this nightmare, though, but he could not get to me. It was as if there was a barrier around Dean and me, not allowing Jackson to rip him off of me.

I felt so bad walking downstairs and waking Jackson up to ask if I could stay on the couch with him or have him lie in my bed next to me. I almost took back the question, but I suggested putting the pillows between us.

The words he spoke after that had my mind racing. Did he just admit that he had feelings for me? I wanted to ask, but I didn't want to scare him off because, right now, I needed him. I felt safe with him and didn't want to lose our friendship. He knew how to lighten the mood in the room and he made me smile with his comment about using the dogs as a divider.

It's as if he already knew almost everything about me. If he had been okay with it, I would have spooned with him all night, but again, I didn't want to scare him off. After waking up from yet another nightmare, I burrowed myself into Jackson's chest and fell back asleep. With his brawny arms embracing me as I drifted back to sleep, I felt protected. I knew he would not let me go.

I hear soft snores just before I open my eyes. Jackson still has his arms wrapped around me, his head gently resting against mine. I feel his warm breath as he exhales. It's tranquilizing.

Without trying to wake Jackson up, I rotate my body so my back is against his chest. Surprisingly, he doesn't wake up. He must be a heavy sleeper. I get fully rotated to where I want to be and back up into him to where our bodies and legs are touching.

After laying there for a few minutes, something pokes me in the ass. Oh, well, I wasn't expecting that. Jackson's hard cock was poking me. After a few minutes, he starts to stir, and then he pulls back suddenly, as if he was doing something that he shouldn't have been doing. I roll over to look at him. "Good morning," I say with a smile.

"Good morning. Were you able to get some sleep?"

I nod.

A sweet smile appears on his handsome face. When I break eye contact with him, his smile fades.

As my eyes trail down his body, I notice that he's adjusting himself. Biting my bottom lip, I try not to laugh. My gaze shifts to his chest where his black t-shirt hung open, revealing his broad chest dusted with dark brown, curling hairs that trailed downward in a tempting line. My fingers were tempted to explore the roughness with my smooth hand.

"See something you like, pretty girl?"

I blink, my eyes snapping back up to his—busted. Instead of looking bashful, I grin, unabashed.

With a quiet smile, he sweeps a strand of hair away from my face, his fingers lingering for a moment.

"If you feel like talking, I'm all ears. If not, I'll be here when you need me."

He leans in to press a light kiss to my forehead.

"No pressure." He adds as he gives my arm a gentle squeeze.

"I am going to get up and get ready for the day. Thanks again for staying the night with me. I don't know what I did to deserve you in my life."

He tilts my chin up, searching my eyes.

"Raven, thank you for asking me to stay. I don't think I would have been able to sleep in my house knowing what you went through yesterday."

His thumb swipes a tear that trails down my cheek.

"I only wish that I could have been here sooner—to stop that monster before he hurt you."

Me too.

I climb out of bed and head into the bathroom. Closing the bathroom door behind me, I lean up against the door and close my eyes.

I probably could have stayed in bed all day with Jackson. Knowing him, he probably would if I asked. A smile crept onto my face at the thought of spending the entire day in bed with him.

There was something special about him.

He genuinely cares.

The thought of him being here only for me to give him hunting permission vacates my thoughts completely. Stripping off my clothes, I toss them into the dirty hamper before turning the water on in the shower. When the water temperature is just right, I climb in and let the water hit my face. Eager to get out of the shower and back into the same room as Jackson, I wash my hair and my body before getting out. When I step out of the shower, my hand reaches for the towel hanging on the towel rack to dry my body off before wrapping it around my body.

When I return to my bedroom, Jackson is already dressed and heads into the bathroom. I grab my phone off the dresser and turn it on. The second my phone screen lights up, multiple missed calls and text messages from my sister appear on the screen. I read Hannah's last message, letting me know she was on her way to my house.

"Shit."

I toss my phone down on the bed and go to throw some clothes on. Jackson walks back into the room when I am only in my underwear and bra.

Realizing he should have knocked, he swiftly turns around and shouts over his shoulder, "Shit, sorry Raven, I should have knocked before coming in."

A burst of laughter echoes throughout my room.

"It's okay. I just need to get dressed. My sister is showing up here in the next ten minutes."

I rush down the stairs to let Nala and Rex outside. When I am walking back into the living room, I look out my front window and see my sister pulling in. The time on my message must have been wrong since my phone was off. Jackson is stuffing his clothes in his bag and acting like he is about to bolt out the door when the door flies open. He freezes and looks at me for our plan of what to tell my sister. I just shrug my shoulders as I head towards the front door.

Hannah meets me in the doorway of the living room and freezes as her eyes widen when she sees Jackson behind me.

"Oh, now I see why you didn't answer me," she says, crossing her arms.

Oh no, she thinks I slept with Jackson. Technically I did, but not in the way she thinks I did. She walks around me and up to Jackson.

"I am Hannah; you must be Jackson. I heard a lot about you."

His eyes dart over to meet mine.

"Eyes here, mister! Right here," as she points two of her fingers at her own eyes.

"Listen, never let Raven shut her phone off. I didn't sleep at all last night. I was half tempted to drive here in the middle of the night."

Jackson nods.

"Yes, ma'am, it won't happen again."

I mouth *thank you* to him; he could have told my sister a thousand excuses, but he didn't. I wasn't ready to talk about what happened yesterday just yet, not even with my sister.

Jackson picks up his bag and throws it over his shoulder.

"I'm heading home for a little while. Can I text you later?"

I nod.

"Yeah, sure. Thanks again."

He smiles and nods.

Before I know it, Jackson and Nala walk out the front door, leaving me alone in my home with my sister. After Jackson and Nala pull out of the driveway, Hannah grabs my hand and pulls me over to the couch to sit down with her.

"So, are you going to tell me why Jackson was here? It looks like he stayed the night."

I knew she was going to ask this question, but part of me hoped she wouldn't. I guess if I tell her; I don't have to tell her everything that happened. At least not now. Maybe I will later down the road.

"Um, well, you remember Dean?"

She leans back, a look of confusion flickering across her face.

"Yes, what about Dean? What does that have to do with Jackson being here?"

Tears pool in my eyes.

"Oh, no, Raven, what happened?"

She pulls me in for a hug, and the floodgates open as I sob into my sister's shoulder.

"Dean came over drunk, asking me for another date. He roughed me up a bit. Jackson just happened to show up to save me. When I eventually got away—I called the cops, and they arrested Dean. I was so upset and scared, I asked Jackson if he would stay with me. He started out on the couch until I had a nightmare, so I asked him to sleep next to me in bed. Nothing happened. Well, other than he held me most of the night because of the second nightmare I had."

Hannah's grip around me tightens, letting me know she was not ready to let me go just yet.

"That is terrible. I am so sorry that you went through that alone. I am glad that Jackson could help you, and I am glad that he stayed here with you. I remember when you had the nightmares after you and Kevin broke up."

Hannah was the only other one to experience my nightmares. When I moved out of Kevin's, Hannah and Henry let me crash with them for a bit until I could get a place of my own. The guest room in their house became my temporary home for the next year. Most nights, Hannah was in there with me instead of in the bed that she shared with her husband.

"I am sorry I turned my phone off, Hannah. I just needed to shut myself out, plus I didn't know if Dean would attempt to call me from the police station."

She pulls away and rubs her eyes.

"Well, you gave me quite a scare. Please just text me next time. It doesn't have to be a detailed message, just short and sweet."

I nod, agreeing that I will not leave her on read again. I am thankful for having my sister here, although I hate that Jackson isn't here. Spending time with Jackson over the past few weeks and spending the night with Jackson, has me wondering if I am starting to have feelings for him. It scares me to get into a relationship after Kevin, but Jackson is not like Kevin, so why am I having a hard time being happy about having feelings for him?

Chapter 22
Raven

It's been a week since I last saw Jackson. We've exchanged a few texts, but he still hasn't come over. Is he avoiding me? Did I do something to push him away?

He seemed embarrassed when he got hard while holding me in my bed. Most of his texts since then have just been asking how I'm doing and whether I'm feeling okay. I haven't brought up hanging out again—he hasn't either. Maybe he just wanted to be friends. Maybe he only said those things that night to make me feel better.

Hannah has been texting me, too, and I've been making sure to respond. The last thing I need is her freaking out and showing up at my door again.

Oh, and Dean has been released from jail. I ended up pressing charges, so hopefully, he got the hint to never contact me again. If he shows up at my door, he'll be arrested anyway—especially since I got a restraining order. And yes, Dean lost his job at the school. Some of my coworkers were supportive, but others—especially Jessie—actually sympathized with Dean. And let me tell you, they were just downright rude to me, even though *he* was the one who assaulted *me*.

Anyway, some of the girls I'm friends with at work invited me out tonight. We are going to the River Bank, the little bar in town. On Friday nights, they have live music. Honestly, I am excited to go out with some girlfriends. Yes, I missed hanging out with Jackson, but I decided I needed some girl time.

When I met the girls at the bar, we ordered drinks and an enormous basket of French fries. They swore up and down that the fries—and the sauce—were the best. I thought they were full of it. I figured they were just drunk when they'd eaten them before. But wow, was I wrong. I'd only had one shot, and I was shoving those fries into my mouth like they were the best thing I'd ever tasted. And the sauce? It was amazing—sweet and salty.

Not only did those fries curb my appetite, they made me thirsty.

So, I wander over to the bar for my next drink, asking the bartender for a margarita. My eyes widen when he sets a gigantic glass in front of me.

"Here you go, sweetheart. By the way, my name's Brody. You must be new to town?"

I nod as I pick up my drink from the bar.

"Yeah, I just moved here a little over a month ago. I'm Raven. It's nice to meet you."

He grabs the towel off his shoulder and starts wiping down the bar.

"It's nice to meet you too, Raven. And the drink's on the house—welcome to River Valley."

Holding my drink up, I smile.

"Thanks for the drink, Brody."

He smiles back and gives me a wink.

"Have a good night, and don't be a stranger, Raven."

Yup, I must have *"I want to get shit-faced tonight"* written all over my face. Or maybe he's already heard the rumors floating around town. Honestly, I wouldn't be surprised—this is a small town, after all.

I don't drink very often, but when I do, I've been told I'm a fun drunk. I take a sip, letting the alcohol slide smoothly down my throat.

The band starts playing *"Craving You"* by *Thomas Rhett*, and I can't help but sway my hips to the beat. One of the girls, Jenna, grabs my hand, joining me on the dance floor. We laugh and dance together with our drinks in our hands.

"I am so glad that you came out tonight," Jenna says as rocks her wide hips back and forth. Jenna is one of the high school teachers at River Valley—she teaches Spanish for the freshman and sophomore classes.

"Me too. Thanks for inviting me. Sorry for not coming out with y'all sooner. I have been enjoying the peaceful life at home."

I'm already feeling pretty buzzed, and I haven't even made it halfway through my drink. Either Brody made this one strong, or I'm just turning into a lightweight.

"Girl, don't worry. I am just glad that you came out tonight."

She holds up her glass of Whiskey.

"To tonight, we are going to have some fun, get drunk and dance until Brody kicks us out."

Laughing, I raise my glass to touch hers.

"To tonight!"

After our glasses touch, we take a nice long sip of our drinks. Jenna's face winces after taking a drink of hers, the sweet, salty taste of mine rolling smoothly over my tongue as it slides down the back of my throat.

Sipping on my drink, I glance toward the door—and that's when I see Jackson walk in with his two buddies, Tanner and Mitch. They head over to a table in the corner and sit down. I avoid looking in his direction. Did he know I was here? Has he noticed me yet? He has to eventually... right?

After the band announces they're taking a break, we head back to our table to sit and chat. I try to focus on the conversation, but every now and then, I can't help stealing a glance over at him. Tanner has a girl straddling his lap, kissing his neck while he runs his hands under her shirt.

Meanwhile, Jackson and Mitch sit there talking, ignoring the couple across the table from them. A waitress walks over and sets down plates of food at their table.

I try to turn my attention back to my friends, nodding along to the conversation, but my thoughts are elsewhere. Is Jackson avoiding me? Did I do something wrong? Does he not even want to be friends anymore?

I want to go talk to him, but I can't seem to move. It's like my boots are filled with sand—anchoring me to the floor. My heart's screaming at me to go, but my mind's keeping me frozen.

Then I see her.

A woman approaches Jackson's table. She's petite, with short black hair that barely brushes her shoulders. She's in a pair of high heels and a black halter dress that is most likely a size or two too small—since it barely covers her ass. Jackson looks visibly annoyed the moment he sees her. She keeps trying to put her hand on his arm, and each time, he shakes it off. Mitch gives her a subtle shooing gesture, clearly hoping she'll take the hint and leave.

Who is she? And why is it bothering Jackson so much that she's talking to him?

I nudge Jenna and ask, "Who's that girl over there?"

She glances over towards the guys, then says, "Oh, that's Gina—Jackson's ex. She must be trying to win him back. I heard she cheated on him with another guy, and then *that* guy dumped her. She's probably regretting it now. Jackson took good care of her… and she ruined it."

So *that's* the woman who cheated on Jackson.

She might be pretty on the outside, but all I see is ugly that she shelters on the inside. Especially now, knowing what she did to him.

Suddenly, my feet don't feel so heavy anymore. In fact, before I even realize it, I'm already halfway across the room, heading straight for Jackson.

What am I going to say when I get there? *Fuck if I know.*

But I know one thing for sure: I have to get to Jackson—and rescue him from this bitch.

He clearly wants nothing to do with her.

As I approach Jackson's table, I hear Gina ask, "Jackson, why can't we talk about this?" His eyes meet mine before looking at her to answer her question.

"Because, Gina, I have no intention of taking you back. You messed up."

Instantly, I have a plan. I know what I'm going to do, and I hope Jackson goes along with it. I walk around Gina's small frame to stand next to Jackson, sliding my arm up and around his neck I pull him in for a kiss. An electric current surges through my body as our lips graze against one another. I feel his hand slide down my back to the curve of my ass.

Thank goodness he is going along with it. I would feel so sheepish if he had pulled away and asked what I was doing. I pull away and look at Gina, who is now frowning.

"Oh, I'm being so rude. My name is Raven, Jackson's girlfriend." I hold my hand out to her, but she looks at me with disgust.

"I know exactly who you are; you're the one who got Dean arrested," she spats.

"He only wanted a second date with you. If you had no interest in him, you should have never gone on the first date with him."

Oh, so the cat is bringing her claws out to play.

"Oh, Gina, would you like to know what I heard about you?"

She doesn't answer, good, because I am ready to tear her the fuck down.

"I heard you weren't happy in your relationship."

Jackson removes his hand from my ass and pulls me onto his lap.

"I also heard that you cheated on Jackson, and the man you left him for dumped you because he found some new piece of ass. And now you want him back? Well, let me tell you something. He. Is. Mine."

I lean into Jackson, running my fingertips through his hair as I pepper his neck with kisses. Jackson groans in approval.

"You wanted to change this man because you didn't like what he enjoyed doing. I, on the other hand, would not want this man to change. He is perfect to me, in my eyes."

Jackson squeezes my leg before turning his head to kiss me. We both get lost in each other as we kiss, forgetting that Gina and his friends are in our bubble. His hand cups my jaw, letting me know he doesn't want this kiss to end anytime soon. As we pull away, he rests his forehead on mine and whispers something that I can't make out.

My plan to get Gina to leave must have worked. We watch Gina throw her hands up and curse under her breath before she storms out the door. Still sitting on Jackson's lap, I feel his hand slide up and down my leg, each time inching up closer to the apex of my thighs. Wanting him to get closer to where I need him most. Satisfaction beams within me that I pissed Gina off. Something about Jackson just made me feel more confident in my own skin.

The band comes back out onto the small stage and starts playing "*Better Together*" by Luke Combs. Grasping Jackson's hand, I slide off of Jackson's lap, pulling him onto the dance floor with me. We only make it to the edge of the dance floor before Jackson's hands are on my hips, pulling me close. I lean into his chest as I continue to sip on my margarita. We sway back and forth to the beat of the music.

I missed Jackson.

I missed him holding me, especially after that night when he held me in his arms while I slept.

I don't want this song to end, because he might leave. And I don't want to feel the emptiness that I felt when he was not with me.

His fingertips push a few strands of hair from my face—his lips brushing against my ear.

"Thank you, Raven—but you didn't have to do that."

I know I was a little drunk, but it gave me the confidence to be bold with Jackson. And no, I don't regret claiming him in front of his ex-girlfriend. Heck, if he really wanted me to be his girlfriend, I would say yes in a heartbeat. But all I have to say back is, "I know I wanted to. I don't like what she did to you." Maybe he didn't see himself being more than friends with me. He avoided me this whole week. If that doesn't scream *I just want to be friends* then I just don't know anymore. But what really confuses me is what he told me the night he stayed with me. Maybe he was just scared to jump into a new relationship. Hell, I would be lying if I said I wasn't terrified myself.

Jackson is different, though, and I have come to learn that over the past couple of weeks, that he is one of the good ones. He has dropped whatever he was doing to help me.

Would he do that for anyone, or did he do it for me because he really cares about me?

He brings me back to reality when he whispers in my ear.

"You know—you just told the biggest gossip girl in town that you're in a relationship with me, right?"

Lifting my head from his shoulder, I look at him.

"So, let them talk. What would be wrong with that?"

He pulls away from me, breaking our embrace, shaking his head at me.

"Raven, I think you have had too much to drink. I think maybe we should wait and talk about this."

Did he really think the alcohol was fully responsible for my actions?

Or does he not see himself in a relationship with me?

It must be embarrassing for him to be seen with me, especially after the whole town knows that I got Dean arrested.

"You know what? I am sorry if I embarrassed you."

Not giving him a chance to reply, I sit my drink down on the bar and walk out the door, not looking behind me. I have no intention of getting in my car and driving home. I know I need to sober up some. All I want to do was sit in my car and bawl my eyes out.

It's raining outside.

Let me clarify, it's pouring. I don't even run to my car. I walk, letting the rain drench my hair and my clothes because at this moment, maybe it will wash away the pain that I am currently feeling right now. When I am almost to my car, someone grabs my hand and spins me around.

I gasp when I see who it is.

"Jackson, just leave me alone!"

He points back at the bar, chest heaving from running.

"I'm not letting you drive after all that drinking."

I pull my hand away from him and turn around and continue walking towards my car.

"Don't worry, I am not. I'm just going to sit in my car until I can drive home," I yell over my shoulder.

"Raven, what is wrong?"

He turns me around and grasps my shoulders, moving some wet hair out of my face. Standing under the light in the parking lot, lighting up Jackson's concerned face. The second I look into his ice-blue eyes, tears fall from my eyes, mixing in with the rain that is hitting my cheeks.

I try again to walk away, but Jackson pulls me in, wrapping his arms around me. My knees feel like they are going to buckle. Torn, unsure whether I should feel upset or relieved that Jackson has me in his arms.

Isn't that what I wanted?

But I don't think I could handle believing just for a second that Jackson wants me, only to find out that he just wants to be friends. However, having him in my life just as a friend should be good enough. I can't imagine life without him in it.

"I don't want to lose you. I don't see my life without you in it. You have been avoiding me all week, and I can't figure out why.

"And when you told me that the whole town would talk about us being together, I thought you were embarrassed because of me."

"Pretty girl," he grabs my chin and lifts my face up so he can look into my eyes.

The expression on his face makes me melt. Desire ignites in his eyes, wild and consuming like a raging fire.

"I don't see a life without you, either. I'm sorry that you thought that."

He rubs his thumb across my cheek as he continues to say, "I am falling for you, Raven, and it scares the shit out of me because I don't want to do anything to make you run."

A rush of relief washes over me. He was worried that I would run.

He continues to say, "It took thirty-two years to find you, and if I am being honest, I am going to use the rest of my life holding on to you."

The next thing I know, Jackson pulls me in for a kiss. We don't care that the rain is pouring down on us. We are already soaked. He deepens the kiss as he lifts my feet off the ground. I wrap my legs around his waist as he spins us around and walks, keeping our lips fused together. Thunder rolls low in the distance, but neither of us flinch.

I feel like I am floating on Cloud 9 in Jackson's arms—his grip firm on my thighs as he carries me across the parking lot. When he stops, he pushes my back up against a vehicle. I pull away from his mouth and realize that it's his truck. Gripping onto his slick shirt, I pull his mouth back onto mine and kiss him like it's my last kiss. I part my lips and allow his tongue to collide with mine. The cold, wet rain should have us shivering—but the heat from his kiss has our bodies buzzing with warmth. He slowly lowers me so my feet are touching the ground, still keeping me pressed up against the side of his truck.

Have you ever been shoved up against a truck and kissed in the pouring rain? Let me tell you, it's fucking amazing. Better than any kiss that I have ever imagined. Both of his hands come up to cup my face before he rakes his fingers through my wet hair.

A moan escapes my lips as he removes his mouth from mine and begins trailing kisses along my neck. Tilting my head, giving Jackson easier access to my neck, silently begging for more.

He rests his head on my forehead; both of us are breathing erratically. I reach up and run the palm of my hand over the stubble of his beard on his cheek and smile.

"I am never going to run. The only way I am running is if it's to you."

My heart skips a beat when he moves me away from his truck to open up the back door of his truck. I climb inside and slide to the opposite end of the truck. I hear the door shut, and before I turn around, Jackson already has his hands on me, pulling me close.

My fingers run through his wet hair before I grasp onto him, pulling his lips down onto mine. Desperate for more contact, I climb onto his lap and straddle him. If I weren't already turned on, the bulge in his pants would have definitely aroused me.

Seeking friction where I need him most, I grind up against his cock that's trying to break free from his wranglers. A low growl comes out of Jackson as I move my hips against him slowly, but with more pressure than before.

"Raven." My name on his lips comes out desperate. I shrug off my coat, letting it fall behind me.

He tugs my shirt over my head and unclasps my bra—allowing it to fall onto the floorboard of his truck. The only things I am wearing are my mini skirt, panties and cowgirl boots. I throw my head back as he caresses my breast before lowering his mouth to suck on my nipple. Being the gentleman that he is, he makes sure the other breast receives the same attention. While he sucks and swirls his tongue around my nipple, I grab onto his hair, making it feel like I am in control of where his mouth goes.

"I want you, Jackson. No, let me clarify that; I. Need. You. Jackson," I whisper into his ear as I reach for his zipper to undo his jeans.

He slides his hand in between my legs, reaching my center where I ache for him, and groans.

"Fuck baby, you are so fucking wet for me."

He slides my panties to the side and dips one finger in to rub tight circles on my clit. My hips buck against his touch.

This man is going to make me lose control. I lift myself up so he can slide his pants and boxers down in one motion. His hard cock bobs free with a bead of precum surfacing at the tip.

I hike my skirt up and slide my panties to the side, but before I sit back down on him, I ask, "Do you have a condom?"

You would have thought he had just witnessed a terrible event with the look that was on his face.

"No, I do not."

He starts to pull his boxers back up. I grab the hand that is on the band of his boxers.

"I'm on birth control, and I had myself tested five years ago."

He lets go of his boxers.

"I am clean, too. Are you sure?"

I nod.

I wanted him inside me; I wanted him to claim me and fill me with his cum.

"Words, Raven, I need words."

Leaning in, I whisper in his ear, "I want you to fuck me, Jackson. I want to scream your name, and you make me come. I want people to hear me inside that bar while I scream your name."

His eyes darkened, heavy with desire—his pupils swallowing those blue irises in a sea of blackness. I line him up with my entrance and slowly sink down onto him. He grips my hips and shoves me down the rest of the way, stretching me around his cock. The slightest pain I felt accommodating his size—pulses into pleasure. Rocking my hips while I adjust to his size, I ride him; he moves his hips with mine, causing friction against my clit. His hands come up to cup my breasts. He runs his thumbs over my pebbled nipples. Pleasure courses through my body. It's almost too much, but I don't want it to end anytime soon.

"Pretty girl, I need you to get off."

A rush of disappointment crashes into me, I lean back, creating distance between us.

Did I do something wrong?

As if reading my mind, Jackson grips my chin and makes me look at him.

"Raven, I want to try something. You're amazing. I dreamt about this for a while."

He kisses me gently.

When he pulls away, I give him a small smile as I climb off of Jackson's cock and sit down on the seat next to him.

"I need your hands on the window."

Listening, I place both hands on the window as he comes up behind me, gripping my hips. He hikes my skirt back up and pushes my panties to the side before shoving his cock back in me. With each thrust, bringing his cock out all the way before slamming back home, my hands slide down the window of the truck.

"You take my cock so well, Raven. You were fucking made for me."

He grunts and brings his hand around to rub my clit as I continue to moan and scream his name.

"Jackson." I scream his name as he sends me over the edge of my first orgasm.

Condensation coats the windows, and there's no doubt that if someone walked by, they'd know what was going on in that back seat.

Especially if they saw my hands pressed up against the glass—sliding down as Jackson thrust in and out of me.

But I didn't care; I was with the man of my dreams.

This man showed up at my doorstep to ask a question. Little did I know I would need him in my life. He cared about me. Jackson was willing to drop everything to help me; we had so much in common. He made me feel happy, whole, and confident. He made me feel like I was worth it.

"Ever since you drove my truck that day, this is all that I have thought about. You looked so fucking sexy driving my truck. I was ready to get out of your car and hop in my truck and take you right then and there."

I adjust my hands back on the glass of the truck window as he continues to pound his cock into my pussy with a punishing pace. I am close to coming again, and he knows it. He reaches his hand back around to rub my clit slowly.

"I need you to come again for me, pretty girl; I want you to squeeze my cock with your tight pussy."

He continues to rub my clit, gradually increasing the intensity as his thrusts become more erratic.

"Jackson," I moan as I reach my orgasm.

He thrust in and out of me a few more times before he fills me up with his cum. Ropes of hot cum coat the inside of my pussy. Claiming me as his. I take my hands off the glass and face him on the seat, feeling his sticky cum between my thighs. He pulls his boxers and jeans up over his cock that was just inside of me. I move closer to him; he puts his arm behind my neck and drapes his hand over my shoulder. He leans in and kisses me on the top of my head.

I have had sex in the back seat before, but typically, my ex had me on my back. Having my hands on the glass made me feel adventurous, knowing that someone could walk by and see what we were doing. Even if they could only see my hands pressed up against the truck window.

Chapter 23
Jackson

What a night it has been. Not only did I just make out with Raven in the pouring rain, but I also had sex with her in the back seat of my truck. I would have been totally fine with her riding me the entire time. There would be no wrong way to do it with this incredible woman. My heart broke when she looked at me like she did something wrong after asking her to get off of me. Her keeping her hands on the truck window and me taking her from behind was a fantasy that I had dreamt about for the past couple of weeks. Every time I got into my truck, all I could think about was Raven and what I wanted to do to her in here.

It killed me when I avoided her all week. I let my past relationship eat at me—allowing Gina's bad decisions take over my head. I knew Raven would never do what Gina did. Any doubts that I had about Raven went out the window after she pretended to be my girlfriend in front of Gina. It felt so right having her in my lap—kissing me with her luscious lips.

Right then and there, I wanted to tell Raven I wanted her to be my girlfriend. After what she said to Gina, maybe she wanted that too. But when I realized she'd had a bit too much to drink, I started wondering if it was just the alcohol talking.

It wasn't until she ran out the door that I realized—I said the wrong things. I was wrong. And I didn't want to let this woman go.

Even though she had no intention of driving home right away, I was so damn glad I ran after her—because who knows what might have happened if she had gotten behind the wheel. I didn't know how strong Brody had made her drink, and I felt nothing but relief when I caught up with her and heard that she planned to sit in her car to sober up.

Instead of her staying in the car, though, we ended up climbing into the back of my truck. And we had a little fun.

I couldn't say how long we stayed there, wrapped in each other's arms while the storm gathered outside my truck. All I knew was this—I didn't want the night to end, and I wasn't about to let this woman out of my sight.

Honestly, I almost didn't come out tonight. I had no plans to leave the house—but the guys talked me into it. I'm going to have to thank them later. If I had stayed home, I wouldn't be here, in the backseat of my truck, with this incredible woman.

I talk Raven into leaving her car at the bar so I can take her home, promising we could come back for it tomorrow or even on Sunday. Truth was, I just wasn't ready to let her go—wasn't ready to sit in silence without her beside me.

The rain hadn't let up. It's still coming down hard, making it tough to see the road, which gives me the perfect excuse to drive slow. To drag the night out just a little longer. Out of the corner of my eye, I watch Raven comb through her dark wet hair—tossing it up into a messy bun on her head. She's beautiful like this— real, unfiltered. And tonight, I'm not letting her slip away.

When I finally pull around the little loop in her driveway, I park as close as I can to her front door so she won't be in the rain for long—not that she seems to care. We're both still soaked from earlier, from kissing in the rain like a couple of reckless teenagers.

Shifting my truck into park, I reach for my seatbelt, but Raven gently places her hand on my arm.

"Jackson, you don't have to get out and open my door. I know we're already soaked, and I'll be inside in like five seconds," she says, her voice soft but certain.

Her hand slides down my arm and settles on top of mine.

"Thanks for bringing me home," she adds.

I place my free hand over hers, letting my thumb trace slow circles across the back of her hand. Her breath catches, and then she leans in, pressing a soft kiss to my lips.

"And thanks for tonight," she whispers, settling back into her seat.

"Thank *you*, pretty girl. Tonight's been one of the best nights of my life."

I let that hang there for a second before adding, "Text me tomorrow—let me know when you want to go get your car. If not tomorrow, we can wait until Sunday. Just promise me if you need to go anywhere before then, you'll text me first."

I mean every word. I'd hand her the keys to my truck, no hesitation. Hell, I'd drive her anywhere she needed to go.

She gives me a sly little wink.

"Sure, Jackson—*if* you'll let me drive your truck."

The thought alone sends a pulse of heat through me. I'm already half gone for this woman, and the image of her behind the wheel of my truck makes my chest tighten.

That's going to live rent-free in my head for a long time.

After tonight, I don't know how I'm ever going to look at that back seat without thinking about her. If her handprints are still on the windows, I'm not cleaning them off. Let them stay. Let them remind me this wasn't just some dream that I fantasised about.

It happened.

She was here.

I was with her.

And I don't want this to become just a memory.

She opens the door and runs up to her house. As I sit there in my truck, I watch her open her purse to search for her keys. Lightning flashes across the sky—causing her key to shine as she pulls it out of her purse.

Part of me really wanted to walk her to her door tonight and kiss her just one more time. I know tonight wasn't an actual date, but I feel like it was the official start of our relationship. I would at least hope so since we had sex in my backseat.

Without hesitating, I kill the engine and jump out of my truck. Rain pelts my skin as I sprint up the stairs just as she slips the key into the lock.

Startled, she spins around, her hand flying to her chest. But the moment her eyes meet mine, relief softens her face.

Stepping closer, closing the space between us in a breathless rush. My hands clutch her face, rough and desperate, as I crash my lips against hers with a fierce hunger.

She melts into me instantly, her fingers curling into my jacket like she couldn't get close enough.

Same, pretty girl.

Our bodies could be skin to skin, and I would still want to pull her closer. My intention was just to give her a kiss goodnight. But I should have known better that my attraction to this woman would have altered that.

Because here I am, shoving her up against her front door, peppering her neck with kisses as I run my hand down her back to grab her ass.

A whimper slips past her lips as I cup the globes of her ass—squeezing, reluctant to let go.

I don't expect her to invite me in, but I would be lying if I said I didn't want to stay here with her tonight. Ever since I stayed with her and she slept in my arms, my bed has felt so empty and cold. I needed her next to me, in my arms. I had never slept through the night until that one night with her. We may have found peace within one another, but our chemistry was exquisite.

I break our kiss but keep our noses close, barely touching, and grin.

"I had fun tonight. I couldn't let you leave my truck without a proper goodnight kiss."

She wraps her arms around my neck and looks up at me; her smile is full of mischief.

"If *that's* a goodnight kiss, I'm curious what you'd do if I invited you into my house for the night."

My smile falters slightly as I pull back just enough to take her in—my eyes lock on hers as she bites her bottom lip.

Damn. That look. She knows exactly what she's doing to me.

I really should go, but my dick is telling me to stay. Desperately wanting to bury myself in this woman all night, just so I could hear her scream my name as she climaxes with each orgasm that we create together. Just the thought has my dick trying to bust out of my jeans. Flipping my hat backwards on my head—one hand up next to her on the door—I lean in to whisper in her ear, "Well if you're so curious, why don't you let me in so you can find out." A gasp ricochets through my ears as she swiftly pushes me away to unlock her door—tugging me far enough inside to slam the door shut behind us.

When she spins back around, she leaps into my arms—wrapping her creamy thighs tight around my waist—and grabs my hat, flipping it backwards on her head with a mischievous grin. Seeing her wearing nothing but my hat is almost too much. It's intoxicating. I squeeze her ass and grin as I carry her up the stairs to her bedroom.

Instead of throwing her down on the bed, I drop us both onto the bed with me on my back, giving her only the option to straddle me—her heated center presses against my cock, ready to bust the zipper on my jeans. She peels her wet jacket off and tosses it onto the ground next to the bed. Running her hands up my chest, she gives me a light kiss, teasing me as she returns to stripping off her shirt.

A shiver runs through her body as the wet fabric glides over her skin and slips over her head. I take the zipper of her miniskirt, not giving her the option to hike it up this time, and unzip it from top to bottom. The skirt falls behind her, leaving her in her bra, panties, boots, and my hat. She reaches behind her back, and within seconds, her bra slips down onto my chest. Her breasts, full and round, come into view—light pink nipples gently pebbled with arousal. Picking up the bra that had fallen onto my chest, I fling it across the room and roll her over, now hovering above her—taking in the sight of the woman lying before me.

She starts to remove the hat from her head, and I quickly grab her hand.

"No, leave the hat. I want to fuck you wearing my hat, pretty girl."

She grins as she reaches for my shirt, giving it a tug. "Well, then—this has got to go. Right. Now." I let out a growl as I pull my shirt over my head and toss it behind me before reaching for my jeans. She grabs the hand that is trying to unbutton my jeans and bites her lip.

"Stand up, Jackson," she commands, her tone filled with demand and desire.

My pretty girl is feisty.

Being the good boy that I am, I stand up. She gets off the bed and drops to her knees in front of me—teasing me by slowly undoing the button on my jeans. Keeping her brown eyes locked on me, filled with desire, she grips the zipper of my jeans while pressing her other hand against my erection, hungry to be freed.

"Fuck, you're teasing me, baby. Now be a good girl and free my cock."

A devilish smirk tugs at the corner of her lips as she unzips my jeans.

Both of her hands gently grasp my jeans, still loosely resting on my hips, and slowly pulls them down along with my boxers, freeing my hard cock. Raven licks her lips softly as I watch her hand slide between her legs; she bites her lip and lets out a quiet moan. The sound alone, has my dick twitching. When her hand comes back up, she wraps it around me, coating my length with her warm, glistening desire.

Her hand moves slowly, tenderly stroking me before she takes me into her mouth. I want to throw my head back, overwhelmed by the pleasure she's giving me, but instead, I lock eyes with my sweet vixen.

She reaches back and squeezes my ass, pulling me deeper, causing her to gag, which only makes me want her more. I cradle the back of her head, guiding her as I thrust into her mouth.

Her eyes flutter, glassy with emotion, and a soft moan escapes around me. One hand stays on my ass, steady and sure, while the other moves between her legs to caress her clit. I feel her getting close; her moans shifting into a steady hum of pleasure that wraps around me. As she chases her release, I hold her head down on my cock, watching her eyes water and hearing her breath hitch as she trembles.

Slowly, I pull away, my cock aching for its own release. I lift her up and lay her down on the bed.

"Spread your legs for me, pretty girl. Let me watch you touch your-self. I want to see you come again."

She slides her panties aside and softly rubs her clit, her eyes lock on me as I stroke myself.

"Good girl," I whisper, my voice low and warm.

Her body shudders beneath my words, and I know she feels every one of them.

Watching her rub her clit in slow, deliberate circles while she watches me snaps my patience.

"Fuck, I need to taste you."

I climb onto the bed and hover over her.

"Let me see that hand, pretty girl."

She brings it up to me, and I take it, wrapping my lips around the fingers she'd just used to pleasure herself. I suck her arousal from them slowly, savoring every drop. Her pupils dilate, swallowing those warm brown depths. Releasing her hand, I lean in and whisper against her ear, my voice low and rough.

"You taste so fucking good, pretty girl—but I need more. You're like a drug, Raven. I'm never going to get enough of you."

She lets out a soft whimper as I trail kisses down her body, each one lower than the last until I reach my destination. I throw her legs over my shoulders, the heels of her boots pressing into my back, and dive in—sucking on her swollen clit that's aching for me.

"Oh, fuck, Jackson," she cries out as I bite gently, then soothe the spot with my tongue.

Her hips jerk when I slide two fingers inside her tight cunt. She's so wet I can feel her heat coating my knuckles. My cock aches, desperate to be inside her, but I'm not letting go yet.

She fists my hair, pushing me harder against her as I suck her clit and curl my fingers inside her in perfect rhythm. I feel her tightening around me, her body beginning to tremble.

"Come for me, baby," I growl, my mouth still on her. "Come all over my hand."

She arches her back, digging her boots into my back as she grips my fingers, coming undone before me. I slide my fingers out of her pussy and trail kisses along her thighs before gently lowering her legs from my shoulders. Raven pulls my hair, bringing my face up to meet her lips. She moans softly when she tastes herself on my mouth.

Pushing me away gently, she says, "Stand up, Jackson."

I obey, even though I'm aching to sink my cock into her. Sitting on the edge of the bed, she kicks off her boots and stands up. She shimmies her panties off and walks past me toward the bedroom door. Standing in the threshold, Raven looks back over her shoulder, silently inviting me to follow.

Before I can get close enough to kiss along her neck, she playfully calls out, "Come get me, Jackson!"

The next thing I know, she's running down the stairs. I follow her, watching as she slips out the back door. She just ran out wearing nothing but my hat. The storm rages on, and she's gone, bare and fearless. The screen door slams shut behind her, slammed by the wind.

Standing in the doorway, I watch Raven sprint naked toward the woods. Thank God it's dark and we live out in the middle of nowhere. I've never stepped outside butt-ass naked before—guess there's a first time for everything.

I push open the screen door and chase after her. It's a good thing I know these woods like the back of my hand. Lightning flashes across the sky, briefly illuminating her as she runs deeper among the trees.

She reaches her gazebo—pausing in the entryway, she turns around and waits for me to catch up. Just inches from her, she spins on her heels and flips a switch inside. Twinkle lights flood the gazebo with a soft glow.

Finally, I have my hands on her wet body, pressing her back into my chest. I place my lips along her neck, and she moves her head to the side, granting me better access. A soft moan escapes her as she whispers my name.

"Oh, pretty girl," I murmur into her neck, my breath making her shudder.

"Do you want me to fuck you out here in the woods?"

She tosses her head back against my shoulder and breathes, "Yes, Jackson."

The words fall from her lips like a prayer, a wish.

She turns, grabs my hand, and leads me over to a seat. "Sit, Jackson," she commands, desire blazing in her eyes.

I settle onto the seat, watching my little vixen, waiting to see what she'll do next. She slips off my hat, pulls out the elastic that held her hair, and combs through her soaked strands before setting the hat back on her head.

Fuck. If I could get any harder than I already am, the sight of her wet, naked, wearing nothing but my hat would make me harder than steel. Her eyes rake over my body before locking with mine.

"So, here's how it's going to go, Jack–son," she teases, drawing out my name. "I'm going to sink my pussy down onto your cock. You don't get to touch me until I say so. Okay?"

Without hesitation, I nod.

She comes over to straddle my lap, hovering her wet heat just above me.

Leaning in, her lips brush my ear as she whispers, "If you're a good boy and do as you're told, I'll let you touch me—anywhere your heart desires."

As she sinks down onto my length, I clench my fist tight at my sides. Every muscle in me is screaming to touch her, but I behave. When she reaches the hilt, a sweet, desperate moan slips from her mouth. Her hands roam up my chest and into my hair as she starts to ride me, sliding up and down with deliberate, teasing strokes.

Lightning crashes outside, flooding the gazebo with a brief golden glow. She throws her head back with a groan, droplets from her rain-soaked hair scattering against my heated skin.

The pleasure is almost unbearable. I want to grip her hips and hold her down when she buries me to the hilt, but my knuckles stay white from holding back.

She grazes her perfect lips along my neck, her breath hot against my skin. She stops moving, her mouth at my ear.

"Touch. Me. Jackson."

The way she says my name rips the restraint right out of me. My hands fly to her breasts, kneading the soft curves, teasing her nipples between my fingertips. My mouth claims hers in a heated kiss as she rocks her hips, riding me harder.

There's no way I'm letting this woman out of my reach. I'd do anything for her. It's crazy—being out in the woods during a storm—but the thrill of chasing her out here and fucking her beneath the lightning has me thinking about doing it again and again. If she wanted me to take her against a tree in the rain, I would.

"Fuck, Raven," I growl, "I could do this all night."

She stops and leans back, her eyes locking with mine, a devilish grin curling her lips.

I reach down between her thighs, my fingers finding her swollen clit. She bites her lip and tosses her head back, gripping my shoulder as she slides up and down on my cock.

"Jackson—I'm yours. All. Fucking. Yours," she cries, her voice breaking as her pussy tightens around me.

She's so close. I press harder, faster, circling her clit until her body shudders under me, and her scream is devoured by the thunder crashing above. Her walls pulse around me as she falls apart, her nails gripping my hair, her whole body shuddering from her release.

I'm right there with her. I grip her hips and drive her down onto me, spilling into her, filling her, claiming her as my cum coats her, marking her as mine.

I'm not letting her go. Ever. We weren't each other's first, but I damn well want us to be each other's last.

Chapter 24

Raven

Holy shit. Can we do that again?

That was insane. Never in my life have I ran outside naked—and definitely never fucked in the woods. But then again, I've never exactly been around any wooded areas in the city. And I sure as hell never wanted to risk getting arrested for streaking.

Out here, though, we were in the middle of nowhere. Or, as my sister would say, "the boonies." I knew what we did was crazy. Jackson sparked a wild side in me tonight. It's a side I have never seen before. He made me feel alive. But God, was it worth it.

We sat in my gazebo, the rain drumming against the roof in a steady rhythm. A couple of blankets lay nearby—thank God—something to wrap ourselves in. It wasn't just crazy that we'd run outside naked in the rain and fucked. It was crazy that we were still sitting out here afterward, bare and soaked from the rain.

The high Jackson and I had been riding was fading, letting the cold slip in. My teeth chatter, my body trembling—not from pleasure this time, but from the chill. I pull the blanket tighter around me, feeling it take the edge off, if only a little.

"Well, I've never done that before," Jackson murmurs, pulling me closer, our naked bodies pressed together for warmth.

Keeping the blanket draped over my back, I stand. Before he can say a word, I swing a leg over and straddle his lap, my head resting against his shoulder. He groans as I settle onto him, his cock pressing dangerously close to my entrance. Maybe this was the best way to keep warm.

His hands find my hips, gliding slowly up and down my curves before stopping on my upper thighs. I lean back, meeting his gaze with a devilish grin. His fingers tighten as he slides them back to my hips, guiding me down onto him.

The stretch makes me gasp, gripping his shoulder with one hand while clutching the blanket in the other. I sink down until he's buried deep within. My lips crash into his, rocking against him in time with the rain's steady beat.

Jackson's tongue traces the seam of my lips, coaxing them apart. His hands cup my breasts, thumbs brushing over my hardened nipples in a teasing stroke. A whimper slips out, and he takes the chance to claim my mouth with his tongue.

The friction builds between us, heat replacing the chill until my whole body is humming. I'm not cold anymore—far from it.

"Yours," I breathe.

"Mine," he whispers against my ear before trailing hot, lingering kisses down my neck.

His strong hands grip my hips, firm and possessive. Each time my pussy swallows him whole, he holds me there for a few intoxicating seconds before letting me lift and ride him again. Lightning flares in the distance, followed by the sharp crack of thunder.

I toss my head back as his hands slide up to cup my breasts, his mouth closing around a hardened peak. His tongue teases and flicks until a jolt of pleasure shoots through me, stealing my breath. My rhythm falters, hips moving in desperate, uneven rolls as the edge draws closer.

Jackson's hand slips between my thighs, fingers sliding through my slick heat until they find my clit. He rubs with just the right pressure—enough to unravel me completely. I cry out as my orgasm hits, my body clenching around him in waves.

He groans, holding me down to the hilt as his release surges into me, hot and claiming. My forehead rests against his, my palms splayed against his chest, feeling the thunder of his heartbeat beneath my hand.

I don't move off him. Instead, I stay there, wrapped around him, his cock still filling me. My arms loop around his neck as I press a tender kiss to the tip of his nose. This might have been the third time tonight, but I'm already addicted to the way I feel when he's buried so deep inside me.

We wait until there is a slight break in the rain before running back to my house. Jackson is on my heels as we bolt toward the door. Once inside, a moan slips from my lips as the rush of warmth envelops me.

Jackson pulls me in for a kiss.

"Let's get to bed. We can warm up faster under the sheets."

He bends down, sliding his arms under my knees and around my back, lifting me easily before carrying me upstairs.

He tosses me onto my bed, then walks over to the dresser to find clothes for me.

With a chuckle, he holds up a nightshirt printed with a bikini body.

"I've never seen one of these before... I might have to wear it myself."

I laugh as he put it back and continues to rummage, pulling out a dark green nightshirt and black shorts. Then he freezes, holding up a pair of underwear... and my pink rabbit.

Oh no. I can feel the heat radiating off my reddened cheeks.

Grinning, he glances at me but—thankfully—sets it back in the drawer without a word. Relief washes through me. As much as the idea of him using it on me was tempting, I wasn't sure I could handle another orgasm tonight. Another night... maybe. The thought alone made my pulse quicken—I always turned it up to the highest setting when I used it.

He hands me the clothes, and I slide the green nightshirt over my head, tugging it down my body before shimmying my underwear over my hips. I meet Jackson's gaze, and his eyes stay fixed on me, dark and entranced. I step into my shorts, dragging them up my thighs; he let out a low groan as I secured them over my ass, letting the elastic snap against my skin.

I bit my lip, crawl into bed, and pat the space beside me. Jackson turns off the light and climbs in, the mattress dipping under his weight. I roll over towards him, molding my body to his. His hand slides down my side, settling possessively on my hip.

We lay there for a while, talking about the small bonfire I was planning this month—just Hannah, Henry, Violet, and Jackson. I didn't tell him why I was keeping it small; maybe I wouldn't have to mention it at all. Jackson seemed especially curious about meeting Hannah's husband, surprised he was so quiet given how outspoken she was. I just told him they worked well together, though I was pretty sure Hannah wore the pants in their relationship.

I don't know what time it is when the conversation shifts to hunting. We talk about out-of-state trips—Tennessee, Montana, even Canada. I love watching him light up as he talks about each one.

My eyelids grow heavy. As I drift off, I swear I hear Jackson whisper, "I think I'm falling in love with you, Raven."

Chapter 25
Jackson

I'm so glad I opened up the back door for Nala's dog door last night—otherwise, I wouldn't be waking up next to Raven right now. I'll head home in a bit to feed her, but for now, I'm soaking up the warmth of her pressed against me.

Thunder usually wakes me in the middle of the night, but last night I slept like a rock. I'm not sure if it was from all the sex we had, or simply because she was beside me. The thought of not having her here every night... it haunts me.

She stirs, rubbing her ass against me, and I instantly feel myself harden. I shift slightly as she rolls over to face me, her fingers tracing lazy patterns through the hair on my chest.

"I had a great time last night," she murmurs.

"I'm glad I invited you in."

I kiss the top of her head, pulling her in closer.

"Me too. Thanks for inviting me in."

I never thought I'd find another woman after Gina—someone who would accept me as I am. But somehow, I found her. She's here, in my arms. And yet... a small part of me can't help but wonder if she's truly happy with me. If one day, she'll tire of who I am and run.

We lay there, talking about our plans for the rest of the weekend.I mention going hunting, and before the words even settle in the air,

Raven asks if I'd mind if she comes with me. I tell her I'd love for her to come anytime she wants.

I'd never craved someone's presence the way I craved hers. The thought of her sitting beside me in the tree stand stirred something deep inside me—something warm, restless, and good. Every minute I spend with Raven feels like something I'll never take for granted.

When we finally climb out of bed—Raven slips into the shower while I pull on my damp clothes from last night. Before heading downstairs, I crack open the bathroom door.

"Hey, I'm going to run home and feed Nala. I'll let Rex out before I leave too. I'll be back soon."

The water shut off, and Raven's head appears from behind the shower curtain.

"Just bring her here. Rex will enjoy having his girlfriend here." She winks and then slides the curtain aside, revealing her glistening body.

I stand there, caught between breathing and staring, taking in every curve as she reaches for a towel. She rubs it through her hair before wrapping the dark green fabric around her. I felt frozen in the doorway, my pulse quickening with the urge to pull the towel away and press her against me.

Instead, I force my thoughts back to Nala, reminding myself I'd be back soon. My feet finally move, carrying me downstairs to let Rex out the back door. He bolts straight for the woods, and I silently thanked the previous owner for putting in a fence out back. Without one, there's no telling where he'd disappear to.

I grab my keys off the little side table before heading out to my truck. Sliding into the driver's seat, memories came rushing back. My eyes drift to the back window, and I let out a low growl—Raven's handprints were still there. I have no plans of wiping them away.

The rain from last night had left its mark—puddles pooling in the yard, the front lawn partially flooded. Pulling into my driveway, I throw the truck into park and step inside my house.

Nala was waiting at the door, tail wagging furiously, probably wondering why I hadn't come home the night before. She pads after me into the kitchen, nails clicking softly against the floor, waiting as I fill her food bowl.

"There you go, Nala. Eat while I hop in the shower and get a bag ready."

After my shower, I pull on fresh clothes, grab my duffel, and toss in a few changes of clothes. As I zip it shut, my mind wanders to the week before Gina left—when I'd bought her a compound bow. I'd hoped it would spark her interest in hunting, or at least give us a reason to go to the range together.

The bow had never been fired. I'd even had a buddy at the bow shop set it up with all the bells and whistles. When he asked if I wanted a special color for the strings, I'd chosen pink and blue. I had the draw weight set low so it would be easy for her to pull back.

Since Raven had been hunting with me lately—and seemed genuinely interested in going more often—I decided it was time to pull the bow out of the closet where it had been hidden for over a year and take it down to her place.

Instead of grabbing my crossbow, I pick up my compound bow, along with the one I want to give to Raven.

After setting the bow cases in the bed of my truck, I walk around to the back of the barn to grab the target for us to shoot at. I toss it into the truck bed, then head inside for my bag and Nala's food, just in case we stay the night. I hoped we would.

Nala follows me out the door, tail wagging, already knowing she is going somewhere. She hops into the passenger seat like it was her rightful throne—my passenger princess. She didn't care where we were going, as long as she was coming with me.

Just as I'm about to pull out of the driveway, I think about bringing our hunting clothes, then decide we can always swing back and change before we head into the woods.

We pull back into Raven's driveway, and I let Nala out of the back seat before grabbing my bag and heading inside. I didn't even think to lock the door when I left, so I step straight in and jog up the stairs.

I find Raven in her room and slip my arms around her from behind, making her jump.

"Raven, it's me—sorry, I didn't mean to startle you. I just let myself in instead of knocking."

She turns, looping her arms around my neck, and pulls me in for a kiss. Every time our lips met, sparks raced through me. When she pulls back, a hint of a smile on her lips.

"What do you want to do today?" she asks.

My smile reaches my ears as I take her hand and lead her downstairs, already knowing exactly what I want to do.

"Where are you taking me, Jackson?" she asks as we step outside, still hand in hand, heading toward the bed of my truck.

I lower the tailgate, but before I could say anything, she gasps and covers her mouth.

"You bought me a bow?"

I want to say yes—but honesty is the best way. Hopefully, Raven would be okay with me giving it to her. I knew she was on the fence about using the hunting clothes I'd bought for Gina—it helped that Gina never wore them. Honestly, I wouldn't want to wear my ex's clothes either.

"Well, no," I say.

"It was supposed to be for my ex, but I never got to give it to her. I was hoping maybe you and I could shoot bows together."

Her eyes lit up, and a smile spreads across her face as she caught my meaning.

"Maybe you could take me hunting," she teases, "and you could watch your cutie in camo bag herself a deer."

"Sounds like the perfect date to me, pretty girl. If you kill a buck, we will have to get it mounted since it would be your first."

She pulls herself up onto the tailgate, legs swinging, then tugs me closer and lowers her lips to mine. When she pulls back, she grins.

"I'd love that. But I have one condition."

I grip her thighs lightly, making her squeal.

"Name it."

She leans back on the bed of the truck, arms behind her, and says, "I don't want to field dress my deer. I kill it, you gut it."

I should probably tell her it's bad luck not to field dress your own deer, but honestly, I am just glad she wants to go hunting with me.

"Okay, but first, let me teach you how to shoot before we even talk about who's field-dressing your deer. You've got to be able to shoot one first."

She pushes me away, already knowing I'm teasing her, slides down from the tailgate, and laughs.

"How hard could it be?"

She holds her arms out as if she were holding a bow and pretends to shoot something.

Grabbing the target from the bed of the truck, I pick up one of the bow cases. Raven takes the other and walks into her backyard.

Watching her carry that bow case, I felt like I was floating.

Finally, I have found a woman who shared an interest in what I loved.

I sit the target down about 20 yards away from where Raven is standing. She has the bow in her hand; the release clipped onto her right hand. I show her how to set the arrow on the string to get it ready. She holds the bow up, and I guide her to clip the release onto the d-loop on the bowstring. Keeping her finger off the trigger, she pulls the string straight back, holding it steady as I help her line up her face—her lips brushing the kisser button on the string.

"Now, close your left eye and look through the peep sight," I say softly. "Line it up with the top sight pin—that's your 20-yard pin. The middle one's 30 yards, and the bottom's 40. Focus on the target, and when you're ready, gently pull the trigger on the release. No rush—this takes patience."

She nods, breathing slowly and deeply, her concentration absolute. I watch as her finger inches toward the trigger. Then—the arrow flies, hitting the dead center of the target.

Her face lights up, grinning ear to ear.

I smirk.

"Well, let's see if that was beginner's luck."

She grabs another arrow, sets it, and aims for the bottom right circle on the target.

"Show me what you got, pretty girl. You might be going hunting with this bow tonight."

She pulls back again, steady and focused, and releases. Another perfect hit. Damn, either she's lying about never having done this before, or she's a natural.

"Okay, let's move back ten yards," I say, using my rangefinder to mark 30 yards between her and the target. I pick up her arrows and set them down nearby. She readies her bow again. I don't remind her about the middle pin—I want to see if she remembers.

She holds steady, lines up her shot, and releases. The arrow pierces the target in the center again.

Raising an eyebrow, I tease, "Are you sure you've never done this before? Because I've never seen someone pick up a bow for the first time and nail the target like that."

She laughs, setting her bow down.

"No, I haven't shot a bow before. But I have shot a gun—my dad taught me to hold a pistol one-handed. One time he made me hold it so long I thought my arm was going to fall off. Holding this bow feels different, though. I can balance it by holding the bow with one hand and the release in the other."

Thank God for this woman. I plan on worshipping her and the ground she walks on for the rest of my days.

She sits down on the ground, looking up at me with that playful smile.

"Well, aren't you going to shoot your bow?"

I nod and walk over to grab my bow from its case. It's been a while since I've shot my compound bow—I've been using my crossbow more on hunts lately. Please, don't let me miss, especially with her already impressing me today.

I notch an arrow, draw back the string with my release, focus on the target, and slowly squeeze the trigger. The arrow flies and lands inside the circle—but far from the center. I frown and pull another arrow, telling myself to calm down. You can't shoot well if you're tense.

"You got this, babe," Raven says softly. "I've only seen you with your crossbow when we hunt."

Her voice soothes me. I take a deep breath, bring the bow up again, and shoot. This time, the arrow hits dead center.

Relief floods me. I just needed to relax.

We shoot a few more times, then pack our bows away.

Our bows. My pretty girl. My Raven.

I love the sound of that.

Chapter 26
Raven

"So, do you want to take your bow out tonight?" Jackson asks, sliding his bow case into the bed of his truck.

Part of me wants to, but another part would just rather sit in the woods with him and not worry about shooting.

"I actually thought about leaving it here today. Maybe next time," I say as I walk toward the passenger side.

His expression dips for a moment, but the disappointment fades once we're both in the truck.

"Okay—next time." He clicks his seatbelt into place, glances at me, and smiles.

"Ready?"

I nod.

"Yes. I promise next time I'll bring my bow. And... thank you again for it."

"Pretty girl, that bow was always meant to be yours. I love that you enjoy shooting it."

He eases us out of my driveway, heading toward the property where he hunts.

"So," he adds, tapping his fingers lightly against the steering wheel, "how's work been?"

"Ever since the Dean situation, I have both friends and enemies," I admit. "I'm just glad not every woman there is still drooling over him. The ones who are, think I tried to take advantage of him."

Jackson's laugh rumbles low in his chest. He steers us off the main road onto a narrow green path leading to the woods. Reaching for the radio, he switches to the music on his phone. His thumb hovers over a playlist labeled: *Hunting*. Scrolling through the songs, he smirks before landing on *Sleigh Ride*.

A Christmas song. In October. I bite back a smile. I'm in no position to judge—I watch holiday movies year-round. Not just Christmas, either. Halloween, too.

As if catching my thoughts, he asks, "Want to know why I picked it?"

I lean over the center console, curious.

"Sure."

I've never known a man who willingly queued up Christmas music.

He taps the steering wheel in a slow rhythm.

"It's a good-luck song. My dad and I used to listen to it on the way to the woods. He swore it gave us a better shot at killing a deer. I didn't believe it... until the year after, when I got my first one after listening to it that morning."

It's the little things that make hunting special for Jackson. It's never just about the deer—it's about the moments, and the people. This was something he shared with his dad, and now he wanted to share it with me. That meant more than I could say.

Honestly, we ought to put a buddy stand in my woods. We could walk out my back door and skip the drive. Maybe I'll tell him that later.

"Well," he says, voice dipping softer, "I'm glad you've still got some friends there. I just wish you never had to go through that with Dean." His hand finds mine as the truck bumps down the grassy trail. "At least he's gone now. I don't have to worry about him being around you anymore—especially after what he tried to pull. Truth be told, I wish that bastard had been locked away for a while."

"Me too," I mutter under my breath.

Jackson is the only one who knows exactly what happened that day. Rumors flew around town about what supposedly happened, and Jackson has probably heard them too—but thankfully, he's never brought them up.

One rumor claimed that Dean stopped by to ask me out on another date, and when he showed up, I was with another man. Supposedly, that man got upset and assaulted Dean. Apparently, he told me to call the cops and roll around on the ground to make it look like Dean had thrown me around. And the best part? Just before the police arrived, he supposedly told me to spin some sob story about Dean trying to rape me.

Another rumor claimed that I went to beg Dean to take me out again, and when he refused—because we worked together—I accused him of attempting to rape me.

I've been called some pretty nasty names, but at least Jackson, my sister, and my friends at work knew the truth: they're just rumors, and nothing that they said happened.

I talked to my therapist the following Monday. We will be meeting virtually every week, and she's been pushing the same thing from the start—I need a support system. People who will pull me out of my head, out of my house, out into the world. People who won't let me spend my nights isolated.

That's one of the reasons I caved and went to the bar last Friday.

And let me just say—I'm glad I did. If I hadn't, I never would've found out who Jackson's ex was. I wouldn't have had the pleasure of getting under her skin that night. And I definitely wouldn't have ended up making out with Jackson in the rain... or having sex with him in the back seat of his truck. Who knows how different things would be if I'd stayed home.

When we reach a stretch of the grassy path hidden from road, Jackson kills the engine and pushes his door open. He slides his hat on, gives me a wink. I can't help but stare at him.

I step down from the truck, shrugging into my heavy jacket as the cold air bites at my cheeks. Jackson hauls his camo backpack from the bed of the truck, the crossbow strapped neatly to the front. Gripping onto the strap, he swings it onto his shoulders, and with a small nod, we start toward the woods.

Today, we're not sitting in the buddy stand.

Instead, Jackson leads me toward something he calls a box blind.

As we get closer, it comes into view—a weathered wooden box raised on a stand, just like the name suggests. Each side has a small window cut into it, perfect for taking a shot without leaving the shelter. The camo paint on the outer walls has begun to chip, fading in places from seasons of sun and rain.

A ladder stretches up the side, its rungs worn but solid under my hand when I test them. Jackson wouldn't bring me here if it wasn't safe. When we've sat in the buddy stand before, he's always been insistent about me wearing a safety harness.

Once, he told me about a friend who fell from a tree stand a couple of years ago—a long, brutal recovery that could've ended much worse. *Lucky to be alive,* he'd said. He's repeated more than once that too many hunters aren't so lucky, and that one bad fall can be fatal.

Jackson lets me climb up first into the box blind. I open the hatch and pull myself inside. It's not warm, but it definitely feels better than the cold October air outside. Jackson said colder days are the best for deer hunting—deer move more to keep their bodies warm.

I walk over to one of the windows and glance down to see Jackson making his way up the ladder, his backpack strapped tight to his shoulders. Once inside, he drops the bag onto the floor of the blind and closes the hatch behind him.

I settle into one of the chairs, watching him unlatch the seals on the windows. He opens them up all of the way allowing the crisp autumn air to filter in.

Leaning over me, his fingertips brush my knee as he reaches to turn on the small heater to my right. A comforting wave of warmth rises, pushing back the chill from the open window.

"Why—is this the first time you're bringing me here? I like the box blind. It's heated. We could just come out here and sit all day."

A soft chuckle escapes his lips.

"Well, I haven't sat in here for a while. Before I brought you, I wanted to make sure it was safe. We don't need it collapsing the minute we get up here."

He nods toward a small trunk in the corner behind me.

"It even has snacks."

He points to a little table nearby.

"I used to keep a few boxes of snacks there, but I learned the hard way—squirrels decided to help themselves one day."

I grin.

"Smart squirrels."

"Smart and sneaky," he says, shaking his head with a laugh.

"They're like tiny ninjas."

I try to keep quiet, but it's impossible not to snicker at the thought of Jackson catching squirrels ransacking his snack stash.

The heater hums softly, mixing with the quiet sounds of the woods—the snap of twigs, the rustle of leaves drifting down. The late afternoon sun casts dappled shadows across the floor and our boots.

"So," I say, "what's your plan if we actually see a deer?"

He smiles, eyes gleaming.

"Patience. And maybe with a little luck, we will be dragging a deer out tonight."

I nudge him playfully.

"And what if I get cold or bored first?"

He grins.

"Then I'll keep you warm."

The easy banter settles between us like a warm blanket, and for a moment, the world outside this little box fades away.

He hangs his bow on the hook in front of us and pulls our Kindles out of his backpack. We can whisper, but even then, we have to keep it to a minimum—deer have excellent hearing.

The box blind sways gently as the wind rustles through the trees. More than once, I look up, expecting to see a deer approaching—only to catch a squirrel shuffling through the leaves blanketing the forest floor.

Birds chirp in the distance, their songs echoing softly off the bare branches.

I could sit out here all day, feeling like I'm in my own little gazebo—minus the books, my comfy chair, and Rex curled up at my feet.

Not one deer shows itself before the sun dips below the horizon.

We stay in the box blind until darkness swallows the woods.

With one foot in the stirrup of his bow, Jackson disengages the safety and holds the bowstring taut.

"Mind pulling that trigger, pretty girl?"

I squeeze the release, watching him slowly lower the bowstring—uncocking the bow. After securing our gear and hanging his bow on the front of his back pack, he swings the strap over his shoulder and opens the hatch.

He climbs down the ladder one deliberate step at a time. When he is halfway down, I follow.

My feet hit solid ground just as Jackson reaches out his hand. Our fingers intertwine, he pulls me close and kisses me before we head down the trail.

Thankfully, I still have a grip on his hand, because I'm far from graceful navigating the woods. A few times I nearly stumble, but Jackson steadies me, keeping me from face-planting on the dirt path.

The woods are peaceful—our footsteps crunching wet leaves, the only sound aside from the soft squeak of our boots. Moonlight filters through the bare branches, faint but enough to guide us back to his truck.

I glance up at the moon, distracted for just a moment—then my foot sinks into a small hole. Twisting my ankle, I collapse to the ground, pulling Jackson down with me. The damp leaves and cold dirt press against my skin, and I wince as a sharp sting shoots up my leg.

"Shit, Raven, are you okay?" Jackson asks, his voice tight with concern as he kneels in the moonlight, inspecting my ankle.

"I'm pretty sure I rolled it," I admit, trying to laugh despite the sting.

"Silly me—not paying attention and stepping right into a hole. I love nature, but I think we have a bit of a love-hate relationship when I'm clumsy."

I glance up at him.

"Are you okay?"

He slides his bag off his shoulders and sets it down carefully before focusing back on me.

"Yeah, I'm good. You, though... can you move it?" he asks, gently probing.

I lift my leg and try to wiggle my ankle, wincing sharply. "I think I'll be okay. Just need a minute before I try standing." I bite back the pain, knowing the throbbing won't fade anytime soon.

"Help me up?"

Jackson jumps to his feet. He grabs his backpack before helping me up—keeping me stable as I steady myself on my good leg.

After this little incident, there's no way we can sneak out quietly—we sound like a herd of squirrels crashing through the leaves.

I keep my eyes on the trail, careful where I step. If my other ankle gives out, the only way out is in Jackson's arms. That wouldn't be so bad, would it? But I'd hate to make him carry me *and* his backpack the rest of the way.

A cramp starts creeping up my calf on the good leg.

"Hey, Jackson... do you think we could take a little break?"

He stops and looks around.

"Sure, let's get to that tree so you can lean against something. Since we're almost at the truck, I'll run my stuff over there and come back for you."

I nod, grateful, as we make our way to the massive tree. I lean against its rough bark, running my hand over the grooves and ridges. It's so wide I can't wrap my arms around it—it must be over a hundred years old. Around us, the other trees stand smaller, younger.

Glancing over my shoulder, I see Jackson coming back toward me.

"Thank goodness you came back," I say, relief leaking into my voice.

"I thought I'd have to drag myself out and hitch a ride with some stranger—and pray they weren't a murderer."

Though it's dark, the moonlight reveals the smirk curling on Jackson's lips. Closing the distance, he leans close and whispers in my ear, "Are you saying I took too long?"

I'm speechless, his warm breath tickling the bare skin of my neck.

He pulls away, and the cold night air instantly cools the spot where his breath once lingered. I reach up and slip his hat off his head, turning it backwards and placing it on mine.

At that moment, I watch the man before me unravel—the same way he did the last time I wore his hat like that. The moonlight casts half his face in shadow, highlighting his devilish smile.

He groans, cups my face, and pulls me in for a searing kiss. His lips part, inviting my tongue inside. He playfully bites it, sliding his hand around my lower back to pull me closer. Then, with sudden urgency, he pushes me back against the tree. The rough tree bark presses firmly into my back, indenting through the fabric of my jacket.

His fingers yank my hair, giving him easier access to my neck, where he trails hungry kisses.

"I lose all self-control when you wear my hat like that, pretty girl," he growls.

His cold fingers trace the inside of my waistband before slipping down the front of my pants. I gasp sharply as his touch meets my center, sliding into my wetness.

He hums, pleased by how ready I am for him, rubbing my clit as his lips crash back onto mine.

"God, Raven... I wish I could bury myself inside you right here, right now," he murmurs, sucking on my bottom lip as he moans against me.

Seeking more friction, I grind against his hand, building toward the edge as he pinches and tugs at my clit.

"When you come, I want you to scream my name. Loud. I want it to echo off every tree around us. I want the people down the street to know exactly who's making you come."

His hand slides up my shirt and beneath my bra, fingers grazing my puckered nipples.

Waves of bliss flood through me. I'm high on Jackson. The throbbing pain in my ankle vanishes, numbed by his intoxicating touch.

My hips buck beneath his hand, the pressure increasing until I scream, "Jackson, don't stop! Fuck, that feels so good!"

The thought that someone might hear us out here sends a shiver straight through me, making my pulse spike and every nerve tingle with heat.

Jackson lifts my chin so I can meet his gaze. The moonlight gives his eyes a different shade of blue—deeper, almost electric.

He lets go of my chin, brushing a stray hair away from my face, then traces my jawline with a finger.

"Come for me, pretty girl."

The intensity coils tight inside me, and I tumble over the edge at those words, riding the wave of my orgasm, every nerve on fire as I chase it relentlessly.

Jackson pulls his hand from my pants and brings his fingers to his lips, sucking off every drop of me. His fingers pop softly as he pulls them away.

"Well," he says with a grin, "I thought I was coming to get you and take you back to the truck so we could head home. Looks like we won't be hunting tomorrow—not after you screamed my name like that. I'm pretty sure every deer in these woods took off."

I swat his arm playfully, laughing.

"You know it was your fault. You could've just came and got me."

He smirks and lowers himself to lift me off the ground effortlessly.

"You know, pretty girl," he says, "you shouldn't have stolen my hat and put it backwards on that head of yours. Haven't you learned by now? It only gets you into trouble."

Surprised, Jackson carries me back to his truck without once stopping for a break. I'm not light—I've always had a little junk in the trunk—and body image has been a struggle for me.

Growing up, I was petite with a nice figure. But once high school hit, it felt like my metabolism took a dive into the deep end. During college, I lost quite a bit of weight after getting into running. I ran numerous 5Ks and felt great shedding pounds here and there.

Then came the knee injury. Recovery became my top priority if I ever wanted to run again. But when Kevin and I got together, the weight crept back on. And he made sure I knew it.

He constantly told me I needed to lose weight and that he never wanted to be seen with me in public unless I wore certain clothes. Once, we were invited to a friend's pool party, and he lied—saying I couldn't make it, that I was sick. He was ashamed of my body and left me alone at home.

I was in a dark place with Kevin.

After I left him, I started eating healthier and doing light exercise again. That's one of the reasons I love where I live now. I can walk every day, and it's great exercise for Rex, too.

When we reach Jackson's truck, he opens the door with the arm supporting my back before easing me into the passenger seat.

"Oh, so I don't get to drive your truck home tonight?" I tease as I slide my legs inside.

He smirks.

"Well, I figured with your ankle, you'd be more interested in being my passenger princess tonight." Winking at me, he closes my door, rounds the hood, and climbs in on the driver's side.

I don't mind being the passenger princess every once in a while. The perks are pretty great: I get to read, nap, and best of all, watch Jackson.

He's staying at my place again tonight. When he went home earlier, he packed some clothes, Nala's food, and a few toys for her so he wouldn't have to come back after hunting. He said knowing our luck, we would get a deer tonight and wouldn't be home until late. Little did he know, I would be the unlucky one, falling and twisting my ankle. But I can't complain about the orgasm he just gave me—I can still feel where the rough tree bark was pressing against my back.

He turns the key and pulls the truck down the path, back onto the road, heading home.

My little house really does feel like home—especially with Jackson there.

"What time do you want to go get your car tomorrow?" he asks.

Oh crap. We still have to pick up my car from town—it's been there since Friday night.

"Umm... I was thinking about sleeping in tomorrow," I say.

"Maybe we can get it after we wake up? I call dibs on driving your truck. You can drive my car back."

A smile spreads across his face.

"Sounds great. As long as I get to drive in front of you while you're driving your car."

I nudge his arm on the center console.

"You just want to watch me belt out songs in your truck."

He laughs and snorts.

"You got that right. Hell, I might put a dash cam in my truck and flip it around so it records you."

A devilish grin spreads across my face. He notices and asks, "What?"

I point to the back seat.

"Are you sure you want a camera recording me back there? Might catch some action."

He laughs so hard he slaps his knee, tears threatening to spill. Then he glances over at me.

"You mean you don't want to make one of those sex tapes?"

Oh good lord, I cross my arms, trying to hold in my laughter.

"No, Jackson, I have zero interest in making a sex tape. Knowing my luck, it'd get out to the world. Plus, haven't you seen the movie where it uploads to the cloud and all their friends see it? I'd be mortified if anyone saw that."

He pats my leg, still snorting.

"I was only kidding, Raven. But I wasn't kidding about recording you singing in my truck."

We pull into my driveway, but instead of unloading his bow and book bag from the truck bed, Jackson comes around and lifts me into his arms. Rex and Nala greet us eagerly at the door as he carries me inside.

"You know I could probably walk now," I murmur, wincing a little.

"Might even be better to start putting weight on it sooner rather than later. Besides, I'm not exactly light."

He smiles softly and sets me down on the couch, leaning in until our foreheads touch.

"If I could, I'd carry you everywhere, pretty girl. Carrying you gives me an excuse to touch you—to feel you breathe. Those are some of my favorite things when I'm with you. You make me feel at peace. You are my home, Raven."

He kisses my forehead before gently helping me take off my boots. I wince when he reaches for the one on my injured ankle. Without hesitation, his hands slid beneath me and he lifts me up again, offering no chance for protest.

"I'm carrying you upstairs," he says softly.

In the bedroom, he helps me slide off my pants so I could change into pajama shorts. Before I could even grasp the zipper, he unzips my jacket and pulls it off my arms. I tug my shirt over my head and toss it onto the floor beside the bed. Holding the oversized t-shirt up, I guide my arms through, and he lowers it down over me.

"I'm going downstairs to feed the dogs and make us some dinner," Jackson says.

"You stay in bed and read. No moving around. I'll bring you an ice pack for your ankle."

I look down at my swollen, purplish ankle and shift myself up against the headboard to sit comfortably. Jackson leaves the room, descending the stairs to tend to the dogs and start dinner.

Sighing, I pick up my Kindle and lose myself in one of Kelli Cooke's fall romance novels until the smell of maple syrup floats up the stairs.

Jackson returns with two plates in hand. I grab an extra pillow and place it on my lap.

Three uneven slices of French toast were stacked high, syrup pooling on top and overflowing onto the plate. I lick my lips in anticipation. Before I could thank him, he hands me a second plate stacked with sausage links and a small dollop of ketchup. He knew my quirks—I hated my food touching.

"I'm going to grab my plate. What do you want to drink?"

"Just ice water, please," I reply, looking up at him. "Thanks."

He kisses my forehead and heads back downstairs.

When he returns, he is juggling his plate, our drinks, and an ice pack. Setting the ice pack on the bed's edge, he wraps it in a hand towel from the bathroom before gently pressing it against my ankle. The cold numbs the pain instantly.

I dig into my French toast, savoring every bite. I was pretty sure I'd only ever told Jackson once that French toast was my favorite food. He'd also learned that ketchup was essential—on just about everything. He cringed when I admitted I put ketchup on tacos, but I told him, technically, ketchup was just like diced tomatoes. He laughed then, but I knew deep down he'd try it next time.

When we are finished, he takes our plates back to the kitchen. Returning, he flips off the lights and slips into bed beside me, pulling me close. I turn to face him.

"So, I've been thinking"

"Would you want to put a box blind out back here? Since you're staying here, it'd make more sense for you to just walk out the back door instead of driving down the road."

He squeezes me gently.

"Really?"

I nod.

"I like that idea. Tanner sells them. I'll call him Monday and let him know I'm going to buy one. I'll even get some comfy chairs for it."

His face lights up as he talks about the plans. I don't know why I'd been so stubborn about letting him hunt on my property, but I was glad he wants to bring me along.

"After everything's set up, you're going to take your bow out. I'll leave mine at home. I'd love to see you get your first deer."

I lean in to kiss him.

"That sounds perfect. I can't wait."

I rest my head against his chest, listening to his fast heartbeat—the excitement of the idea thrumming between us. I smile as my eyelids grew heavy, drifting off to sleep to the steady rhythm of Jackson's heart.

Chapter 27
Jackson

Before my eyes even open to let the sunlight wish me good morning, I notice the spot beside me in bed is empty. The sheets are cool where she should be. Blinking awake, I scan Raven's room and spot the bathroom door closed.

I slide out of bed, padding toward it just as the rush of water fills the air. A small smile tugs at my lips—maybe I can convince her to let me join.

I ease the door open, and Raven's head appears from behind the shower curtain, damp strands clinging to her cheek.

"Sorry, I was trying to be quiet. I hope I didn't wake you," she says softly.

Her eyes track me as I push the door wider and step inside. In one smooth motion, I strip off my sweatpants and boxers. She's still watching, lip caught between her teeth, a playful smile curving her mouth as her fingers clutch the curtain like it's the only thing keeping her steady.

"Can I join you?"

She nods, her gaze lingering on my cock as I step toward the shower. When I stop in front of her, her eyes finally lift to meet mine.

"You alright in there, pretty girl?" I ask.

She bites her lower lip and smiles before taking my hand and pulling me in with her. The moment our bodies meet, I wrap my arms around her slick, wet frame.

"Well, good morning to you, too," I murmur, pressing a kiss to her forehead.

Her arms loop around my neck as she rises onto her tiptoes, bringing her wet lips to mine. My hands trail down the smooth plane of her back until they find the soft curve of her ass. She breaks the kiss with a smile, and my eyes drift down to her ankle—still a little swollen.

"How's the ankle this morning? You seem to be putting some pressure on it today," I say.

Her hands slide from my neck down my chest, fingers curling playfully in my chest hair. Her eyes flick back up to mine.

"I'm not going to baby it, Jackson. I'm a tough girl," she replies.

Smirking, I reach for a bottle of shampoo and squeeze some into my palm. Raven's eyes dart to what I've picked up.

"Did you not see the other shampoo? There's one that doesn't smell so fruity," she says.

I lather it between my hands, pretending I'm about to work it into my own hair—then instead, I start massaging it into her thick, wet strands. The moment her shoulders loosen and her body melts further into mine, I know I've done something right.

A soft moan slips from her lips as I work the shampoo in, my fingers massaging her scalp. Grabbing the showerhead from its mount, I rinse the suds away, warm water cascading over her hair and down her back.

Raven turns to grab the loofah hanging in the shower and passes it to me along with a bottle of body wash. While I return the showerhead to its place, I pour the gel onto the loofah, working it into a rich lather before gliding it over her skin.

She faces me, letting me trail bubbles from her shoulders down to her toes. Water trickles over her chest, washing away the foam almost as quickly as I spread it. I turn her gently, running the loofah down her back, and press a slow kiss to her neck.

She arches into me, her ass brushing against my now-hard cock. I let out a sharp hiss. I had no intention of burying myself inside her in the shower, but damn—she makes it hard to keep control of myself.

I work the lather over her lower back, sliding down to the curve of her ass. Leaning close, my lips brush her ear.

"Greedy for my cock this morning, pretty girl? It's not even eight yet."

Without a word, she shuts off the water, snatches the loofah from my hand, and hangs it back up. Stepping out of the shower, she glances over her shoulder—her eyes saying *follow me*—and wraps herself in a towel.

Without looking away, I grab the towel next to hers and dry off quickly before trailing her out of the bathroom, never letting her out of my sight.

In seconds, I'm on her tail, following her into the bedroom—jealous of the towel clinging to every curve as she walks. She stops beside the bed, and I close the gap until there's barely an inch between us, desperate to get my greedy hands on her.

Before I can touch her, she lets the towel fall in a slow, deliberate drop to the floor. She spins before I can grab her hips, shoving me down onto the bed.

Propping myself up on my elbows, I keep my eyes locked on her as she moves to the nightstand.

She digs through a drawer and pulls out a small black object. With a click of the button, her head tilts back, wet hair snapping against her back as a moan escapes her lips.

Fuck.

She walks back, tossing a remote control for a butt plug onto the bed beside me. I pick it up, glance at her, and press the button. Another moan pours from her as pleasure ripples through her body. My girl is ready to play this morning—but there's no way I'm letting her climb straight onto my cock. We're going to have some fun first.

Raven straddles my hips, but before she can line me up, I grip her waist and guide her pussy to my face. She squeals, grabbing the headboard as she hovers above me. With the remote still in my hand, I turn up the setting. Her hips buck, and I pull her down onto my mouth.

My hands roam her thighs, feeling goosebumps rise under my touch as I suck her clit. The combined intensity of my mouth and the plug vibrating in her ass has her grinding against my face like she's chasing every bit of friction she can get.

She cries out my name when I spank her ass, and I slide two fingers deep into her tight, soaked pussy. The vibration hums against my hand as I curl my fingers right where I know she needs me. Her lust-filled eyes meet mine, and I take her clit between my teeth, tugging gently before sucking the swollen bundle of nerves.

My free hand cups her breast, fingers teasing her hardened nipple until another shiver rolls through her. That's all it takes—her pussy begins to tighten around my fingers. She bites her bottom lip as if holding back, so I press the remote again.

Her mouth opens in a silent scream, her walls clenching down hard. I slow my pace, rubbing her clit as I ease her down from her orgasm.

When she finally lifts off my face, she slides down my chest, her wetness smearing against my skin, making my cock ache and throb for her. She lines herself up, hovering at my tip—then pulls back, leaving me painfully desperate for her.

"Everything alright?"

She doesn't answer— instead she just crashes her lips against mine, groaning as she sucks herself off my mouth. Her hand wraps around my cock, and a devilish smile curves her lips."

"Everything is perfect."

She swings a leg over me, straddling my hips but facing away. I grip her waist as she lowers herself, my cock sinking into her inch by inch. The added pressure from the plug sends a deep, vibrating hum through her, and I can't resist grabbing a handful of her ass.

When she's fully seated, she starts rocking her hips, my cock sliding in and out of her slick heat. Her head tips back, wet hair sliding down her spine, and her hand slips between her thighs to rub her clit. Watching her pussy swallow my cock was enough to send black specks dancing across my vision—it was pure intoxication.

"Raven," I growl, my voice rough. I want to hold out until she's tipped over the edge again. I've always made sure my partners came first, if not twice.

"Pretty girl, I love it when you play with yourself while riding my cock. When I fill that tight pussy up with my cum and we go get your car, I want people to *know* you've been claimed. You're mine, Raven."

I thumb the remote, turning the plug to a higher setting. Her hips jerk and grind, moving erratically as the orgasm tears through her, her voice breaking on my name. Her walls clamp down around me, milking my cock as my release spills deep inside her.

Her body shudders, still trembling when I finally turn off the plug. She eases off me and curls up on my chest, her breathing ragged. I kiss her forehead, wrapping my arms tight around her.

"Ready to get dressed and head into town to get your car in a bit?"

She props herself up on an elbow, teasing, "Will there be enough people up and about to know I'm yours?"

Rolling her under me, I cage her between my arms.

"If not, we'll just have to do it again," I murmur, kissing the tip of her nose.

I climb off the bed, pull my clothes back on, and head downstairs to take care of the dogs while Raven finishes getting ready.

Walking out the front door, Raven snickers as she runs around to the driver's side.

Her ankle must feel a lot better.

She climbs in and waits for me to get into the passenger seat before holding out her hand for the keys. An infectious smile spreads across her face when I place them in her palm. Turning the key, she quickly turns the dial on the radio—looking for her desired station.

Buckled up and ready to go, we pull out of the driveway and head towards town. Out of the corner of my eye, I watch her roll down the window, hanging her arm out as the breeze tousles her hair. It's definitely a little warmer out, especially for October. I feel completely at ease in the passenger seat, watching her drive my truck into town with a smile on her face—one that's perfectly mirrored on mine.

She reaches over the center console for my hand. Intertwining our fingers together, I give her hand a gentle squeeze.

"Are you enjoying being the passenger princess this morning, Mr. Jackson?" She ask, chuckling. I lift our joined hands and press a kiss to the back of her hand.

"I sure am. Does my pretty girl enjoy driving my truck?"

Focusing on the road and biting her bottom lip, she runs her hand down the steering wheel.

"I'll admit, it's definitely different compared to my car. But I definitely like it. Might have to trade in my little car for one of these."

I would prefer she didn't. The only truck I want to see her driving is mine. But if she really wanted to get her own truck, I would support her decision. I know if there was something I wanted, she would support me.

"Well, if that's something you want to do, find one you like, and we'll check it out."

"Really?" She beams.

"Thanks, I appreciate it. I may know how to change a tire, but I don't know much about cars. With my luck, I'd buy a piece of junk and it would die on me within a few days."

I never understood dealerships and why they would sell people cars that didn't run well. Dealerships often took advantage of women. I remember the car my sister bought on her own. I offered to go with her that day, but she insisted on doing it alone. It wasn't even five days later that the engine went out. Thankfully, she was able to get it fixed for free after talking to the dealership.

Raven pulls into the parking lot next to her car.

"Want to go in and get breakfast? They started serving breakfast on the weekends."

I already know her answer when she unbuckles her seatbelt and hops out of the truck. Raven walks around the hood, taking my hand as we enter the bar. Sunlight illuminates the room through the small windows on the west side of the building.

We're greeted by Brody—the bartender here—as we walk through the door. After taking a seat, he stops by to hand us our menus. I slowly set mine down and wait for Raven to decide what she wants before calling him back over.

Raven sets her menu down and asks, "So, what are you getting?"

I run a hand down my beard before replying, "I'm going to get the pancake special. Are you getting your French toast? I haven't had it here yet, but I've heard it's really good."

She covers her face like she's embarrassed. Gently peeling her hands away one by one, I say, "There's nothing wrong with getting the same thing everywhere you go. When I used to go to Lucy's Diner in town, I'd get the same thing every time. Hell, there were times I didn't even have to say my order—they'd just bring my coffee to the table and let me know my food was already being made. That's one of the perks of living in a small town like River Valley."

But in a small town, everyone knows who you are and what your business is—and they love to gossip, especially when it's just a rumor. I remember all the things they were saying about Raven. Every time I heard someone talking about my girl, I made sure to tell them what really happened. Well, I left out a couple of details; I'm sure Raven wouldn't want the whole town to know that Dean was attempting to rape her before I pulled in. That is something I hope to never witness again.

I know it's a small town, but I hope I never cross paths with Dean. He mentally and physically hurt my girl. I never really cared for him as a person, but I never would have thought he'd go that far to hurt someone. Thankfully, he is not allowed within a certain distance of Raven, so as long as he follows the rules, we won't have a problem.

Brody comes back over to take our order before attending to more customers further down the bar.

The jukebox in the corner stops playing, and I spin around in my seat, walking over to pick the next song. As I flip through the tracks, I feel an arm wrap around my waist, and out of the corner of my eye, I see Raven resting her head on my shoulder.

"Which song are you looking for?" she asks, watching me flip through the list a second time.

"Just looking for the perfect song to play."

She covers her mouth, trying to stifle a laugh.

"Do you have a special song you listen to while eating breakfast?"

Smirking, I nudge her.

"If you must know, I do, in fact, have a special breakfast song," I say jokingly.

When I decide which song I want to listen to, I drop my quarters into the slot and press the button for the one I want. Wrapping my arm around Raven's waist, I turn and walk with her back to our seat. As *"Better Together"* by Luke Combs begins to play, I let go of her waist and reach for her hand.

She looks up at me with those deep brown eyes, and instantly I knew she could tell exactly what I was about to ask. She nods and links her hands behind my neck, pulling us closer. We sway to the music, letting the rhythm guide us across the open floor.

I lean in and whisper, "I was actually trying to find the perfect song to dance with you before we ate. I didn't get to dance with you much the other night."

She giggles, her smile lighting up her face.

As the song ends, Raven begins to pull her hands away from around my neck. I glance over and see Mitch at the jukebox, giving me a wink. I nod back—this dance wasn't over yet. Grabbing Raven's hands, I place one on my shoulder and held the other in mine. Resting my free hand on her hip.

As *"Slow Dance in a Parking Lot"* by Jordan Davis begins to play, we move together across the floor. I look over at Mitch and smile. He might've been through a tough time with his fiancée, but he was always there for me.

Raven and I sway gently to the beat. I slide my hand off her hip, giving her a spin before placing it right back on her hip and pulling her in even closer. Our bodies press flush together. She looks up at me, and I lean down to kiss her. The warmth of her mouth sent a spark through me, and as we rock back and forth to the music, I moved my hand to the small of her back, pulling her even closer—even though we couldn't possibly be any closer than we already were.

Lost in the moment, in the music, in her, I forgot the world around us. When the song ends, Raven pulls her lips from mine, snapping me out of our little bubble and reminding me we weren't alone.

Looking toward the bar, I notice Brody walking over to our seats with our food. As we head back, I catch sight of a few women sitting in the corner, whispering and watching us. One of them laughs, and Raven's head turns immediately at the sound.

I squeeze her hand and wrap my arm around her.

"You okay? We can leave if you want."

She shakes her head and sits down at the bar, picking up her fork without meeting my eyes. She fidgets in her seat, cutting up her French toast but never taking a bite—just moving the pieces around on her plate.

I look toward Brody and wait until he looks my way. When our eyes meet, I mouth, *box.*

Nodding, he grabs a couple of takeout containers from behind the counter and sets them down in front of me. As I reach into my pocket to hand him my card, he waves it off, mouthing, *don't worry about it,* before glancing at Raven, who now had her face buried in her hands.

"Thanks, buddy," I say as I open up the boxes and carefully slide our food inside. I rub Raven's back gently.

"Hey... let's get out of here," I say with a soft smile.

"I know the perfect place we can go to eat."

When Raven follows me out the door to the parking lot, I remember the reason we came into town. With how much her demeanor has changed in just the last five minutes, I'm not sure she's up for driving. I take her hand and gently spin her around to face me.

"Raven, I know it's something you probably don't want to talk about. Just know that I'm here—and I'll always be here."

I brush a stray piece of hair from her face, tucking it behind her ear. A single tear rolls down her cheek, and I reach up to wipe it away before it falls.

"So, we have two options," I continue.

"We can take my truck home together, or you can drive it and I'll take your car. If you're not up to driving, you could drop me off at work before heading to school. Just... don't forget to pick me up," I add with a small grin.

That earns a soft smile from her. She kicks at the gravel and silently holds out her car keys. I hand her mine in return, and she climbs into my truck. I watch her drive off before getting into her little car to follow.

The whole way home, Raven is on my mind. I want to ask her questions, to help her open up—but I'm afraid of pushing too hard and driving her away. That's the last thing I want.

I want her to know I'm here, that I'll listen whenever she's ready. No pressure. Just presence.

When we pull into her driveway, she doesn't get out right away. As I open her door, I see fresh tears running down her face.

"Baby, come here," I say softly.

"Let's get inside."

She nods and takes my hand as I help her down from the truck. Without thinking, I scoop her up into my arms, close the door behind us, and carry her inside. She wraps her arms around my neck and buries her face in my chest.

Once inside, I carry her to the living room and sit down on the couch with her still in my arms. I brush a few wet strands of hair from her face, tears still trailing down her cheeks.

God, I wish I could take this pain away. I'd give anything to erase that day from her life. It brought us closer, sure—but I'd rather we had grown closer a different way. A safer way. She should never have had to endure the emotional and physical trauma that Dean put her through.

I'm willing to be patient, to build something strong and lasting with her, one step at a time. I'd do anything for Raven. She's my world.

"If you want to talk about it, I'm here," I say quietly.

"If not, we can just sit here and cuddle on the couch. Whatever you need. I'm here for you. Always. You know that, right?"

She nods against my chest, wiping her tears with the back of her hand.

"Thank you," she whispers, her voice shaky.

I lift her chin, wanting her to look at me.

"Anytime, pretty girl. I'll always be here for you. You are my world."

Closing my eyes, I press a soft kiss to her forehead. I scoot us over to the end of the couch so I can stretch my legs out along the cushions. Picking up the remote from the side table, I flip through the channels until I find something worth watching. I settle on a show and set the remote down.

When the program returns, Raven peeks up to see what I've picked. A smile spreads across her face.

"So, not only do you like to go hunting, but you also like to watch it?" she teases.

I chuckle.

"Well, that's where I get all my tips and tricks."

She grabs my hand resting on her leg and laces her fingers with mine.

"So... do you want to go turkey hunting with me in the spring?" I ask, giving her hand a gentle squeeze.

"I don't care what we hunt," she says softly.

"If I'm with you, that's all that matters to me."

This woman quite literally fell into my lap—and I'll thank God every single day for that.

The breakfast we brought home from the bar ended up going to waste since I never carried it in from my truck. By the time Raven worked up an appetite, all she wanted was popcorn.

So, while she sits on the couch, I pull her popcorn maker out of the cabinet and start popping some for us.

Standing with my hands on the counter, I glance at Raven, who sits upright on the couch, her eyes fixed on the hunting channel. On the screen, a father and son are deer hunting in a buddy stand in Kentucky. A large trophy buck makes its way into view, and the father coaches his son through the process, preparing him to take the shot.

When the deer is finally in the boy's line of fire, the boy pulls the trigger. The buck runs a few yards before collapsing in a nearby bean field. The excitement on the boy's face was something any father would cherish. The camera crew follows them out into the field, capturing the boy's reaction as he approaches the deer. He is visibly shaking from the adrenaline, but the huge smile on his face says it all. They take several pictures—some of just the boy and his buck, others of him and his dad together.

Before the show ends, the father and son come back on screen to talk about the hunt, expressing their gratitude to the Make-A-Wish Foundation, which had made the experience possible. The boy had been diagnosed with cancer the year before.

Raven quietly wipes away tears while the father talks about everything they had been through. My own eyes begin to well up as memories of my mom come rushing back—memories I haven't let surface in a long time.

I was only thirteen when she was diagnosed with cancer. I saw what she went through every day—chemo, radiation, the exhaustion. She tried to stay strong for my sister and me. Dad focused on taking care of her, so I felt like I had to stay strong for my sister, especially near the end, when things got really bad. I prayed every day that Mom would be cured, but I guess God had other plans. She passed away when I turned fifteen.

The buzzing of the popcorn maker pulls me back to the present.

I grab a large bowl from the cabinet, pour the popcorn in, and set the bowl from the machine aside to cool. Grabbing the bowl of popcorn, I walk over to Raven and hand her the bowl before sitting down beside her. Wrapping my arm around the back of the couch, I scoot closer until our bodies touch.

As the next show starts, Raven says softly, "That was so sad. I can't imagine having a child and then hearing they have cancer. The thought of my nieces going through something like that... it just ties my stomach in knots."

She pauses for a moment, then adds, "My grandmother had cancer. She passed before I was born, so I never got the chance to meet her. But my mom always tells me I remind her of my grandma—that we could've been twins, personality-wise."

She turns to look at me.

"Hey... what's wrong?"

She gently wipes a tear from my cheek. I lean into the warmth of her hand as it rests there.

"My mom had cancer too," I say quietly.

"She passed when I was fifteen. It was really hard on all of us."

Her thumb brushes softly along my cheek, grazing through my beard.

"Oh, Jackson," she whispers, "I'm so sorry. I didn't know. If you want to talk about it, you can. If not, I completely understand."

I place my hand on top of hers, still pressed against my face.

"Not today,"

"But I'd love to tell you about her one day. I'm thankful for the fifteen years I had with her—even though the last two were so hard. After she passed, I struggled a lot. But even though my dad and sister were going through the same grief, we leaned on each other. Her death brought us closer in a way. It taught us to be grateful for every day, and to love each other that much harder. We may have lost Mom, but we still had each other. That meant everything."

I look down to see tears trailing down Raven's cheeks.

"Oh, pretty girl... please don't cry," I whisper, brushing my thumb under her eye.

"How about we go for a walk once we finish our popcorn?"

She nods, smiling faintly.

Standing at the wood line in Raven's backyard I pull my turkey slate call out from my coat pocket, and move the striker in small oval motions on the slate call—imitating the sound of the turkey yelping.

"What's that?" Raven asks as she stands next to me. I hold the call out to her and she takes it.

"It's a turkey slate call. That's what I use for turkey hunting. Here, hold the call like this in the palm of your hand, grip the striker like a pencil and put pressure on the call and make an oval motion."

Raven does what I tell her to do until she is making the same sounds that I was just doing.

"That's it, so tell me something. Have you ever messed with one of these? Sometimes it takes a few times for a beginner to get the right sound."

She scrunches her nose and shakes her head. Raven looks back down at the call and makes the sound again.

"Well, let me tell you something. When I was learning how to use this call, it took me a couple of hours before I got the hang of it."

She hands the call and striker back to me and starts to walk down the path into the woods, looking over her shoulder she says, "I am just full of surprises aren't I?"

Tucking the call into my pocket, I run after her. She squeals and darts through the woods. The constant crunch of leaves beneath our feet fills the air as we race toward her gazebo. She beats me inside, but by the time I catch up, I'm doubled over, trying to catch my breath. Raven, on the other hand, looks like she could keep running without a care.

She settles into her little seat that she calls her *cozy seat* and makes room for me to sit next to her. I lean back against the wood and open my legs so she can lie between them. Wrapping my arms around her, I rest my head on top of hers. The scent of her strawberry vanilla shampoo drifts up to my nose. I close my eyes and listen to the sounds of nature mingling with her breathing. It's soothing, and I never realized needing to hear her breathe was something I couldn't do without—until now.

Chapter 28
Raven

Yesterday was rough, hearing those ladies laughing. I knew that they were talking about me. I was thankful for Jackson taking me home and just holding me. My feelings for Jackson over the past week have grown stronger. I knew I was falling for him, but I think that I am starting to fall in love with him. I am pretty sure I have heard him say that he loves me, but I was half asleep when I thought I heard those words. The way he acts around me screams that he does. I love how good we are together. We always enjoy doing what the other likes to do, and just being physically with one another. The sex is great. The man always made sure that he got a few orgasms out of me before coming inside of me. I never really experienced an orgasm with a man until I was with him. My vibrator used to be the only thing that helped in those situations. Right now it's just collecting dust in the drawer of my nightstand.

Even though we went and got my car yesterday, Jackson ended up taking me to work today. We both worked in town, so it made perfect sense to carpool instead of driving separately. He adjusted his hours, so he made sure he was back at the school to pick me up when it was time for me to leave.

Walking out of the school, I look to see that Jackson is parked in one of the spots just a few rows away. Jackson looks up from his phone and sees me walking towards him. When I get to his truck I open up the door and toss my stuff in the back seat.

"Hey pretty girl. How was your day today?"

I climb into his truck and reply, "It was good. So, did you call Tanner about getting the box blind for my woods?"

While I wait for him to answer, I roll down my window to hang my arm out, letting the wind flow through my fingers. He grabs my other hand and places a kiss on it before he says, "I sure did. It's already paid for. But we need to go pick it up. Are you okay to head there now to get it?"

He's really excited about getting this, and I can't fight the urge to not pick on him. "I don't know—we might need to head home to let the dogs out."

He quickly turns to look at me. The look of disappointment on his face, all because he has to wait just a few extra minutes.

"I am just kidding. They will be fine. However, I do think I need to install the dog door on my back door very soon. It's been hanging out in my closet. Know anyone that can help me with that?"

A smile forms on his face as he flips his hat backwards on his head.

Smirking, he says, "I think I might know someone that can help you with that. But—I think he might be on the way to get a box blind, so he will have to check his schedule."

I sigh.

"Oh well, I was hoping that you would be able to do it. I would hate to have another man come into my life."

His head whips around to look at me.

"I think his schedule just cleared up. He can get the job done after he gets the box blind set up." He says as he turns onto his buddy Tanner's road.

"And yes, I think Nala and Rex will be okay for a little longer." I say with a sly look on my face.

"I knew you had to be joking. But yes, I will put in the dog door when we get home." He says with an exaggerated grin.

As we get closer, Jackson talks about his plans for where he is going to put our new box blind. He knows just the spot where he wants to put it, too. I can't help but laugh when he talks about knowing the exact tree he wants it on. He did tell me about his friend who used to live in my house—mentioning that they used to go hunting all the time until his friend moved away. He then tells me that the owner before me was a hunter as well, but wanted to keep the property to themselves.

When we pull into Tanner's driveway—I look over towards the house to see him walking towards us as Jackson backs up to the navy blue pole barn. Cutting the engine, Jackson climbs out and lowers the tailgate.

"Hey Raven, I see he finally convinced you to put one of these in your woods," Tanner says.

Jackson smirks and walks into the barn. Resting my elbow on the truck door, I say, "actually it was my idea. I figured since he has been staying at my house a lot that he should put one out back instead of driving down the road."

He smirks, "well Raven, he is lucky to have you. I don't think I have ever met a woman who supports their partner's hunting obsession like you do."

Jackson walks out of the barn with a large box and slides it into the bed of his truck.

Shouldn't every partner be supportive—well within reason? The way I see it, hunting is a way to help control the population. If there were no hunting, our world would be overpopulated with these creatures. Yes, they are pretty to look at, but I would rather see a hunter kill a deer instead of seeing the deer become roadkill on the side of the road.

"Well, Tanner, if you must know, I actually enjoy going out and sitting in the woods with Jackson. I took my hunter's education class already."

My comment seems to shock him.

"Well, Raven, I hope Jackson knows you are a keeper. Gina never did any of this for Jackson. It's good to see him happy again," Tanner says, winking at me.

Jackson slides the last box in, slams the tailgate shut, then circles the truck to my window and shakes Tanner's hand.

"Thanks bud. I really appreciate it."

Tanner lets go of Jackson's hand and says, "No problem, enjoy it."

He points at Jackson.

"Hey, do you have a tree picked out already?" Tanner asks with a wink.

"You know, I was telling Raven that I did on the way over here. She laughed at me when I told her that."

Tanner smirks.

"Listen, Raven, it sounds weird, but you have to make sure you put these things on the right tree. First, you have to make sure the tree is in a good area. Second, you have to make sure the tree is going to support it."

Rolling my eyes, I laugh at them. Jackson knows I'm just messing with him.

He leans in to kiss me before asking, "Are you ready to head home and put this thing up?"

Smiling back at him, I nod.

"See you later, thanks again," Jackson says as he walks around his truck to get in.

Tanner waves as he walks back towards his house and says, "No problem, bud, enjoy!"

Buckling his seatbelt, Jackson puts his truck in drive to head back home. Putting my hand on the center console, Jackson reaches over to lace his fingers with mine. The smile on his face makes me ecstatic. I am looking forward to unfolding more memories after we get this box blind set up behind my house. Watching him get excited about walking out my back door to go hunting was gratifying. I can't imagine what my life would have been if he never would have showed up on my doorstep.

Would we have eventually run into one another?

All I knew was that I was thankful that he had shown up that day. I thought I was broken after my last relationship—instead I felt like I was pieced back together, thanks to Jackson. He squeezes my hand, giving me a worrisome look.

"What are you thinking about in that pretty little head of yours?"

As he continues glancing between the road and me, I reply, "I was just thinking about the day we met. I am thankful that you walked into my life. I can't imagine what would have happened if you had never shown up on my doorstep. Especially if things went south with Dean. I probably would have high tailed it out of River Valley."

Jackson pulls off on the side of the road and faces towards me. He lets go of my hand, to cupping my face, "I am thankful every day that I stopped over at your house. I didn't know what I needed in my life until I met you. You make my world better just by breathing." Jackson says as he grazes his thumb over my cheek.

My breath hitches at the words, causing me to melt—leaning in, he presses his lips to mine. This kiss didn't feel like any other kiss we shared. It felt like a promise, a craving that could not be denied.

He pulls his lips from mine, and if I am being honest, I am already missing the touch of his lips on mine.

"If I had never shown up on your doorstep that day, it would have been worth the wait until our paths crossed. You would be worth the wait. I thank God every day that I don't have to wait though." Jackson whispers the words like a prayer.

He sits back in his seat.

"Are you ready to head home and help me set this up in the woods?" He asks while putting his truck back into drive. I nod as he pulls back onto the road, heading home.

Jackson turns into my driveway and stops beside the backyard gate. He hops out, swings it open, and eases the truck through. Pulling up to the green path that disappears into the woods, he hesitates, weighing whether the truck can pull down the path.

Giving him the green light, he pulls back into the woods until he stops the truck next to a cluster of trees.

"That's the tree I want it on," he says as he points over to the trees.

He is going to have to physically point it out because I see multiple trees in the direction he is pointing. Before I even get out of the truck, Jackson is already lowering the tailgate to pull the boxes out of the bed of his truck—laying them in a stack off to the side of the path.

It took a couple of hours to put the box blind together. The pile of boxes that once contained the building materials formed a nice sturdy box blind sat in a heaping pile. This one is massive. It stands on four legs, ratchet straps cinched tight around the tree to keep it steady, even when the wind picks up. The metal is painted in a camouflage pattern that blends in with the trees behind it.

I feel Jackson wrap his arms around my body, linking his hands around my waist.

Pulling me in, he whispers in my ear, "Want to go up and check it out?"

Moving my neck to the side, he kisses me in all the right spots. I pull out of his embrace and run toward the ladder. He chases after me, and I squeal when he smacks my ass as I climb up.

Once I reach the top, I look down to see Jackson climbing the ladder. Before he gets to the top, I gaze out into the woods. Gripping the railing, I shut my eyes and listen as the wind whistles through the trees and the creek's water flows gently below.

Jackson stands behind me, running his hands down my body before turning me around. My eyes are still closed, but I can feel his hands pulling me close to him. Feeling a hand push a few hairs out of my face, he silently demands, "Open your eyes, pretty girl."

The first thing I take in when I open my eyes are his icy-blues. Looking closer, I notice a tinge of amber fleck visible in the iris of his left eye—something I'd never noticed before. I run my hand through his beard, feeling him lean into my touch. Wrapping my arms around his neck, I press my lips to his.

Next thing I know, Jackson is lifting my body off the platform—my muscles tense for a moment, knowing how high up we are, but I know we're safe. Wrapping my legs around his waist, he carries me inside the box blind.

Shutting the door behind us, he presses me up against it. The grooves in the door shoot pain up my back—but lust overpowers it, leaving me craving more. I tilt my head to the side as Jackson peppers my neck with kisses.

"I love it when you wear these," he growls, grabbing my tight pencil skirt. "You gave me one hell of a show when you climbed up here—" His hand slides deliberately up my skirt, fingers teasing my bare skin—"teasing me."

I moan, heat pooling deep inside me as his fingers slip between my slit. Pulling them out slowly, I whimper, desperate for more of his touch.

"Do you want me to do dirty things to you in here, pretty girl? Want me to fuck you hard against this door? So every time we come back, this moment will be burned into your mind—just like it is in mine."

I grind my hips against his hard cock, aching to be freed, but he holds my hips firmly in place. His pupils darken with need.

"Not yet, pretty girl. Patience."

Dropping to his knees, he hikes my skirt high, ripping my soaked underwear off and stuffing them into his back pocket. Bare and exposed, he lifts one of my legs over his shoulder, and he dives in, burying his mouth exactly where I need him. The roughness of his beard and the warmth of his mouth formed the perfect contrast,—sending shockwaves through my body.

Sucking fiercely on my clit, my hips jerk uncontrollably with waves of pleasure. I grab his hair, holding him tight, desperate to keep him there. My legs would give out if not for the one draped over his shoulder.

He looks up at me with a wicked, devilish grin, then starts kissing and nipping the inside of the leg draped over his shoulder. His beard teasingly brushes against the inside of my thighs as he peppers the tender part of my thigh with kisses. Gasping, he slides two fingers deep inside me, returning to suck my clit with wet, teasing pressure.

His fingers pump steadily, while his teeth gently clamp around my clit, driving me wild and making me let out animalistic moans I've never made before.

"Fuck, you're so fucking close. Your pussy is squeezing my fingers tight."

He rubs my clit slowly, pressing just right to push me to the edge. Then he pulls his fingers out, and I whimper, aching for him inside me.

As if he read my mind, he presses his fingers back into my entrance, this time adding a third. I groan and grind my hips down hard on his hand, feeling my walls stretch deliciously.

"Jackson, I need—"

He slides his fingers in and out with slow, steady strokes, his mouth clamps onto my clit as his other hand slips beneath my bra, his thumb teasing my hardened nipple. His piercing blue eyes lock on mine as I unravel, chasing my orgasm.

He rubs my clit in slow circles, easing me down after I come hard all over his fingers.

Breathless, I lean against the door as he lowers my leg from his shoulder, keeping his hands firmly on my hips so I don't collapse. He stands, cups my face, and pulls me into a searing kiss.

Parting my lips, he groans deeply as his tongue slides into my mouth. He grabs my hands, intertwining his fingers with mine and presses them against the rough doorframe of the box blind, holding me tight.

"Hello? Anyone up there?"

I freeze, eyes wide, wondering who's outside the box blind—in my woods—at my house.

Jackson peeks out the window to see who it is.

"It's Mitch," he whispers, adjusting himself in his jeans.

Moving away from the door, Jackson opens it and walks out onto the platform while I make myself more presentable.

"Hey Mitch, I didn't know you were going to swing by today," Jackson says as he climbs down the ladder.

God, I hope *freshly fucked* isn't written all over my face when I walk out of here.

Taking a deep breath, I exhale and step onto the platform. Leaning on the handrail, Mitch looks up and says, "Oh hey Raven, so what do you think of it?"

Well, considering Jackson just orally assaulted me in this thing, it definitely has a dual purpose.

But I can't say that, so I just reply, "It's really nice. We'll definitely stay cozy in here."

Jackson chokes on some water he's drinking when I mention staying cozy in the box blind.

"You alright there, bud?" Mitch asks, patting Jackson on the back.

"Anyway, Tanner said you guys picked this up today, so I figured I'd swing by to see if you needed some help. But I see you got it all set up yourselves."

Just as I'm about to start climbing down, Jackson talks to Mitch to keep him distracted so he doesn't see under my skirt on the way down the ladder.

Hopping off the last step, I walk over to Jackson's side.

"So I heard it was your idea to put this up in your woods. Jackson's been eager for years to hunt here again. He was pretty butt hurt when you told him no a few weeks ago."

Jackson puts his arm around me, pulling me close.

"Well, you see Mitch, I just needed to take her out into the woods a few times to get her hooked."

Mitch looks at us both with a smile.

"I'm so happy for you two. You're exactly what Jackson needed, Raven. It's good to see him truly happy again."

Mitch pauses, clapping his hands together.

"Well, I think I'll head out. You guys have a nice evening."

He walks up the path toward the house.

We wait a few minutes until Mitch is out of sight so he won't hear us.

"Well, that was a close one," Jackson says, pulling me in close.

"Do you think he suspects we were doing anything up there?" I ask, wrapping my arms around his neck.

Jackson shakes his head.

"Nah, I don't think so. Even if he did, who cares?"

I give him a quick kiss, and he gestures toward the stack of boxes.

"I think we should clean up before it gets too dark. Plus, we need to get inside to take care of Nala and Rex. They were probably going nuts when they saw us driving through the yard."

Jackson gathers the empty boxes and tosses them into the truck bed. I scoop up his tools, open the back seat, and set them on the floorboard.

Shutting the door, I run around the truck, beating Jackson to the driver's seat. He slaps my ass as I climb in.

Sitting down, I turn to face him. He wedges himself between my thighs, running his hands up my skirt—his thumbs lightly brushing against my bare pussy—reminding me he still has my torn panties in his back pocket.

Grabbing his hat off his head, I flip it around backwards. My sweet, sexy Jackson wearing his hat backwards is sexy as hell.

Chapter 29
Jackson

Raven was having brunch with her sister this morning before their parents came for a visit. She mentioned that this was the first time that her parents were coming to visit her since she had moved to River Valley.

She said Hannah finally convinced them to come visit. I am not sure why her parents had to be convinced to come visit their daughter, but I don't know too much about them. Raven doesn't talk about them much; however, she mentioned that they were retired, so it's not like they didn't have time to come visit their daughter.

They chose not to.

When Raven told me last night that they were coming, I couldn't tell if she was excited or nervous about them coming to visit. When she got up this morning, she was all over the house, organizing things, cleaning rooms. It was like she wanted to make sure she pleased her parents. Like she didn't want to give them something to complain about while they were here.

As if Hannah could sense Raven's silent distress call, she showed up around 10:00 this morning to take Raven out to brunch. When they walked out the door and left, I continued to work on some of the housework, hoping that Raven would be able to relax and enjoy her brunch with Hannah.

After I felt like the house was spotless, I pull out my phone to give Tanner and Mitch a call. I scroll through my contacts and call Tanner first. It rings until his voicemail picks up. Maybe he had someone over last night. If he were out hunting, he would have texted me.

I leave Nala and Rex in the house and get in my truck. Scrolling through contacts, I find Mitch and tap call. I hold the phone to my ear as it rings.

"Hey Jackson, what are you up to?"

Rubbing the back of my neck, I reply, "I was calling to see if you and Tanner wanted to come to my house for a little bit. Raven is having brunch with her sister before her parents come over—and I figured I would find something to do to kill some time. We could shoot some clay birds if you wanted to." I hear some shuffling around through the phone.

"Yeah, I can leave my house here in a few minutes. I will be right there. Have you called Tanner yet?"

Putting my truck in park, I shut the engine off and get out.

"Actually, I tried calling him before I called you. He didn't pick up."

Shutting the door to my truck, I continue, "I just got home, so I will get everything out that we need."

I hear a door creak open on his end.

"Okay, Jackson, see ya in a few minutes," Mitch says before we hang up.

"So, Jackson, the other day when I showed up out of the blue, what was going on up there?" Mitch says, waggling his eyebrows at me.

Well shit.

I had a gut feeling that he might have heard something. Raven wasn't the quietest when I was eating out her pussy in the box blind that day.

Letting out a chuckle, I say, "Yeah, Raven and I were fooling around up there." I say with the biggest smile on my face.

"I kind of figured, but I didn't want to embarrass you guys—I almost turned around and left, but when I stopped hearing noises, that is when I decided to say something. I am happy for you bud, it's good to see that you found someone that makes you truly happy," he says as he pats my back. He stands next to me—waiting for me to throw the clay bird in the air for him to shoot.

"Yeah, I definitely don't plan on letting her go. I've never met a woman who accepts me for me. I thought my future was with Gina. Now, I can't imagine what my life would be without Raven in it."

Mitch pulls his gun up to get ready. I count down before sending the clay bird into the air. Within seconds of it soaring through the air, Mitch shatters it. He rests the gun on his shoulder and turns to face me.

"So you get to meet her parents today? You said you already met her sister, right?"

Sitting back in my chair, I nod.

"Yeah, I get to meet them today. I have met her sister though. She is pretty nice. Hannah and Raven seem to be really close."

Rubbing the back of my neck, "I have a bad feeling about her mom and dad, though. Raven's mood flipped last night when she found out they were coming to visit. This would be their first visit since she had moved to River Valley. I guess her sister was the one to convince them to come visit."

Holding up another clay bird, I ask, "Ready for another one?"

Mitch nods as he raises the gun back up, waiting for me to release another.

"Three, two, one," I say as I pull the trigger, flinging the clay bird into the air.

"Thanks for coming to kill some time with me. We need to do this more often."

He winks at me.

"You know, if you didn't hunt or spend all of your spare time with Raven then you would have time for your friends," he says in a non-serious tone.

Mitch and I were like brothers. We grew up together, so we always picked on one another.

We only get to shoot for thirty more minutes before Mitch has to go home. Lacy has been blowing up his phone, demanding to know where he is and insisting he get home. I want to grab his phone and tell her the world doesn't revolve around her, but I know those words would just make things harder for him. After he leaves, I put the guns and the clay bird thrower away.

Looking down the road toward Raven's house, I see her car isn't back yet, so I decide to head back instead of waiting.

As soon as the door cracks open, Nala and Rex try to squeeze their heads through to greet me. I walk around the house for one final inspection, making sure everything is tidy. When I reach the living room, I plop down on the couch, grab the TV remote, and flip through the channels. Nothing looks good, so I settle on the news since it's noon. I lay my head back against the cushion, close my eyes, and drift off to sleep.

"I have something to tell you." I say, as I walk towards the front porch.

Raven sits on the porch swing on my front porch, looking out into the field across from my house. She turns around to look at me, with a tortured look on her face.

"I have something to tell you too."

Walking up the porch steps, I walk across the porch to sit on the swing next to her. She turns her head as soon as I sit down. Refusing to look me in the eye. A million thoughts race to take over my mind.

"You go first." Raven says, still avoiding eye contact with me. I grab her hand.

"Please look at me, pretty girl."

She doesn't move.

Taking a deep breath and exhaling, I say, "Raven, I wanted to tell you how much you mean to me. You make me the happiest man in the world. Would you marry me and be my wife? I promise to love you and cherish you until the day that I die."

Raven's hand fidgets in mine. I look down at her hand as she pulls it from mine. I follow her hand, watching it land on her body, except it's not her body.

I slowly look up and gasp.

"Oh Jackson, I knew you would finally come around. Of course I will marry you." Gina says as she hops off of the swing and straddles my lap.

I try to move but can't. I feel paralyzed as Gina wraps her arms around my neck and brings her lips to meet mine. Still unable to move, all I feel is her lips on mine. She opens her mouth and licks my lips, coating my lips with her saliva.

"Get off of me!"

I try to yell, but instead it comes out as a whisper. I send up a silent prayer as I keep trying to move, but no part of my body will move, not even a flinch.

She stops licking me and says, "Jackson! Jackson! Jackson!"

Feeling my shoulders shaking, I open my eyes to see Raven hovering over me. Thank goodness it was only a dream.

I pull Raven down onto my lap, latching my arms around her, not wanting to let go. Her breathing soothes me, which helps me slow my breathing down to a normal rate.

"You okay, Jackson? You were having quite the nightmare," she says as she runs her fingers through my hair. Her touch alone calms me.

"Yeah, I'm okay now. Just glad it was a dream." She studies my eyes, making sure I am okay before she gives me a light kiss.

"Hey you two, get a room!" Hannah huffs as she walks through the living room.

Chuckling, Raven climbs off of me and says, "My parents will be here in about 45 minutes. Hannah said that Mom texted her when we were on our way back home."

I get up from the couch to follow Raven into the kitchen.

"Well, did you get some beauty sleep, Jackson?" Hannah asks, walking into the kitchen from the dining room.

"I am pretty sure I was just resting my eyes."

Hannah smirks.

"Oh please, you could definitely tell that you were having a nightmare."

A chill went down my spine. She was totally right that I was having a nightmare. And I hope I never have that one again, or else I will never want to sleep. It was bad enough that it would be hard to avoid Gina when I was in town. And now Gina has crept into my unconscious mind once again while I was sleeping.

"So, I think we are just going to order pizza when my parents get here. I think they would really like Louie's Pizza," Raven says, grabbing the takeout menu that she kept on the fridge.

"Can't go wrong with pizza, plus it's nice that it can be delivered," I say, walking over to look out the window.

As it got closer to the time that Raven said her parents would be here, I start to get a little nervous myself. Not only am I nervous to meet them, fearing what they will think of me, but also nervous for Raven. This was a big deal for her. I know I am going to stand by her side the entire time they are here. That is one thing I love about us. We support one another.

Hearing a car come down the driveway, I walk to the front window to see a green car parked out in the driveway. Raven's mom was the first to open up her door to get out. She was petite. Shorter than Raven. Her short, curly silver hair bobs with each step she takes. I can't make out what they're saying, but she keeps turning her head to talk to Raven's dad as they walk toward the steps of Raven's front porch. I pad over to where Raven is standing, waiting for the doorbell to ring. But it never does, instead, the doorknob turns and the door swings open.

"Well, we finally made it," Raven's mom says as she places her hands on her hips after coming in the door. Raven's dad trails behind, looking around the house as he stands behind his wife.

"Thanks for coming. I was thinking about ordering pizza for dinner. The little pizza place in town delivers, so we can eat it here," Raven says nervously.

I watch Raven's mom rake her eyes around Raven's house like she is doing an inspection.

She turns to look at Raven's dad to remark, "Huh, we come all this way and she just wants to feed us a pizza. No home-cooked meals or hey, let's go out to eat at a restaurant. I doubt there's a restaurant anywhere in this small town."

I really wish she were *joking right now.*

Honestly, I am trying to rack my brain to figure out why she wants them here at all if they are going to treat her this way. I know they are her parents, but my first impression of them is that they don't treat Raven well. Before Raven can reply to her mom, her eyes fall on me.

"I thought it was just Hannah joining us?" She asks, walking over to me.

"Mom, this is Jackson. He's my boyfriend." *Boyfriend..* I love how that sounds rolling off of her tongue.

We really haven't discussed titles or anything, but I am ecstatic to hear her call me her boyfriend. I reach out my hand to her mom. Instead of taking my hand, she lunges at me, wrapping her arms around me. "It's nice to meet you," I say, patting her back. I look over at Raven, who shrugs her shoulders at me.

"Are you the man who is going to give—"

"Okay, Mom. That's enough," Raven yells, cutting her mom off.

Well, now I am curious about what she was going to ask.

Her mom lets go of me, glaring at Raven.

"I was only asking if this handsome fella was going to be the one to make beautiful grandbabies with my sweet daughter one day. I told you we aren't getting any younger."

I let out a little chuckle, then look at Raven. Her face is bright red. I would give her anything. I know we haven't been together for very long. Our relationship was fairly new. But I just have a feeling that she is *the one* for me. If she wants kids, I would ask how many? The sight of her belly swollen with my child fills my mind. Hell, I am surprised her birth control hasn't failed yet. And if she doesn't want to have kids, I would be fine with that, too. As long as she is in my future.

"Mom, just drop it. Jackson and I just started dating. Don't start planning our wedding just yet."

Her mom looks like she's about to say something, but instead she walks right past me and plops down onto the couch.

"Jackson, this is my dad," Raven says, gesturing to her dad. He towers over me. However, he doesn't intimidate me.

"Nice to meet you, Mr. Catz. I heard that you like to go fishing."

Holding out my hand, he gives me a nice firm handshake.

"You can call me Pete," he says in a gruff voice.

He slowly makes his way over to sit down next to his wife. Raven looks over at me, rolling her eyes before walking over to sit down on the loveseat. Hannah follows her, sitting next to her.

"I will call and order the pizza," I say as I walk into the kitchen.

Pulling out my phone, I lean on the counter that overlooks the living room and dial the number to order the pizza.

"So, Hannah, I am surprised you didn't bring the kids with you. We will probably come over to visit tomorrow if that is okay?" Raven's mom says as she picks at her pizza on her plate.

I can't believe the conversations happening around this table. Raven's dad doesn't say much, unless his wife asks a question that gets him to reply, "yes, dear." But Raven's mom never asks Raven what she's been up to since moving here, or how she likes her job.

If anything is said to Raven, it's that she moved away from her family. If I recall, Raven mentioned it's only an extra five to ten minutes compared to where she used to live in the city.

I never hear her mom mention Raven having kids again. But with the way she keeps looking at us, I know she's thinking about saying something.

Thanks to Raven's mom, I learn quite a bit about Hannah. Occasionally, I look over to see a mixture of hurt and annoyance on Raven's face.

My parents loved my sister and me equally. They never talked to us the way Raven's mom talks to her.

I rest my hand on her leg and give a gentle squeeze, letting her know I'm here for her.

No more than an hour after we finish eating, we say our goodbyes to Raven and Hannah's parents as they rush out the door. Her mom says they have to get home for a TV show they want to watch.

Not only am I relieved, but I can tell Hannah and Raven are, too. As soon as the door shuts, Raven goes to lock it.

"I am so glad they are gone. I am okay if they never come back to visit." Raven says as she walks over to wrap her arms around my neck.

"I am sorry you had to go through that, Jackson. Mom doesn't treat Raven that well. Hell, I had to bend Mom's arm backwards just for her to come," Hannah says as she kicks back in the chair.

"Well, there's no place I would rather be than here with you. I would rather have been here with you than sitting out in the woods." I say while rubbing her back. Her tense body relaxes in my arms.

"Okay, lovebirds, I will get out of your hair. Henry is probably pulling what little hair he has left since I have been gone all day."

She grabs her purse, pulls her keys out and heads to the door. She turns around and waves at us.

"See you two later. Don't do anything I wouldn't do," she says. Winking, she spins around and walks out the door.

Her sister is something else.

I know it seems like her parents favor her more, but at least Raven and Hannah are close. If my parents acted like that and I wasn't close with my sister Luna, then I probably wouldn't have any contact with them.

I am so thankful for the relationship that I had with my parents when they were alive.

Chapter 30
Jackson

I hardly go out during hunting season—let alone to any bonfires—since by the time I'm climbing out of my tree stand, it's dark, and I usually end up going straight to bed when I get home.

Raven's friend Violet is in town visiting and we are having a bonfire tonight. I could go hunting this evening and then walk to the bonfire when quitting time comes. Instead, I decide to help Raven prep everything before our guests arrive.

We prepare the spare bedroom for Hannah and Henry and set up an air mattress in the living room for Violet. As we head to the kitchen, Raven mentions that things might get a little crazy between the three of them since there will be alcohol involved. She doesn't go into detail on what they do. I want to ask what happens, but I decide not to.

Violet, Hannah and Henry walk in the door while we are preparing some of the food. The girls jump in to help and send me out the door with Henry. We set up a few tables, get the fire going, and return to the house to help them carry things out. When we walk back inside, the countertops in Raven's kitchen are filled with finger foods—marshmallows, chocolate bars, and graham crackers for making s'mores.

Grabbing the large platters of finger food, Henry and I walk outside to sit them on the tables next to the coolers filled with beer and moonshine.

While Henry and I set up the chairs around the fire, Raven, Hannah, and Violet carry out the supplies for the s'mores.

"Hen–ry—," Hannah sing songs, "—get the shine out. I brought out the shot glasses!"

Hannah sits the shot glasses down on the table while Henry pulls out the jar of moonshine. He twists the lid off and pours the clear liquid into each shot glass. Henry is a quiet soul compared to Hannah. Hannah is like the life of the party. Her husband, on the other hand, could be a fly on the wall, he could blend in and you wouldn't even know that he was in the room. I wonder what they have in common. The two of them seem completely different.

Anyway, we pick up our shot glasses.

"Thanks, Raven and Jackson, for hosting this little bonfire," Violet gestures towards the fire, "and thank you for allowing us to crash here after we get a little tipsy. Jackson, I am sorry for what you may witness tonight."

She winks at me.

"Here's to a good time!" we all raise our shot glasses up.

"Cheers!" We all shout in unison.

Raven wasn't kidding when she said that the three of them can get a little wild when alcohol is involved. I didn't think it was the smartest idea, but the girls wanted to play hide and seek in the woods.

Henry and I are the seekers. It's dark and hard to see walking through the woods, but when we hear giggles, we follow them and find Hannah and Violet right away.

The only one that needs to be found is Raven.

"Henry, if you want to take Hannah and Violet back out to sit by the fire, I will find Raven."

When I look over towards him, he nods, and he starts to walk away with Hannah and Violet.

"Oh—Jackson, when you find her, tell her we will be ready for another round of shots." Hannah says, slurring her words.

Violet and Hannah grasp Henry's hands and run, dragging Henry out of the woods.

Shaking my head, I think they need to be cut off soon.

Or now...

Heading deeper into the woods, I occasionally stop to listen—hoping to hear movement that would point me in the direction of where Raven could be hiding. I thought eventually I would hear some giggling. I get all the way down the creek and peek in her gazebo. Pulling my phone out, I turn on the flashlight and shine it inside.

Not in here.

Where could she be?

I walk down one of the deer trails that leads to the blind that sits along the creek.

As I get closer, I stop to listen. I hear some shuffling around in the direction that I am heading. How did I not know that there was a possibility that she would hide in there?

Thank goodness she chose not to climb up the ladder to the box blind since she had been drinking. That would have been a nasty fall if she tried to climb up there.

I find myself standing outside the ground blind, waiting a few minutes before unzipping the door to go inside.

Pulling the zipper to open up the ground blind, I hear Raven snickering. I peek my head inside to see Raven sitting in the chair, looking over her shoulder at me. Her phone screen lights up the blind, allowing me to see the grin displayed on her face.

"Took you long enough. I figured you would have found me ten minutes ago."

I step in and sit down in the chair next to her. It's dark, but the moonlight from the moon shines in through the open windows.

"Well, if you must know, I went to see if you were hiding in your gazebo first."

Nudging her in the arm, "Hannah and Violet were found within the first few minutes. They could not stop giggling. I told Henry to take them back to sit around the fire so I didn't have to worry about them tripping and falling in the woods."

She tosses her head back and laughs.

"That was probably a good and a bad idea, Jackson. I can only imagine what Hannah and Violet are putting him through right now, especially with how much they had to drink."

Smirking, I picture Henry trying to keep his wife and Raven's friend out of trouble.

What could possibly happen that could be that bad?

With how much they had to drink, I am surprised they haven't passed out yet.

Surely, whatever happens tonight, they won't remember.

I start to stand up, but Raven grabs my wrist and says, "Sit with me for a bit."

I sit back in my seat and listen to Raven's breathing, along with the sounds of nature around us.

"Nature was always my go-to when I needed to get away from the world. It's a space where I can relax and escape reality. I never thought I would enjoy spending time out in nature with someone until I met you, Jackson. I am really thankful to have you in my life," Raven says, the moonlight hitting her face just right for me to see her genuine smile.

I wish I could slow down time right now, because I could sit out here with Raven all night.

But I know that eventually we have to go back up to the house. We probably shouldn't leave Henry to deal with Hannah and Violet all by himself.

We start making our way down the trail that leads toward the house. As we get closer, I hear snickering and moaning.

Moaning?

What the hell is going on?

The closer we get, the louder the sound grows. I'm not sure what we're about to walk in on, but I hope it's nothing I don't want to see. These three have been out here by themselves for a little over half an hour—who knows what happened while we were gone.

Raven stops walking and grabs my hand, turning me to face her. "Thank you, Jackson, for another great night," she says before standing on her tiptoes to press her lips to mine in a short, sweet kiss. She pulls back, takes my hand again, and we walk the rest of the way until we're back in Raven's backyard.

I'm not entirely sure what I expected to walk into—especially after Raven warned me it would be a bad idea to leave the three of them alone with alcohol involved.

I wasn't even to the edge of the woods before I had to turn my head to avoid searing the scene into my memory forever. From the quick glimpse I got, Henry and Hannah were going at it like they were trying to make a baby. They'd found a large blanket somewhere and spread it out in front of the fire. Luckily, it wasn't close enough to actually catch fire.

Not only is Hannah riding Henry's cock, snickering and moaning at the same time, but she's also not the only woman enjoying him right now.

At this moment, I wish we were still in the ground blind, snuggling together. If I were still out there with Raven, I wouldn't be seeing her best friend Violet making out with Hannah—while sitting on Henry's face.

Even after snapping my gaze away as fast as I could, the image was already burned into my brain. I stop dead in my tracks, suddenly hesitant to step into Raven's yard.

"Uh, Raven?"

I am about to ask her what we need to do, but before I can finish my question she says, "Oh shit, not again."

I whip my head around to look at Raven, not sure if I was hearing her right. Did she really say, not again?

"What do you mean, not again?"

She tosses her head back and puts her hand on my shoulder.

"Well, Jackson, this isn't the first time this has happened."

Keeping my eyes on her, "I kind of figured that out when you said, *Oh shit, not again.*"

She bites her bottom lip as she looks over at the scene that I am trying to avoid looking at.

"Yeah, when Hannah and Violet get drunk together, they can get a little freaky in the sheets. Or in this case, out in the backyard. Hannah somehow convinces Henry to have a threesome. He's a pretty quiet dude, so I am uncertain if he actually enjoys it or if just fears he is going to make my sister angry. I am not sure why I even got the air mattress out for them. I knew something like this was going to happen. The three of them will just end up in bed together."

In the distance, Hannah screams out Henry's name, and I burst out laughing.

Shit, I can't believe this is happening right now.

"Totally understand if you want to head inside while I deal with this," she gestures towards the threesome that is happening in her backyard. "I can guide you past them if you want to close your eyes."

I take her hand, but instead of closing my eyes, I focus my line of sight on Raven. My eyes rake down her body, stopping at her ass. Watching it sway back and forth as she guides me to the house.

I stop walking and tug her back, spinning her around until her hands are on my chest and my arm is wrapped around her waist.

Tilting her chin up, "I can help you if you want me to. You don't have to do this alone." I graze my fingers over her jawline. She leans into my touch, like she fears I am going to take it away any second.

"That would be great, Jackson. Because let me tell ya, these three can be a pain in my ass when I try to interfere." She grabs my hand that is on her cheek and we make our way towards the trio.

"I have to warn ya, Henry might get a little possessive, so it might be a good idea if I handle Hannah and Violet and you handle Henry. If you want to turn back now, you can—judging by the look on your face, you look like you are regretting this decision."

Shaking my head, "I will never regret helping you, Raven. I am just trying to rack my brain around how Henry gets possessive of Violet. I can understand why he would be with Hannah."

Raven shrugs her shoulders, insinuating that she doesn't really know why either. When we are literally right next to them, Raven leans over to tap Violet on the shoulder.

She turns around to look at Raven and me with her glassy eyes.

"Oh no, Hannah, Rave–n and Se–xy Jack–son have either come to poop on our party, or they are here to join us."

Hannah makes eye contact with me and smiles. Her eyes are also glassy.

"Oh, do Jackson and Raven want to come play with us too?" Hannah asks as she grabs both of Violet's breasts with her hands and claps them together.

Rubbing my hand over my face, wondering how in the hell we're going to get these three inside, especially when Hannah was still bouncing up and down on Henry's cock. But then an idea pops into my head that will help both Raven and me get these three inside fast.

"No, Hannah, it's time to go inside. I heard that there is a bear in the woods. It's about to come this way."

Hannah freezes, and her eyes widen.

"Bears! Oh shit, Violet, Henry, we gotta go! A bear is coming after us!"

If the alcohol didn't take over her brain, she would know better that there aren't any bears in Raven's woods. In fact, I have never seen a bear around River Valley.

But that doesn't stop the three naked bodies from hightailing it into the house, leaving their clothes behind next to the blanket.

A burst of laughter echoes in Raven's backyard. She grabs my arm and tugs me towards her.

"I would say that was not funny, but it was pretty funny seeing them run like their lives depended on it. Let's go inside, though. We need to make sure they make it into the guest bedroom and not onto the air mattress downstairs. Or worse, let's make sure they don't end up in our bed."

I like the sound of that, *our bed*.

The fire is starting to go out, since it doesn't look like the trio that was currently fucking in Raven's backyard put any wood on it to keep it going.

I grab the bucket of water I carried out earlier and dump it on the fire. The small flames hiss as the water splashes over them. Raven picks up the food sitting on the table while I grab the tray of shot glasses and walk toward the house with her.

"In the morning, I will come out and grab the coolers. I think they will be okay out here overnight. Unless you think that bear is going to stop by for a drink?" I say, jokingly.

"I have to admit, that was pretty clever. And funny. But I could have gone without seeing Henry full naked."

I toss my head back, letting a low rumble of laughter roll from my chest.

"Well, next time maybe we will tell them that they need to get dressed, so the bear doesn't try to take their clothes. We could tell them that the bear is going to try to dress up and walk around town. Think they would believe that?"

"Maybe, especially if they truly thought there was a bear in my woods," she says as she gestures back toward the tree line.

When we make it into the house, we are glad to see that Hannah, Henry, and Violet are not downstairs in the living room. I sit the tray of shot glasses down on the countertop and hear some noises coming from upstairs.

Raven grabs my hand and pulls me toward the stairs.

"What are your plans to get them out of our room if they are in there?"

She stops midway up the stairs with a smirk on her face.

"You mean you're not going to tell them that a bear is coming up here to get them?"

I pull her down to the stand on the step just above me and kiss her.

"Careful, Raven, that mouth of yours is going to get you into trouble."

Her breath hitches, but our little moment is interrupted when we hear Violet or Hannah moaning and Henry grunting upstairs.

We ascend the stairs, and Raven notices that the guest bedroom is closed. She walks up to the door and presses her ear to it.

"Yup, they are in there getting it on." She says as she gestures towards the door.

Raven turns around and says, "And if they don't slow down anytime soon, Hannah will be popping out another niece or nephew for me."

I follow Raven into her room and close the door behind me. Her room is not soundproof. It's like the walls are paper-thin. You could hear it out in the hallway, but in Raven's room it was so much louder. Raven reaches into her nightstand and pulls out a little box containing earplugs. She grabs two out for herself and then hands me a couple.

"Here, you might want these."

I put the earplugs in. They help, but I can still hear them in the room next to us. At least it's not as loud. This is definitely not how I thought the night would have ended.

Raven slips into her short shorts and an oversized t-shirt and slides into bed. I strip off my pants and shirt and climb in next to her. Lifting the sheet, she backs into me so I can wrap my arms around her.

She turns around to face me. Pressing her lips to mine, I rake my fingers through her hair. She tosses her leg over mine, trying to get her body closer to mine. My pretty girl breaks our kiss, allowing our noses to touch.

"I just want to let you know that I don't share," she says as she looks down at my lips.

Running hands along her body, "I don't like to share either, this right here," my hands sliding up her shirt, "is all mine. No one is allowed to touch you like I do."

A whimper sounds from her lips that form an O shape when my fingers brush up against her skin while I slowly bring my hand out of her shirt.

She's mine, and I am hers.

I will forever choose her.

Chapter 31

Raven

"So, where do you want to sit today?" Jackson asks, running his hand up and down my thighs, which are draped over his lap.

If he gets any closer—the only place we will be sitting is in this spot with me on top of him.

"We could go sit up in town and hand out candy. It is Halloween after all," I reply—standing up, I turn around to straddle his lap. His hands land on my hips—slipping up my shirt—spreading goosebumps up my sides from his touch.

"Hate to break it to you, pretty girl, but if you're wanting to do that we should have went to the nearest Walmart to buy candy. The candy aisle at the grocery store in town was wiped out. How about we go to the haunted caves in town?"

"Haunted—caves?"

That's the last thing I wanted to do on Halloween night. Haunted places, whether they were pretend, weren't really my thing. The last time Hannah took me to one—I was 16, and she was 18. She told Mom that she was taking me to the movies. I was okay with going to the movies, but as we drove past the theater and out to the middle of nowhere—I realized that not only did she lie to Mom—she lied to me as well. That night was a disaster. Hannah held my hand the entire time we walked through this haunted corn maze that eventually had us walking through a two-story home. Any little sound or movement I caught out of the corner of my eye, had me jumping—shreiking—or climbing up Hannah's back. We weren't even half-way through when she kept telling me to calm down, that it wasn't real. She could tell me that it wasn't real all she wanted to, but when that big giant guy with the facemask came out holding a chain-saw. I bolted. I don't think I had ever ran that fast in my entire life. I found a closet to hide in—thankfully, no one was in there with me. When Hannah finally found me five minutes later, curled up in the fetal position. I was so scared to walk through the rest of the house. Thankfully, the worker that told Hannah where I went sent us through the emergency exit, or as I called it, the chicken shit exit. After that night, Hannah never invited me out again to engage in any Halloween activities until my nieces were old enough to go trick or treating. I was totally okay walking around with them, watching them fill their buckets full of cand y.

"Yeah. There's an old mine under the town. They hold tours on one side of the mine and a haunted cave on the other. I used to volunteer there growing up. Luna and I used to be the ones who would randomly walk behind people in the room that had strobe lights in it."

A shiver rolled down my spine.

"Hey, you okay?" Jackson asks.

His eyes snapping up to mine—watching me—he brushes his finger-tips up and down the side of my arms.

I tuck a few strands of hair behind my ear.

"Uh—yeah. I just don't really do the scary stuff—I mean—it's been a while."

He searches my eyes, waiting to see if I have more to say or if I am really going to uncover the truth. *Honestly, I should just tell him about it. He would understand.*

"Let's go," I say.

Here's to not telling him the truth.

Maybe it won't be that bad. Jackson will be there by my side.

What the hell was I thinking?

I can't go through with this.

I just need to turn around, tell Jackson so we can go back home.

But how am I going to tell Jackson that? He actually seemed excited about going into this *haunted cave.*

Tiki torches light up the path to the cave. We have been standing in line for about 15 minutes, and we are still pretty far from the entrance. Anxiety builds within me the longer we wait. I honestly don't get why people want to come to these types of places to have someone scare them. Is it really fun to have someone in a mask grab you or yell "boo"—because let me tell you, it doesn't seem fun to me.

After 30 minutes of waiting, we finally reach the booth that is taking money so we can get scared out of our pants. Right then and there I—almost say hey let's go home. But every time I open my mouth, nothing comes out. Even if I want to say something, its already too late. Jackson is handing over the cash for our entry fee.

Shit.

Too late now, Raven. Now Jackson is going to see Raven, the scaredy-cat.

Jackson waves to a few people at the entrance before we head in.

"Hey Jackson, have fun!" The man wearing a clown costume yells.

"Oh, we will, won't we? Hope we get the shit scared out of us tonight," he says, giving my hand a gentle squeeze as he looks over at me.

The flame from the tiki torch flickers a light across Jackson's face. Little does he know I will most likely get the shit scared out of me.

Relax, Raven, you're with Jackson. He won't let anything happen to you.

Taking a deep breath, I nod, letting out an awkward laugh.

"We sure will. Can't wait!"

Next thing I know, we are stepping into the cave.

Into the *dark* cave.

With this being my very first time, I had no clue what to expect. I had no clue what I was about to walk into.

Not sure if it's because we are underground or my chest is just constricting. But it's hard to breathe down here. I feel my heartbeat thrumming through my body as we walk along a flimsy bridge.

Thankfully, Jackson hasn't mentioned that I'm gripping his hand too tightly. If I could see, my knuckles are probably white from holding on like it's my lifeline.

I shriek when something—or someone—brushes against my foot as we walk along the bridge. Jackson might be laughing now, but if he truly knew this wasn't fun for me, he wouldn't be laughing.

When we finally reach the end of the bridge, our feet touch an uneven path, half-swallowed by shadows. It winds forward, drawing us into a room glowing with light—or rather, fire. The flames hiss and flicker, casting long, dancing shapes across the walls.

Jackson is close beside me as we pass a cluster of small figures—children, dressed as ghosts.

Maybe this isn't so bad after all... or maybe that's what they wants us to think.

The kids can't be older than ten. They are wearing white sheets over their heads, eyeholes crudely cut out, dark eyes peering from within. One of them suddenly darts in front of us, bouncing on their feet before letting out a sharp, gleeful "Boo!"

Not wanting to disappoint the little ghost—I throw my hand to my face and scream. The little ghost throws its arms in the air, spins wildly, and vanishes into the smoky room, giggling as it runs.

"You made that kid's night, pretty girl," Jackson says, kissing me on the cheek.

A group of tiny ghosts yell, "Gross," in unison in their ghost like tone.

The next room we walk into has flashing strobe lights, casting erratic shadows across the walls. A man steps out in front of us, staring—his face hidden behind a mask streaked with blood. He tilts his head to the side, eyes starring right into my soul. Then he shifts his gaze to Jackson and slowly pulls something from behind his back.

When he raises it, my eyes widen.

Oh shit. No, no, no!

The man is holding a chainsaw. He lifts it above his head and presses a button—bringing the machine to life with a deafening roar. At first, I feel paralyzed, fighting with my own mind, trying to convince myself that it's not real. But my logical side is overruled.

I tug on Jackson's hand, but my grip slips from my sweaty palm. The anxiety that had been building until now suddenly bursts. A blood curdling scream rips its way up my throat. My vision narrows—what do I do next? I run.

I have no idea where I'm going. Darkness swallows me as I continue to run. I know I won't find a closet to hide in down here. Behind me, I hear Jackson shouting my name, and a few of the volunteers yelling at me to stop. But my legs don't listen. They carry me deeper into the cave, farther and farther from Jackson. The voices that were yelling, fade to a whisper.

Then, I trip. I fall—face-first into the dirt. The contact with the ground wasn't sudden; it felt as if I fell a couple of feet.

It's pitch black. I can't even see my own hand in front of my face. I know it's there, but the darkness swallows it. Not even bothering to move, I just sit there, crying, waiting for someone to find me.

If they find me.

Chapter 32

Jackson

Oh my God, this was an awful idea.

I should have known, with the way Raven tensed up when I mentioned the caves. It was written all over her face.

Everyone was evacuated from the caves while the rescue squad searches for Raven.

My Raven—the one who ran off into who knows where. I wanted to run after her.

Still, if I had kept up with her and been with her this whole time, she wouldn't be alone. But if I did and never found her—then what? We both would be lost.

Mitch was the one holding the chainsaw. If I had known, I never would have come here. Or at least, I would've shaken my head at Mitch when he looked at me.

Even though we've only been searching for an hour, it feels like forever. I *have* to find her. I'm not leaving this cave without her.

"Jackson, I'm so sorry," Mitch says as we walk through the cave—thin string attached to our belts so we don't get lost—our flashlights cutting through the darkness ahead.

"Dude, I had no clue she'd freak out like this. I wish we'd just stayed home. When I mentioned the caves to her, her body tensed at the idea. I've gotta find her, Mitch."

"Hey—we'll find her. She couldn't have gone too far."

I hope he's right. The thought of something happening to her makes my chest cave in.

Hopefully, she's okay... wherever she is.

After tonight, we are never coming back here again.

"So, have you heard from Tanner? I feel like he's been MIA lately."

I huff a laugh. "Nope. But we know how Tanner gets around this time of year."

"Yeah, I just feel like he's really been keeping his distance. After you left the bar the other night, he took a girl home—but I haven't heard anything since. The only reason I know nothing happened is because I drove by his house and saw him getting into his car."

"Well, maybe tomorrow—or in a day or two—we'll go over to his place and talk to him. I'm sure he's fine."

The farther we head into the cave, the colder it gets. It only makes me worry more, knowing Raven came here tonight wearing only a hoodie and jeans. The cave floor becomes more jagged, forcing us to lift our feet higher so we don't trip.

"Did you hear that?" Mitch asks, shining his flashlight across the cave.

A quiet whimper echoes off the stone walls.

"Raven! Is that you?"

Picking up the pace, I stumble a few times over loose rocks, barely able to run. I stop just in time at a ledge. I shine my flashlight down a three-foot drop and there she is—Raven—curled up in a ball, her eyes shut.

When Mitch catches up, he exhales, "Oh, thank God."

He's got that right.

I found her.

She's safe.

I hand Mitch my flashlight and jump down over the ledge, landing next to her.

She flinches as my feet hit the ground.

"Shh, pretty girl. It's just me. Come here."

She lifts herself up and crawls into my arms. I wrap them around her, never wanting to let go again after being so terrified.

"I'm so glad I found you. I was scared out of my mind when I couldn't. But you're safe now. Are you hurt?"

She nods.

Before she can speak, I ask, "Where?"

She lowers her hand and rubs her ankle—the same one she rolled in the woods over a week ago.

"Oh, pretty girl, you've got the worst luck with this ankle. Let's get you home."

I lift her off the cold ground. She shivers in my arms. Mitch leans over to take her so I can climb back up. Once I'm out, he hands her back to me. He takes off his jacket and drapes it over her as we head back the way we came.

"This is so embarrassing," she murmurs.

"I should have told you. I'm so sorry."

"Hey, there's nothing to be embarrassed about. Though I wish you had told me—we could've stayed home."

She doesn't say anything. She just stays quiet.

"Hey, talk to me. What's going on in that head of yours?"

Her body shifts in my arms. She rests her head against my chest and says softly, "I was just thinking about what would've happened if you never found me."

The flashlight flickers across her face, just enough to show the tears running down her cheeks.

"Oh, pretty girl, don't cry. I would've looked for you until I found you. I wasn't leaving this cave without you in my arms."

"I don't deserve you," she sobs into my chest.

"Yes, you do. We deserve each other. You and I—we are meant to be, pretty girl."

When we finally see the glow from the haunted caves' entrance, a wave of relief crashes over me. *Thank God this nightmare is over.*

"She has been found—I repeat, she has been found," one of the rescue team members repeats into a handheld radio.

After the medics examine Raven, they tell her she'll need to take it easy for a while after rolling her ankle again. I help her into my truck, and we drive back to her house.

She stays quiet the whole ride, her hand resting in mine. Every so often, I glance over at her to make sure she's okay. When our eyes meet, she offers a small smile, silently telling me she's alright.

This night could have ended so much worse. Her injury could've been serious. Hell, what if she'd fallen into a deeper hole and... died?

I take a deep breath, slowly exhaling.

Thank God it's just a rolled ankle.

I can't imagine my life without her.

I've been meaning to tell her that I love her. I know we haven't been together long... but what if I never got the chance?

I need to tell her. I guess I've just been waiting for the right moment.

But how will I know when the right moment will be?

Chapter 33
Raven

When I heard Jackson yell my name in the cave, I knew he would find me, eventually.

He was so close.

I would be safe soon.

Even though Jackson had me in his arms, carrying me toward the cave's exit, my heart was still racing—faster than a horse trying to win the Kentucky Derby.

After the medics checked me over, we went home. But my thoughts wouldn't stop. They raced through my mind like a wildfire. I felt so ignorant for running away. *What the hell was I thinking, running from a guy holding a damn chainsaw?*

Exactly—you weren't thinking.

I knew I needed to tell Jackson the truth when we got home. Why I reacted the way I did. I should've been honest from the beginning. I also needed to tell him how I felt.

I'm in love with Jackson.

But after tonight, I wouldn't be surprised if he wanted nothing to do with me. Who would want to be with someone who can't even face their fears? I should've stood my ground, screamed like everyone else walking through those haunted caves. Instead... I ran.

Taking a deep breath, I watch him round the front of the truck. He opens my door gently.

I turn my legs and let them dangle out. His hands reach for mine—steady, warm, familiar.

"Raven, let's get you inside. Then we can talk, okay?"

I nod.

A tear escapes my eye, but Jackson catches it with his thumb.

Is this the end?

"Hey," he whispers, his voice tender, almost breaking.

"It's going to be alright. You're safe now."

His words tremble at the edges, like they're holding back more than just fear. I look up, and under the moonlight, I see it—tears welling in his eyes, glistening in the silver moonlight.

Jackson helps me out of the truck like I'm made of glass, careful not to jostle my swollen ankle. His hand never leaves mine, not even as we step onto the porch and he unlocks the front door. It creaks open into the quiet warmth of home, and for the first time since the cave, I feel like I can finally breathe again.

Rex and Nala lift their heads—not even bothering to get up from their beds.

He guides me to the couch, eases me down onto the cushions, and props a pillow behind my back. Then he kneels in front of me, still holding my hands like he's anchoring me—afraid I might slip away again.

"I'm okay," I whisper, even though the words feel like a lie.

Jackson shakes his head gently.

"You don't have to say that. Not to me. Tell me what's going on. Please."

My throat tightens.

Tell him. Tell him everything.

"I was scared," I begin, my voice barely audible. "Not of the guy with the chainsaw—not really. I mean, yeah, that too... but it started when I went to a haunted corn maze with Hannah."

He stays quiet, just listening. His eyes never leave mine.

"Hannah and I—we went to this haunted maze that eventually led into a house. When a guy came at us with a chainsaw, I freaked out and ran. She found me later hiding in a closet. I just... I don't do scary things well, in case you haven't noticed."

Jackson's jaw tightens, but he doesn't interrupt.

"I didn't tell you because..." I pause, struggling to keep my voice steady.

"Because I knew it was something you were excited about. And I didn't want to ruin it. I understand if you don't want to be with me anymore."

He reaches up and gently brushes his fingers along my cheek.

"Nothing like that would ever change how I feel about you," he says softly.

"I just wish you'd told me. You mean everything to me, Raven. Do you have any idea what it did to me, not knowing where you were? Thinking something might've happened to you? I would've searched day and night until I found you."

Tears prick my eyes again.

"But I ran. I left you."

"You were scared. It's okay to be scared of that kind of stuff—it makes you human. And you're here now. That's what matters."

I stare at him, the storm in my chest finally starting to quiet.

"There's something else I need to say," I whisper.

He tilts his head, eyes soft.

"What is it?"

"I love you, Jackson. I know we haven't been together that long, but tonight made me realize... if something had happened, and I never got the chance to say it, I would've regretted it for the rest of my life."

His breath catches. For a moment, he just looks at me—like he's memorizing every detail of my face.

Then he smiles, and it's the softest, most real smile I've ever seen.

"I love you too, pretty girl. I think I've been waiting for the perfect moment to say it. But you know what? This moment—right here—is exactly right."

He leans forward, pressing his forehead against mine, and I close my eyes, breathing him in.

Warm. Steady. Safe.

In his arms, the cave feels a million miles away.

Right where I'm meant to be.

Chapter 34

Jackson

Waking up next to Raven—the most beautiful girl in the world—feels like I am on cloud nine.

I have no desire to move. Not because I'm still tired, but because this—this exact moment—is perfect.

Too perfect to risk disturbing her.

Her hair is pulled up in a messy bun, with a few loose strands trailing across the pillow. I just want to lie here all day, taking her in.

Last night, we told each other we were in love. My heart filled with bliss the moment when she said those words.

She starts to stir, her eyes fluttering open.

"Good morning, pretty girl," I sing-song with a smile.

She presses her lips to mine, our foreheads still touching. "Good morning," she whispers.

"Feel like going for a walk later?" I ask, brushing a few stray hairs from her face. "If your ankle is bothering you we can just stay here."

"Yeah, I'd love to take a walk. I love you."

Cupping her cheeks, I search her eyes—full of warmth, full of want—and say, "I love you too."

Raven insists that we listen to Christmas music while we get ready for our walk. Every year, when the clock struck midnight on Halloween and November 1st began, she mentioned that she would start playing Christmas songs. I kept reminding her that we can't just skip over November. Not only is Thanksgiving in November—but so is my birthday.

Raven mentions having another bonfire to celebrate my birthday. Jokingly, I tell her we didn't need a repeat of last time. Although, looking back now, it *was* funny—the fact that Henry, the quiet one, ended up with two women to himself. I'm just glad Raven has little to no interest in sharing me with another woman.

Raven grasps my hand and tugs me out the door into the crisp November air. It feels as if the temperature dropped drastically overnight. Sunshine shimmers through the leafless branches swaying gently in the wind.

As we walk through the woods, a breeze dances past us, and the sound of Nala and Rex's paws kicking up wet leaves echoes ahead—already running deeper into the woods.

Raven lets go of my hand, gives me a playful smile, and runs with a limp to her gazebo that is now in view. Her long brown hair sways from side to side as she runs down the path. Laughing, I jog after her, not able to go too fast with the small bag over my shoulders.

"You never told me what you packed," Raven says, curiosity in her eyes as I reach the entrance of her gazebo.

"It's a surprise—now close your eyes."

She shuts them tightly, scrunching her nose dramatically to show they're closed. I wave a hand in front of her just to make sure, then unzip the bag. One by one, I pull out the items: a couple of thick blankets, a thermos of hot chocolate, two books, and a small box.

Gently placing my hands on her shoulders, I guide her over to her seat. "Sit for me, pretty girl."

A laugh escapes her.

"Oh, do I know why you want me to sit?"

I shake my head, laughing as I catch her playful pout.

"No, not this time."

With a smile tugging at my lips, I slide the contents of the small box into my back pocket before tucking the box itself back into the bag. I spread a blanket over her lap and pour the hot chocolate into the mugs I'd packed. I hand her one, placing it carefully into her waiting hands.

"Can I open my eyes now?" she asks, peeking with one eye.

"Not yet," I say. Sitting beside her, I place the book in her lap and lay mine next to me.

I lean back, smirking.

"Okay—now you can open them."

Her eyes flutter open. She glances down at the book on her lap, then peers into her mug, watching the steam rise in soft swirls.

"Uh, Jackson, this is really sweet and all, but... is this the surprise? We just did this the other day."

A mix of nerves and excitement tightens in my chest. My palms start to sweat—and not from holding the mug. Was this too fast? Maybe. But after last night, I knew I couldn't wait any longer.

"Have you read these books before?" I ask, gesturing to the ones resting on our laps.

She shakes her head.

"No—but I've been meaning to."

"Well... the characters in these books fall in love pretty quickly—kind of like us."

Her gaze drops to the cover in her lap, then lifts sharply to meet mine. My heart's beating faster now.

"Raven," I say softly, taking the mug from her hands and setting it on the little side table. I take her hand in mine.

"I know we've only known each other for about a month. But the day I met you—and learned how much you loved the outdoors—I knew I had to get to know you better. And over these last few weeks, I've fallen head over heels for you."

Her eyes begin to shine, but I press on.

"You're a craving I never knew I had. After last night—after the thought of something happening to you—I realized I've waited too damn long to say this: I love you."

Reaching behind me, I pull the ring out of my back pocket and hold it in my palm.

"I know it's not much, but I bought it for you, pretty girl."

I keep my gaze locked on hers.

"Raven, my pretty girl—will you make me the happiest man in the world... and marry me? Because my hunt ended the day I found you."

She doesn't hesitate.

Tears spill down her cheeks as she nods, her voice shaking with emotion.

"Yes, Jackson. Yes. Yes. Yes!"

Sliding the ring onto her delicate finger, I cup her face in my hands, brushing away the tears running down her rosy cheeks.

"I love you, pretty girl."

"I love you too, Jackson. This was the best surprise."

Yes, it was.

And I'm just thankful she said yes.

Epilogue
Raven: One Year Later

Breathing erratically, my body starts to shake. My eyes stay locked on the big buck stepping out into the cornfield straight ahead of me. He catches me off guard. Here I am sitting quietly, reading on my Kindle, when I look up—and there he is.

After what felt like hours, he finally starts to move, inching his way toward the west side of the field before turning down the green trail that leads straight to me.

Jackson takes my Kindle's page-turner—so now the only thing in my hand is my bow.

Slowly, I rise to my feet. My legs tremble beneath me, adrenaline surging through every nerve. I wouldn't be surprised if the twelve-point buck notices me with how much I was shaking.

He keeps walking, unaware. I raise my bow, carefully and slowly, preparing to draw the string. But I don't pull back just yet—he's still too far out.

I wait.

My breath comes in short bursts, heart pounding so hard I can feel it pulsing in my ears.

Twenty yards.

That's my window.

I draw the string back, anchoring the kisser button against the corner of my mouth. My eyes shift through the sight, lining up the correct pin.

My entire body is coils with tension, but my focus is razor-sharp. He steps into the shooting lane.

This is it.

Aiming just behind his shoulder, I drop the pin down a touch—just like Jackson taught me.

"Always aim a little low. They'll drop when they hear the shot."

I inhale and exhale slowly, doing everything I can to stay still, stay quiet. My finger hovers over the release trigger. The bow feels heavy, but my grip is steady. I take one last breath, then pull the trigger.

The arrow releases with a sharp twang.

Time slows as I watch the fletching slice through the air. Then—impact. The buck bolts, crashing into the woods with my arrow lodged deep in his side.

Still trembling, still breathless, I watch him disappear into the trees.

We sit in the buddy stand for about ten minutes, though it feels like hours. Still shaking, I hook my bow onto the rope and lower it to the ground before climbing down.

Jackson walks out into the cornfield where I'd shot the deer and found a few small spots of blood. I met him on the trail where the deer had ran, and together we follow the blood trail, each spot growing larger with every step.

Jackson keeps his eyes glued to the ground, but mine scan ahead, searching for any sign of the deer. We crest the hill, and there it is—lying in the creek at the bottom.

"Deer like to run toward water when they're shot," Jackson says, hopping off the bank and into the shallow creek to check out the deer.

"Still not sure why, but they do."

It took both of us to pull the massive buck out of the water.

"You know," Jackson says, catching his breath, "I've never killed a deer this big before. And you know what they say—your next deer has to be even bigger. You'll never want to shoot anything smaller than this big boy."

He pulls out his phone to call Mitch to help load the deer into the truck, but Mitch doesn't answer. So he tries Tanner, who eventually picks up and says he'd be there in ten minutes.

"Stop by the house and grab the side-by-side," Jackson says into the phone.

"No way we're dragging this thing out by hand."

After he hangs up, Jackson comes over to stand by the deer.

"Alright—picture time. Get down there and hold his head up."

Grasping the antlers, I feel how stiff the body has already become. I look up as Jackson snaps a few pictures.

Lowering the deer's head gently, I stand back up and say, "I think I'll call him Wilber."

Jackson laughs—until he sees the look on my face.

"You're serious? You just named your deer?"

Smirking, I place my hands on my hips.

"Well, there's a first for everything. You nickname deer based on their antlers. Mine deserves a name. Wilber suits him."

He pulls me in and kisses my forehead.

"That's true. So does this mean you're going to name all the other deer heads in our house?"

Tapping my finger on my chin, I tease, "Hmm... we'll see."

About ten minutes later, Tanner arrives in the side-by-side. Someone is sitting in the passenger seat, but I can't make out who it was—until they get closer.

It's Jackson's sister, Luna.

"Luna?" Jackson asks, surprised to see his little sister climb out of the side by side.

Tanner jumps out of the side by side and helps load the deer in the back.

"What are you doing here? I didn't know you were coming into town."

"I'm moving back up here," Luna says, walking over to stand beside me as we watch the guys lift the buck. I wrap my arm around her and pull her into a hug.

"Well, welcome home. We are happy to have you here."

As I say those words, I notice Tanner smiling—just a little. Then I look over at Luna. She was smiling too.

Hmm. Interesting.

"Whew," Tanner says, closing the tailgate.

"Raven, I think you just killed the biggest deer in River Valley."

"I told her that," Jackson adds, picking up my bow.

"Also told her the next deer's has to be bigger—there's no going back now."

He turns to me.

"Why don't you and Luna head back to the house? Tanner and I'll walk out."

I grab my backpack off the ground and place it between Luna and me in the side-by-side.

"See you boys at the house."

We climb in and drive towards the house.

After Jackson and I ran off and got married at the courthouse a year ago, we sold both our houses and bought land on the outskirts of town. That's where we built our new home.

Now, Jackson and I don't have to drive anywhere to go hunting—we can walk out the back door. Hell, our bedroom has a balcony that gives him a clear shot right from the window if he wants to kill a deer, wearing his boxers. It has always been a dream of his to own a property where he could just walk out his back door.

After everything that happened with Dean, I just wanted a fresh start. I talked to him about moving in with me, but the memory of that day—what Dean did—still haunted me. We needed something new. Something ours.

When we told my parents that we'd gotten married, my mom was furious. She wanted a traditional wedding and was especially upset that she hadn't been there. When she found out Hannah had been there, she lost it.

Hannah, Henry, Violet, Tanner, Luna and Mitch had been our witnesses the day we said "I do."

Who would've guessed that the man who showed up one day asking for hunting permission would end up being my husband?

Jackson and I love each other for exactly who we are. We've never tried to change one another. We both had to survive some pretty dark chapters before finding each other—but in the end, we got our happily ever after.

Thank You for Reading

Thank you for reading **Cutie In Camo**!

If you liked reading Jackson and Raven's story, please let me know and share with others by leaving a review on **Amazon, Goodreads,** social media, etc.

Follow me on TikTok at: **@Rebeccagulleyauthor2319** and tag me in any post regarding Cutie In Camo!

Be on the lookout for Tanner and Luna's story.

Also by

Cutie in Camo
A Long Time Strutting(Releasing 3/28/26)
Caught Under The Mistletoe (Releasing 7/1/26)
Second Shot (Releasing 11/17/26)

Acknowledgements

Thank you so much for reading Jackson and Raven's story. It means the world to me that you picked up this book and chose to spend your time with these characters.

To my beta readers—Katie, Porsche, Luci, Taylor, and Deishima—thank you for your honest feedback and for cheering me on through every draft.

To my husband—thank you for pushing me to the finish line when I needed it most. You promised you'd read this once it was published... so enjoy it, sweetheart, front to back.

To my parents, who have always encouraged me to chase after my dreams—thank you.

To authors Jessica Booth and Breanne Bergie—thank you for your advice and guidance throughout the writing and publication process. Your support helped me bring this dream to life.

To Meribeth Richards—thank you for the late-night talks, advice, and for letting me bounce ideas off you, along with helping my brain dig a little deeper.

To the ARC readers who signed up and believed in this story before it was even published—thank you. Your excitement and early support mean more than I can put into words.

And finally, to the readers—thank you for picking up my debut novel and giving it a chance.

About the author

Rebecca currently lives in a small town in Ohio with her husband, two kids, and four dogs. When she isn't spending time with her family, you can usually find her with her nose buried in a book or supporting some of her favorite indie authors on social media. She graduated from Wright State University in 2017 and has always enjoyed creative writing. Never in her wildest dreams did she imagine she would become an author—but that changed after reading several novels in different genres by her favorite authors, which inspired her to write about her husband's lifestyle: hunting.

After graduating from high school, her husband introduced her to hunting. She quickly fell in love with the peaceful setting and experienced the thrill of the hunt firsthand when she harvested her first deer in 2013.